# THE
# RUDDERHAVEN
## SCIENCE FICTION AND FANTASY ANTHOLOGY
### III

Edited by

Douglas Rudder

RudderHaven
3014 Washington Ave
Granite City, IL 62040

Published by:
RudderHaven
3014 Washington Ave
Granite City, IL 62040
USA

First Softcover Printing, July 2015, RudderHaven
(ISBN 978-1-932060-16-4)

Edited by Douglas Rudder, C. K. Deatherage, Sheri Rudder, Becca Rudder
Cover Art and Design: Douglas, Sheri, and Becca Rudder
Nebula image Courtesy NASA/JPL-Caltech
Landscape image Courtesy Jon Sullivan/PDPhoto.org
Illustration in "Love at First Site" by C. S. Marks

Printed in the United States of America

ISBN 978-1-932060-16-4

# *Acknowledgements*

Thanks to all of our authors, editors, and everyone who made this book possible, and to our families and friends for their support and encouragement.

Special thanks to our readers. We hope you enjoy the characters, worlds, and stories we have presented to you. If our stories have sparked your imagination, touched your hearts, or tickled your sense of humor, then we count it a success.

# *Contents*

**Science Fiction**

**Fantasy**

**Fantasy Novella**

## *Saving Faith*

### Douglas Rudder

She's gone. It happened so fast. Faith stepped through the portal to . . . wherever it led . . . and disappeared. We all saw it: the creature charging, the intense light interference, and then the portal collapsed—with Faith on the other side.

Dr. Craighead and the scientists scrambled to re-establish the portal, or bridge, or whatever they wanted to call it, while I dashed down the corridor to the ship's stores to assemble another survival pack, ignoring the stiffness in the left side of my body as I ran. Panic battled with the fury coursing through me. The image of that beast thundering behind Faith like a huge, wide-bodied rhino burned in my mind. Faith had run for all she was worth, but just as she reached the edge of the energy "bubble" of the bridge, it flared with incredible intensity—and vanished.

My heart hammered in my chest as I burst through the door of the storeroom. With a trembling hand, I grabbed a backpack from the locker. It slipped from my grasp and thudded on the floor. I bit back a curse, hissing through gritted teeth.

I grasped my forehead and inhaled deeply, trying to slow my pounding heart. If I was going to be of any use to Faith, I needed to calm down. It was a challenge. I had been on the battlefield, had seen both enemies and buddies fall in combat, had steeled myself against the pain and terror of war, and had come to grips with the impairment left behind by my own wounds. But the thought of finding Faith's broken body, of what that monster might have done to her, ripped through my heart like an armor-piercing round.

She should not have been on that side of the bridge at all. Major Jacoby and the Expeditionary Team should have gone through first to clear the way and establish a perimeter for the researchers. But Jacoby's team was still a good twelve hours away by shuttle, having been deployed to the *USS Gregory* two days earlier.

The *Gregory* was one of three ships in the area, about five million miles beyond the orbit of Mars. The other two ships in the exploration group for Project Breakthrough included our ship, the *USS Pathfinder*, and the *HMS Saint George*. The *Gregory* had been considered the ship most likely to establish a functional Einstein-Rosen bridge first. They boasted the most prestigious and experienced science staff in our small fleet.

But they did not have Dr. Faith Overby. A specialist in theoretical astrophysics and quantum mechanics, her passion for E-R bridge theory as a means to explore deep space became almost legendary among the Project scientists. Her brilliance amazed her colleagues, and her enthusiasm amused them as outbursts of "booyah!" often followed her epiphanies and successes, sometimes accompanied by a little happy-dance. Our science team's motto became: "You just gotta have Faith." They were right.

As the *Pathfinder's* Supply Officer, I interacted with all of the ship's departments, including the research team. That's how I got to know Faith.

She would drop by on occasion to requisition equipment and supplies. Sometimes she would linger and chat about the Project for a while. Much of what she said zipped right over my head (my reflexes were *not* fast enough to catch it), but that didn't faze her a bit. It did not matter that my knowledge of astrophysics was pretty much nonexistent. I became a sounding board for her, a neutral outlet for her to bounce ideas off of. It seemed to help her organize her thoughts. I didn't mind; the excitement that radiated from her during our talks was, well, kind of attractive.

Before long, I started spending more time in the lab, first under the pretense of delivering supplies, then because of real interest, both in the Project and in spending more time with Faith. I had no illusion of anything serious coming of it, but I enjoyed her company. Our friendship was just that, a friendship. She lived and breathed the Project. The Science department head, Dr. Niles Craighead, often had to shoo her out of the lab to get some rest. I doubted a personal life was even on her radar.

One of the large holds on the *Pathfinder* had been reconfigured to house the research lab and equipment for the Einstein-Rosen bridge. Desks, workbenches, and computer consoles took up much of the area around the entrance, while the guide ring which would act as the access point to the E-R bridge dominated the center of the hold.

The guide ring was massive, about five meters in diameter and two meters in thickness. The inner ring shone with a silvery sheen. Plates of darker metal covered the outer rim and edges of the ring, with a metallic coil running through a half-sleeve encircling it. On the far side of the interior ring, the glassy surface of the emitter array picked up the subdued lights of the research bay.

I remember the first time I approached the ring close up. It towered over me like a great mechanical monument, majestic and mysterious. We were about to open a gateway to the unknown. I stood there like a spellbound kid, until a hushed voice startled me out of my reverie.

"Amazing, isn't it?" I hadn't even heard Faith come up beside me.

"Yes, it is," I agreed.

She gazed at the aperture, as if she could see strange new worlds beyond it. "This is where a new age of space travel begins. It's like looking into the pages of history not yet written."

"Ah, a scientist *and* a poet."

Faith shrugged. "Being a scientist doesn't mean I can't appreciate the artistry of the universe around us."

"True." I waved my good hand at the guide ring. "How close are we to firing this thing up and seeing what's on the other side?"

Her lips compressed into a thin line. "If only it were that easy." She looked up at me, and then gave my sleeve a tug. "Walk with me, George. I need to stretch my legs a little."

I glanced down. "They look about the right length to me."

"Hush, George."

I hushed. We strolled in silence for a while, out beyond the guide ring to the empty, quiet end of the hold. Soon she stepped a little closer and looped her arm through mine as we walked, resting her other hand on my elbow. While she gathered her thoughts, I basked in the warmth of her nearness.

Finally, she spoke. "An Einstein-Rosen bridge is, by its very nature, inherently unstable. A traversable bridge, doubly so, because it requires a much larger amount of exotic matter than current science can find or generate."

"Exotic matter?"

"Negative energy. It creates negative pressure to push back the naturally occurring positive energy and hold the bridge open."

"Well, my mom always told me to accentuate the positive."

Faith rolled her eyes and gave a wry smile. "The cosmos accentuates the positive enough already. That's the problem. In order to open *and* stabilize the bridge, we need to find a way to stimulate the formation of enough exotic matter and inject it into the field in the right amounts. We need to regulate the flow to achieve the proper balance between positive and negative density."

That one I remembered from our talks. "Zero-point energy."

She raised her eyebrows. "You *have* been paying attention." She closed her eyes and sighed. "That's the part that still eludes us."

"You'll figure it out," I said, squeezing her arm

against my side with my elbow. "After all, 'you just gotta have Faith.'"

"Oh, shut up."

*   *   *   *

Two days later, Faith had a "booyah!" moment, and a new, highly improbable technology was born. She huddled with Dr. Farris and the engineering team to hammer out the design specs. In just over a week, the Einstein-Rosen bridge array had been upgraded and was ready for a field test.

The entire research and development team showed up for the test, which seemed a bit chancy to me should something go wrong. But this was their baby, and they all wanted to be there for the birth. A good part of the off-duty ship's crew—including me—were on hand as well. First Officer Kelleher was there, representing the Captain. The Captain and the rest of the crew were patched in at their duty stations via video monitors.

We were situated behind a transparent safety screen. An anti-radiation field had already been activated on the near side of the guide ring, with a thick metal alloy plate ready to drop into place if needed.

Faith manned the control board, with Hank Baumer, one of the engineers, at her elbow. He had helped design the system and functioned as Faith's backup for operating the bridge. Dr. Craighead stood across from her as she ran through her pre-test checklist. They conferred briefly, and Faith nodded.

Dr. Craighead stepped away from the control board and faced the crowd. All systems were go.

As he launched into a "We stand on the cusp of history" speech, I surveyed the group gathered in the lab.

All of their faces reflected eagerness, along with a variety of other emotions, ranging from expectation to hope to apprehension. This was the critical stage, the culmination of their efforts about to be put to the test.

Craighead nodded to Faith. "It's your show, Doctor. You may proceed when ready."

With the slightest hesitation, Faith flicked a series of toggles on the board and then activated the system. A deep thrum filled the chamber, and all eyes turned toward the guide ring. A breathless anticipation hung over the room. The emitter array on the far side of the ring began to glow, gradually getting brighter as the pulsating thrum intensified.

A cheer went up as a shimmering, luminescent sphere sprang to life from the guide ring. The sphere glowed blue, with streams of light swirling through it and bright flashes flaring up sporadically, like some kind of alien fireworks display. A hissing crackle accompanied the flashes, loud and sharp.

"Dr. Overby?" Dr. Craighead's voice rose above the din.

"Just a moment," Faith called back.

Tearing my eyes from the roiling lightshow, I glanced back at Faith. She stood at the control board, light from the energy field flickering across her features, reflecting from her eyes as she made adjustments. A little smile danced at the edge of her lips. She had never looked more vibrant, more beautiful. This was her moment, her dream becoming reality.

The flashing diminished and she straightened up. "That's got it," she said and looked up. Her eyes widened, her lips parted slightly in astonishment. A hush descended on the room.

The energy bubble had calmed down and become semi-transparent. The bright flashes gave way to smaller sparkles, but they no longer fully obscured the view beyond the sphere.

I don't know what I expected to see, but this was not it. I guess since we were in a ship in space, I expected to see space. But there were no stars, no nebulae, no planets hanging against the blackness. There, framed by the swirling glow, was a planet's surface.

A rocky outcropping jutted up through straggly grass directly ahead through the opening. The ground appeared to slope away beyond the outcropping, but I could not tell if it was a hill or steep drop-off. Beyond the edge, a plain stretched out, though we could not see too far through the haze of the bubble. To the right, barely visible behind the edge of guide ring, a cliff rose toward the sky. The landscape seemed perfectly aligned with the E-R bridge, as if we could step right through the opening onto the alien planet.

The really weird part was that we could see both the deck of the ship and the ground of the planet through the bubble, but it was impossible to pin down where the deck ended and the ground began. One of the physicists, a Dr. Mizrachi, attributed the phenomenon to quantum effects within the field. According to their theory, the E-R bridge should consist of two spheres connected by a throat or tunnel. We only saw one sphere. Mizrachi posited that we were actually seeing both spheres simultaneously and not seeing the tunnel at all.

While the mechanics of that effect may have been the greatest thing since the apple conked Sir Isaac, it was the practical application—exploration—that peaked my interest. As soon as the bridge had been opened and stabilized, Captain Showalter had sent a message to the *Gregory* requesting the Expeditionary Team to join us. Their estimated transit time was eighteen hours.

Eighteen hours! An alien planet sat right there, its surface tantalizingly close—and we had to wait. Not that we could just dive in anyway. Despite our desire to begin exploration, a whole raft of tests needed to be performed on this side of the bridge before we even considered sending anyone or anything through it. The time might fly by for those who actually had tasks to do. For those of us not on the research team, not so much.

Faith ran herself ragged, flitting from station to station. Her primary responsibility revolved around the bridge operation itself, but she had a hand in several tangential processes as well—plus an insatiable drive to understand everything. Yet, in the midst of it all, her gaze was often drawn to the energy sphere and to the alien landscape beyond.

Other than a couple of quick supply runs, I really didn't have much to do. The part of bystander rankled me. It's not easy to sit on the sidelines when you used to be involved in the action.

My inner grumblings were interrupted by a thump on the shoulder from one of the lab techs, a guy named Izzo. "Hey, Peebles! Dr. Overby sent me to get you. She figured you'd want to see this."

"What's up?" I asked as I fell in step with him.

"We got the green light. They're prepping T-RED for launch."

My pulse rate bumped up a notch. T-RED stood for Telemetry-enabled Remote Exploration Drone, and represented the first phase of our attempts to traverse the Einstein-Rosen bridge. Now we were getting somewhere.

People began drifting toward the guide ring as word spread about the impending launch. Izzo and I joined the flow. Down near the ring, the techs gave the drone a final check, while Dr. Craighead spoke with the engineer who would be controlling the drone.

Faith stood at the bridge controls once again, giving instructions to Hank Baumer. She paused and scanned the gathering crowd. Her eyes lit up when she saw me. She grinned and gave a quick wave. While she wasn't doing a happy-dance outwardly, I'll bet she was bouncing like a kangaroo on the inside.

A couple of hours later, the situation had changed. Dangerously so.

The first tense moment came when T-RED penetrated the energy sphere. Thrusters angled down and a little forward, the drone hovered slowly into the bubble, sensor and camera arms extruding from the small craft's surface. As it touched the edge of the field, the same flashes and crackles that had marked the initial activation of the E-R bridge flared violently, starting at the drone and rapidly spreading throughout the sphere. The cacophony assaulted my eardrums, and the flashes made it difficult to see the drone and totally obscured the alien planetscape.

Faith's fingers flew over the controls, fiery resolve blazing from within. Like a Valkyrie with lightning in her eyes, she bent physics to her will. That bridge would not *dare* collapse, not on her watch.

Gradually, the interference lessened. While smaller sparks still popped around T-RED, the field itself returned to its previous state. At Dr. Craighead's signal, the drone started forward again. About two-thirds of the way through, the drone seemed to falter, then stabilize again.

"Sorry about that," the engineer running the drone said. "The signal is erratic."

"That's quite all right, Evan," Dr. Craighead responded. "We are dealing with the unknown. Bobbles will happen." He shifted his attention to Faith. "Dr. Overby, can we compensate for the signal fluctuations?"

"I'm tweaking as we speak, Doctor. But I'd rather keep modifications to a minimum; it's knife-edge balanced already."

"Understood. Do what you can."

No further hitches interrupted T-RED's historic voyage. Silence descended on the lab as the drone approached the far side of the bridge. I could feel myself tense up with anticipation, leaning forward, almost willing the little craft on. Then T-RED was through, floating in the air of an alien world.

The ovation in the lab dwarfed the earlier one, practically shaking the bulkheads. Much backslapping and hugging ensued. We had done it. We had pierced the veil of space and placed a man-made drone on a world outside of the Solar system. I was seeing Faith's "pages of history" being written before my eyes.

Unfortunately, that's about as far as history made it for T-RED. Communication with the drone's onboard computer was iffy at best. The signal strength did not diminish, but it lacked coherence. The signal seemed almost warped when passing through the Einstein-Rosen bridge. Faith chalked it up to quantum effects within the field, explaining that the radio waves themselves were injecting positive energy that caused a fluctuation of the positive/negative balance.

I took her word for it. What it boiled down to was that they could not control T-RED well enough to explore or even take soil or plant samples. If the drone's radiation and atmospheric sensors had not already been enabled before passing through the E-R bridge, the attempt would have been a complete wash. As it was, they would have to wait until T-RED returned before they could do a full analysis of the recorded data.

After several attempts, Evan the Engineer did manage to extend the drone's landing gear and lower it to the ground, which effectively turned T-RED into a six-wheeled land rover. This led to one final test: rolling the drone home through the bridge.

It worked, although Faith had to stabilize the field again when the drone entered the bridge. The flashes weren't as pronounced this time. The little guy rolled across the floor of the energy bubble. It was strange to watch. First, dust came up under the wheels as they still apparently made contact with the ground through the field. Then suddenly there was no dust and T-RED wheeled across the deck plates of the ship. We never even saw the transition. Finally, the drone popped out of the guide ring and rolled into a small decontamination chamber.

Faith locked her control board and headed down to join the rest of the researchers gathered together to go over the data captured by T-RED's sensors. I snagged a chair from a nearby desk and plopped down, settling in for the long-haul. Once the scientifical types started poring over the data recorded by the drone, I doubted they'd come up for air for quite a while. Still, I wanted to be there when Faith got a break, to congratulate her—and maybe see if she wanted to head down to the galley for a cup of coffee.

At first, she was like the kid in the proverbial candy shop: all smiles, eyes alight with the joy of discovery, chattering like a magpie with anyone nearby as she took notes and shared her analyses. But a little while later, she seemed to withdraw a bit, and her conversation appeared to become more serious. Every so often, her wistful gaze would return to the Einstein-Rosen bridge and the world beyond.

Before long, Faith was in earnest discussion with Dr. Craighead, with the rest of the researchers looking on. A couple of the others added an occasional comment, but Faith and Craighead did most of the talking. The conversation became more animated—almost heated—on both sides; I resisted the urge to go down and listen in, but boy did I want to. Whatever they were arguing about, the majority of the research team seemed to be lining up with Faith. Something was up, and with a hollowness forming in the pit of my stomach, I figured it couldn't be good.

Finally, with obvious reluctance, Dr. Craighead gave in. He and Faith left the group and headed over to where First Officer Kelleher stood chatting with another crewman. Visually, it was almost an instant replay of the last discussion, only it was Kelleher's turn to face Faith's impassioned discourse. Kelleher looked skeptical, but more receptive than Craighead had been. After a brief discussion—mainly because, from what I could see, Faith didn't let him get a word in edge-wise—they left the lab together.

\* \* \* \*

"George?"

My head snapped up with a jerk. I guess I dozed off in my chair. Blinking the gumminess of sleep from my eyes, I shifted myself into a more upright position. Faith smiled down at me, her eyes bright with excitement. Just behind her stood Dr. Craighead, his face an impassive mask. No, not quite impassive. A slight tightness of the skin around his eyes indicated that he was less than thrilled about something. That place in my gut was no longer hollow; a knot was slowly forming to fill it.

I tried to keep my tone light as I stood up. "Congratulations, Faith." I smiled, gesturing to the bridge. "How does it feel to poke a hole in the universe?" Okay, that sounded lame. It was the best my sleep-fogged brain could come up with at the moment.

She grinned and gave me a quick hug, which caught me flat-footed, but I enjoyed it anyway. "It's wonderful! I've always dreamed of this moment, yet now that it's here, I can hardly believe it's real."

"It's real," I said, glancing at the alien vista. So close, and yet so far. "If only the Expeditionary Team were here to get the ball rolling. That planet needs exploring."

Faith and Craighead exchanged glances. Wariness crept into her features as she looked back at me, not quite making eye contact.

"About that," she said slowly, "we've decided—and the Captain concurs—that based on the data we received from T-RED's sensors, we're not going to wait for Major Jacoby's team to get started."

"Are you people insane? You don't know—"

"Wait, please!" she cut me off, reaching out her hand. "Let me explain."

My jaw muscles flexed, but I managed to respond with a civil voice. "Make it good."

She shook her head and gave me a sidewise look. "Oo-oo-oo, you're a toughie. Okay, here's what we've got." She held up her thumb. "First, the atmospheric readings from the drone show that the planet has a human-breathable atmosphere. No unusual radiations or dangerous microscopic organisms." Next, she extended her index finger, which made her hand look disturbingly like a pistol—pointed right at me. "Second, we don't know for sure how long we can keep the bridge open; it uses a lot of power. Therefore," she speared me with a glare, "it is worthwhile to send someone through to take the samples T-RED was unable to gather. This person can take further readings and images to give the Expeditionary Team valuable intelligence to enhance their mission to make it safe for the research group."

Remind me never to match wits with a genius. That last part was clearly designed to appeal to my military background. "And what lunatic did they get to go?"

A rosy flush tinted her cheeks. "Me."

For a wonder, I didn't scream. "Why you? You're not a botanist or geologist."

"It's her privilege, Mr. Peebles," Dr. Craighead answered. "It was her discovery and expertise that solved the riddle of creating a traversable Einstein-Rosen bridge, a feat many deemed impossible. If only one can go, it will be her." He looked hard at me, maybe as hard as I was staring at him. "The Captain's decision is final."

Faith touched his arm. "Please, Doctor, let me handle it. I can do this, George. I know how to run the scanning equipment and the samplers. It will all be done within the vicinity of the bridge, so that if something comes up, I can get back quickly."

If something comes up. Did she even have a clue about what that meant in an unknown wilderness? But she wasn't finished with me yet.

"Now," she continued, "just one more thing." She caught the corner of her lower lip in her teeth, then said, "I need to requisition a survival pack. Can you put that together for me?"

*You've got to be kidding me.* Not only did she want to do something incredibly idiotic, she wanted *me* to equip her to do it. "Fine," I growled. "I'll prep two. I'm going with you."

Her eyes softened. "George, you know you can't. You were taken out of active duty for a reason." She reached down and took my left hand in hers, giving it a gentle squeeze.

I barely felt it. My army career had ended abruptly when a shell went off near my position. My left arm and leg had been pretty chewed up, and my left side paralyzed for a while. Aside from the scars, my body mended with time—and lots of surgeries—but my left leg and arm were still not full strength, and my hand was almost useless from nerve damage. I could still use it for simple things, but it was permanently numb, like I had been out in the cold for too long—only it never thawed. It had very little dexterity and almost no grip. I could feel pressure, even pain sometimes, but that was about it.

But I wasn't ready to give up yet. "It's Jacoby's job

16

to check things out first, not yours. He'll be here in a few hours. Wait for him."

"We may not *have* a few hours," Faith answered. "The bridge isn't entirely stable. You saw what happened when the drone passed through it. We have to take the chance while the bridge is still open."

"But that's exactly why you shouldn't go!" I snapped. "It could destabilize at any time. What happens if you get caught on the other side or worse yet, *inside*, when it falls apart?"

She looked up at me through her eyebrows, her eyes large, almost pleading. "I've waited my whole life for this, George. Don't take it away from me."

All the things I wanted to say, all the arguments, the logic, died in my throat. How could I look in those eyes and crush her dreams? I wanted to take her in my arms, to hold her, to protect her.

Instead, I turned my face away, closing my eyes against the moisture building up in them. My response was slow in coming; I didn't want the trembling in my chest to sound in my voice.

"Go through, take your samples, and come back. No exploring. Limited exploring," I amended, catching her expression when I opened my eyes, "near the bridge."

For a moment, I thought she was going to argue, but then she nodded. "All right, George."

"I mean it, Faith. Don't take any more risks than you have to. Be safe . . . and come back."

"I will," she said softly. She tossed me a smile. "I'll tell you what, after I get back, we'll order dinner and take it down to the lounge for tonight's movie. All right?"

"It's a date," I said, then realized how that sounded. "I mean, not a 'date' date, just—"

She pressed her fingers against my lips and drew closer. "Yes, George, a 'date' date." I can only imagine the stupid look I must have had on my face, because she tilted her head and laughed. "I'm tired of waiting for you to ask. Goodness knows I've given you plenty of opportunity. I'll see you when I get back."

Only she didn't come back.

\* \* \* \*

I sealed up my survival pack and hooked a coil of rope to it. Setting it aside, I stepped over to the weapons locker and keyed in the combination. The hunting rifles tempted me for a second, but with only one good hand, there's no way I could fire one accurately. I bypassed them in favor of a semi-automatic handgun. Ramming a clip home, I tried racking the slide, but failed miserably. My left hand didn't have enough grip or strength to pull the slide, and trying to pin the gun against my side to use my right hand was too awkward. I'm lucky I didn't blow a hole in my ribcage while I fought with the blasted thing.

Then my eyes lighted on a revolver near the bottom of the locker. I snatched it up, along with its holster and ammo belt. With a smile of grim satisfaction, I swung the cylinder out and, cradling the gun in my left elbow, began loading it.

A motion at the periphery of my vision caught my attention. Dr. Craighead stood in the doorway.

"How long have you been standing there?"

"Long enough." He regarded me coolly. His eyes dropped to the revolver, then flicked to the semi-automatic, and then back to me.

"Don't start, Doc," I said.

He lifted an eyebrow. "I said nothing."

"Good," I replied and resumed my task. "How long until they can get the bridge back up?"

"Not too long, I would venture."

Something in his tone set off warning bells in the back of my mind. "You don't sound too thrilled about it."

"I'm not," he replied. "It was a mistake to let Faith go through before Major Jacoby's team arrived." He paused, a trace of uncertainty crossing his features. It passed quickly, and his expression settled into the serenity of a man reconciled with making a difficult, but necessary, decision. "I do not think it would be prudent re-establish the bridge just yet."

With a flick of my wrist, I flipped the cylinder closed and pointed the revolver straight at his balding forehead. "You'll open the bridge, or I'll put a bullet in your brain."

He didn't even flinch. His eyes met mine with a calm, measuring gaze. My bluff had been called, and he had won.

I lowered my arm, shifting the gun barrel away from him. "We can't just abandon her, Dr. Craighead." My voice sounded pleading, almost child-like, in my own ears. "I—we can't lose Faith."

He frowned, and for a moment he looked almost as despondent as I felt. "We cannot discount the possibility that we may have already lost her."

"I don't believe that!" I snapped.

"You *won't* believe it," he shot back.

"I *don't* believe it. Until we know for certain, we have to assume she's still alive. We have to go after her."

"When Jacoby gets here—"

"We can't wait for Jacoby! Don't you see? Every minute, every *second* we delay counts against her." I cinched the holster around my waist. "Get that bridge up; I have to go."

He held up a hand. "Why you, Mr. Peebles? Why not one of your shipmates, someone more—"

"Able-bodied?" I said darkly. Faith had used that one on me, and I had caved. Never again. My body may have been damaged, but I still had my life. And I was going to live it.

Even if it killed me.

"I'm sorry, Mr. Peebles . . . George. I didn't mean that the way it sounded."

"Sure you did. But it doesn't matter," I said, forestalling his reply. It was time to shift tactics. "Tell me, Doctor, when we reopen the bridge, what are the chances that it won't open at exactly the same location on the planet's surface?"

His brows furrowed, wrinkling his forehead. "If our calculations are correct, it should be relatively close to the original location. However, factoring in planetary rotation and our relative positions, there is a chance that it will not be exactly the same place."

I nodded. "That's my thinking as well. Here's the deal: This is a civilian vessel. The ship's crew is trained for shipboard duties. They do not have training in wilderness survival and tactics. I do. I'm the only one on board qualified to run a search-and-rescue mission under these conditions. I can do this, Dr. Craighead."

"That's what Faith said before she left."

"Yes, sir. If I'm wrong, you can still send Jacoby through when he gets here." I managed a feeble smile.

"I'm just a supply clerk; the ship can do without me. I'm expendable. Faith isn't."

Craighead looked at me for a moment, and then nodded. "Very well, Mr. Peebles. I will inform Mr. Baumer and Dr. Farris that we will activate the bridge." He headed for the door, then paused and glanced back at me. His eyes were rimmed red. "I care for her, too, George. If I had ever had a daughter . . . Bring Faith back, Mr. Peebles."

"Will do, Doctor." I slung the survival pack over my shoulder and followed him out. One thing still bothered me. "I can't for the life of me figure out why the Captain let her go without waiting for the Expeditionary Team."

"History, Mr. Peebles." Craighead's visage darkened. "He wanted to cement his place in history as the Captain of the first ship to discover and explore a new world outside the Solar system, and feared we could not sustain the bridge long enough to wait. He rushed his decision without weighing the cost."

I had no words.

\* \* \* \*

"That's the best we're going to get," Hank Baumer shouted over the staccato of the energy field.

While not nearly as bad as the first time the E-R bridge sprang to life, there was still far more flashing and popping than when the drone had passed through. I could only hope that there would be no damaging effects to objects passing through it—namely me.

Peering through the interference, I tried to pick out landmarks. The outcropping we had seen before was not visible, but there were a couple of other formations that looked familiar. It must be the same plateau. It had to be.

"Perhaps we should wait," Izzo said as he adjusted the straps on my survival pack behind me. He gave it a firm tug to make sure it was solidly in place.

"No," I replied. "It's time."

Izzo held up his fist for a fist bump. "Good luck, George."

"Thanks." I nodded to Dr. Craighead, who was assisting Hank at the bridge controls. "This is it," I whispered under my breath and started forward.

Approaching the glow of the energy bubble, I reached a tentative hand out. When my skin came in contact with the energy, I felt a tingling in my fingers, enveloping my hand as I reached in. The flares increased, snapping against my skin like firecrackers. I jerked my hand back out with a startled yelp.

"Are you all right, George?"

I held my hand up. "Not a mark. I'm fine."

With that, I drew a breath and plunged in. Inside the sphere was surreal. It looked—and felt—like I was inside a pyrotechnics display. I picked up the pace, hurrying as best I could toward the landscape ahead, cringing at the abuse my eardrums were taking from crackling pops. Once, I thought I heard somebody call my name, but I was not about to turn back now. The die had been cast, and I was going through.

The clump of my boots against the deck suddenly changed to the crunch of dirt and sparse grass, though I could hardly see anything through the flashing at this point. Both the sound and light interference were heavy now, and I knew the portal was about to collapse again. The edge of the sphere lay just ahead. I lurched forward and threw myself through the curved wall.

I tumbled to the ground in a puff of dust and did a shoulder roll, coming up in a crouched stance, one knee on the ground. I took stock of my surroundings. The bridge was gone, but I expected that. A cliff wall rose from the ground beside me to the right, with another cliff beyond it, split off by a chasm between them. Straight ahead, the semi-arid land dropped away into a craggy terrain that ran to another mountain range in the distance, broken up by scraggly grass and an occasional twisted, gnarly tree.

A deep, rumbling growl sounded behind me. Still crouched, I slowly turned my head to find its source—and froze. Just off my left shoulder, about ten meters out, stood a mutant rhino-monster like the one that had chased Faith. The creature stood on four short, thick legs, beneath a wide, heavily-muscled body. Its head was broad and flat, with a wide, lipless mouth filled with long, pointed teeth. It definitely was *not* an herbivore. Horns curved out wide on either side of its mouth, hooking forward into cruel barbs. Another horn protruded like a long spike straight ahead from a ridge atop its skull, clearly useful for impaling its prey. Amber eyes glared out from beneath the blotchy gray skin of its brow. Its hide looked thick and durable. I doubted my revolver would even tickle it.

It huffed and growled again, louder this time, pawing the ground, head lowering in preparation to charge. I was caught between Scylla and a hard place, a monster and a cliff. The cliff face was closer than the creature. If I could reach it before the beast caught me—and did horrible things to my anatomy—I might just have a chance.

I sprang to my feet, stumbling as I tried to get my

balance, and raced toward the cliff. I might run like I have a flat tire, but that didn't slow me a bit, not with several tons of sudden death dogging my heels. The ground shook as the beast pounded after me. Its footfalls grew louder as I neared the cliff wall. I took the last few feet with a flying leap, hitting the wall, and clawing my way up the side of the cliff.

A tremendous *whomp!* sounded beneath me, rattling my teeth and jarring me to the core with the impact, nearly causing me to lose my one-handed grip. Rocks and dirt cascaded down around me. One rock clipped the side of my head, causing me to see stars. But I held on.

I glanced down in time to see the creature tear its horns out of the cliff face, rending a huge divot of dirt and rock loose and scattering debris with an angry shake of its head. It looked up at me with baleful eyes and let loose with a powerful, wide-mouthed bellow. I could feel the heat of its breath—and smell the fetid halitosis erupting from that nightmarish maw. The stench almost accomplished what the impact couldn't, but I managed to cling to the rocks in spite of it.

The sound of his bellow reverberated from the surrounding cliffs, echoing across the valley and out onto the plains. Luckily, this fellow wasn't built for climbing. He thumped his flat feet as he paced back and forth at the base of the precipice.

A different sound rose in response from the plains below. It was almost like a chorus of bleats and the distant thunder of many hooves. The rhino-thing swung its head around and took a few steps that direction. It glared back at me one more time, but seemed to decide that meat on the hoof would be better than waiting for the wall-mounted morsel to drop down. With one last snort, he turned away and headed for the sloped side of the plateau, barreling down it toward his new prey.

I waited until its footfalls dwindled in the distance before sliding down the cliff side to the ground. Aside from a few scrapes and bruises, all my pieces and parts seemed to be intact. The side of my head was a little tender from where the rock bounced off my skull. I probed the spot gently with my fingers, and they came away sticky with blood. The wound wasn't bleeding profusely, so I just let it be.

My eyes swept the plateau, looking for anything that could lead me to Faith. An object on the landscape caught my eye. The outcropping we had seen through the E-R bridge jutted up from the ground about thirty meters from where I stood. I was in the right place—which meant the beast that chased me was most likely the same one that attacked Faith. A wave of dread washed over me, the imagery of those powerful, spike-toothed jaws descending on Faith's slender form haunting my mind's eye.

Keeping my revolver at the ready, I explored the plateau, peering behind every stone, shrub, and boulder, but came up empty. No body, no sign of recent carnage.

What I *did* discover during my survey, back where I thought the original Einstein-Rosen bridge had opened, was a hodge-podge of scuffs and tracks in the dirt. Unfortunately, the earth there had been trampled enough by our hammer-footed predator that any tracks Faith might have left behind were pretty much wiped out. Only one small footprint remained in the midst of the jumbled mess.

I dropped down on my knees beside that footprint. *Let her be alive. Please, let her be alive.* I began to tremble, breathing heavily. I knelt there for a moment, silently, not thinking, not imagining.

And accomplishing nothing. It had been a tough day. It might even get tougher. But that didn't matter. What mattered was saving Faith. She was out in this alien wilderness, lost and alone, probably terrified out of her wits, not knowing if rescue would ever come. After that grand speech about being the only one aboard ship with survival training and military skills, I just sat here wallowing in self-pity instead of doing what I came here to do.

Drawing one more shuddering breath, I rose to my feet. "Enough of the pity party, numbskull," I muttered. "Focus on finding Faith."

There had to be some trace that showed what direction she went. After the bridge collapsed, with that monstrosity on her tail, what would she have done? The cliff loomed before me, but farther out than where I came in at. It did not seem possible that she could have outrun the rhino-beast in a straight dash. I looked down the slope to my right, using the small binoculars from my survival pack. It was pretty barren, with nowhere to hide and no evidence that Faith had been caught there.

That left the drop-off into the chasm between the cliffs. Could she have made that run without getting caught? The ground nearer the chasm was more broken up by boulders and bushes than the rest of the plateau. The creature's size and momentum would keep it from being able to change direction quickly. If Faith had cut at a right angle after she lost the bridge, she might have been able to reach that area ahead of the beast. A little broken-field running, utilizing the rough terrain, *could* have gotten her to the edge of the chasm first.

"Okay, George. Now you've got a starting point."

I headed off toward the edge of the plateau, watching for signs of Faith's passage while trying to stay aware of my surroundings. I was acutely cognizant of the fact that in a strange wilderness environment, I was the prey, not the predator—as the beastie I had already tangled with demonstrated. That's an aspect of survival that you learn quickly, or you don't survive.

I reached my destination without picking up her trail, much to my disappointment, although I was not entirely surprised. I could only guess at her angle of approach based on where I thought she started from. Stepping to the brink, I knew Faith had not come this way. The embankment dropped away far too abruptly for an inexperienced climber to attempt, especially one without climbing gear. But I did not give up hope, not yet.

Several meters along the plateau to my left, the descent sloped out just a bit. The grade would have been too sharp for that horn-headed behemoth to trundle down, but a human could climb or slide down it without too much trouble, if one was careful. I took off at my best imitation of a trot. Even before I got there, I knew I hit pay-dirt.

The marks in the soil indicated something had slid over the edge not too long ago. My heart raced as I whipped out my binoculars and scanned the base of the plateau, almost afraid of what I might find. But there was no crumpled body in the rocks below. What I saw next caused my racing heart to do a stutter-step: a trail led away from the plateau, across the ravine.

Grabbing the rope from my pack, I quickly and securely tied it to a nearby boulder and started down. I could have gone down without the rope, but after I found Faith, we'd need to get back up again, assuming that's where the bridge would appear when Craighead's people got it open again.

If they got it open again. That thought sent icy fingers up my spine. What if they couldn't reactivate the bridge? What if too much time had passed and their calculated congruency no longer matched up with our location? We could be stranded here indefinitely.

I glanced at my watch and did a double-take, then grimaced. It had only been a couple of hours since I came through the portal, though it seemed *much* longer. I brushed my sleeve across my face, wiping the sweat from my eyes. My hair was dripping wet, and perspiration trickled down my back. Not only was the day growing warmer, the physical exertion was beginning to take its toll. My body was no longer accustomed to it, outside of the gym anyway.

The rope played out a couple of meters from the ravine floor, so I slid the rest of the way down. The slope there wasn't too bad; it would be relatively easy to climb back up to the rope when the time came.

The ravine cut between the two cliffs to my right. The cliff on the other side of the chasm extended about half-way out parallel to the plateau, tapering down to a rocky spur as it merged into the plain below. The tracks I had spotted from above led toward the end of that spur. After taking a swig of water from my canteen, I started off again.

I had only taken a few steps when I dropped to one

knee and scooped up an object from the dusty earth. It was a small strap and clip—from one of the pouches on Faith's survival pack! I closed my fist around the strap and clasped it to my chest, breathing a prayer of thanks. It must've gotten torn loose during her slide down the embankment. It was the first real evidence that I was on the right track.

The fatigue I had felt just moments before gave way to a renewed vigor as I surged to my feet and resumed my quest, my stride light and swift. The trail was sporadic; the terrain ahead was broken by hard, dry ground, patches of tall, scraggly grass, and a scattering of stony debris. But the occasional stretches of crumbled earth revealed that the trail continued in the same direction.

A breeze swept through the ravine, warm but welcome. The dust swirled and shifted a bit, not enough to hide the tracks, just to make them less distinct. That thought brought me up short. I knelt to examine the tracks again, feeling my brows furrow. Thus far, I had seen no solid footprints, just irregular, trailing scuffs in the dirt. A closer look revealed why. It looked like something was being dragged along. Could Faith be dragging her survival pack? Some of the marks seemed to fit that scenario. But there was a secondary set of drag marks, kind of splayed out and wispy, almost like she was using branches to mask her trail. Why would she do that?

She wouldn't. The markings did not sweep back and forth across her back-trail, they just continued straight along the path. These marks were not created by a branch, they were created by a thick, hairy tail. My suspicions were confirmed seconds later when I spotted a print in the dirt, almost cat-like, but with longer, more dexterous toes—tipped with vicious claws.

Something was stalking Faith.

I broke into a dead run, pulse pounding, desperation driving me recklessly forward. I rounded the end of the spur and slid to a stop, eyes transfixed on the scene before me, stomach churning in horror.

A creature crouched in the dust about fifty meters ahead. It was a little smaller than me, but its body was long, with hard, lean muscles. Aside from coarse hair at the base of its skull and its wide, fanned-out tail, it had no fur, just black skin, blazoned with reddish-brown spots. Both its build and movements were a bizarre blend of big cat and—otherworldly. There's nothing earthly to compare it too.

It hunched with its back to me, forepaws ripping at something on the ground in front of it. Bits and pieces from Faith's survival pack lay scattered across the landscape.

White-hot rage burned in my veins, and with a cry of anguish, I raised my revolver and fired—into the ground about a half meter from the creature. Even in my frenzied state, some small corner of my mind did not want to chance hitting Faith, alive or not. I wanted to chase the beast from that spot, either to scare it away or to blow its ghastly head off.

The creature jerked and whirled to face me. It glowered at me with red eyes, its sharp, needle-like teeth barred in a lipless mouth, like a demon spawned in the pits of the netherworld. With a snarl, it sprang toward me, bounding across the terrain between us with startling speed.

I dropped into a marksman's stance, instinctively going for a two-handed grip with my bad hand, then sliding my gun-hand to brace it across my left forearm. Drawing a bead on those red eyes, I squeezed off a shot. The creature gave a cry of pain as the bullet grazed its shoulder. Its stride faltered briefly, but still it came, bouncing and juking wildly over the broken ground, a predator intent on killing its new prey.

Two shots later, the monster lay dead.

I remained poised for combat, panting, unable to tear my gaze from that vile corpse. Finally, I closed my eyes and lowered my weapon. What had to come next terrified me. Slowly I raised my head, forcing myself to look at what the creature had been rending, afraid of what I would see. I could feel my eyes widen as my stomach lurched, disbelieving my own senses.

Lying in the dirt, mutilated almost beyond recognition, were the shredded remains of Faith's . . . survival pack.

That's it. Faith was nowhere to be seen. Holstering my gun, I reached for my binoculars and surveyed the debris. There was no blood, no tracks leading away from that spot, nothing. She had never been here, had never come this way. It didn't make any sense; I had scoured the plateau and had found no other tracks leading away. Where could Faith have gone?

How could I be so blasted dense? Faith and Dr. Craighead had called it. A half-crippled supply officer had no business out here playing soldier, no matter how noble his intentions, or how well he had performed in that role in the past. Now my ineptitude had most likely cost us both our lives.

A whisper of sound was the only warning I had before a spine-jarring weight crashed into my back, slamming me to the ground. Claws raked across my backpack and needle teeth snapped centimeters from my cheek. It hadn't occurred to me that these things might hunt in pairs. Pulling my elbows under me, I managed to heave myself up just enough to allow room to draw my revolver, grunting with the effort. I reached across my body, thrusting the gun up beneath my left armpit until I felt the barrel strike the beast's flesh, and pumped my last two rounds into the creature's torso.

With a screeching wail, it reeled off me and writhed madly in the dirt, pawing at the wounds in its side. The wounds were not lethal; it wouldn't remain sidetracked by its injuries for long. There was no time to reload, so I did the next best thing: I ran.

As I dodged around the spur, I could hear the beast scrambling to its feet behind me. I knew I'd never make it across the ravine alive, not at the speed that thing could travel. I needed to find a defensible position. I scanned the cliff face beside me and spied a ledge about seven or eight meters up. The climb didn't look too difficult, which was good and bad—my pursuer looked to be a better climber than me. I could only hope that his wounds would hamper him enough to give me a fighting chance.

I almost made it. I had my elbows up on the ledge, pulling myself up, when I heard the creature scrabbling up the cliff wall below me, rapidly closing on my position. Bracing myself on my left elbow, I quickly drew the revolver, swung out the cylinder, and began loading it.

Claws tore into my calf above my boot, sending a searing pain up my leg. I screamed, striving against the urge to black out. I flipped the cylinder closed, pointed the revolver point blank at the creature's face, and pulled the trigger. Nothing happened. The cylinder had failed to lock in place; I knew I was dead. The beast's claws dug deeper into my flesh as it dragged me backward toward those ghoulish teeth, rising up for the kill.

A crack like a rifle shot rang out. The creature's head snapped back, blood spurting from its skull. A second shot blew a hole in its chest, and the creature toppled backward, careening from the cliff face and plunging to the ravine floor below.

I collapsed against the ledge, gasping from the burning slashes in my leg, teeth clenched against the pain. My eyes sought out my rescuer. At the top of the plateau, blonde hair streaming in the breeze against the deep blue sky, stood Faith, hunting rifle still at her shoulder, the look of an avenging angel on her face.

I blinked, not comprehending what I was seeing. Faith had been unarmed when she passed through the portal. Where did that rifle come from? A few seconds later, Izzo appeared at her side, pistol in hand, watching their backtrail. Then First Officer Kelleher stepped into view, hunting rifle held at the ready.

Even as darkness took me, a weak laugh escaped my lips at the irony of the situation. I had crossed the Einstein-Rosen bridge to an alien planet seeking Faith, to protect her until I could return her safely to the *Pathfinder*. But as it turned out, the guy who tried to be her erstwhile protector ended up being saved by Faith.

\* \* \* \*

Faith never was trapped on the planet. She made it to the bridge before it collapsed the first time. According to theory, if one were inside an E-R bridge when it collapsed, that person would be destroyed. However, from her perspective, the E-R bridge remained open until she got back to the ship. From our perspective, it had been down about an hour before Craighead's team re-established the connection. Apparently, we had passed each other in the anomaly without ever seeing one another. It was as if we traversed different tunnels between the two ends, or perhaps different "lanes" of the same tunnel. Faith said to toss it in the bucket of "quantum effects" along with the other oddities. She was sure they would figure them out in time.

I got all this from Izzo while I recovered in the ship's infirmary. He said Faith was just as incensed when she found out they let me go through to find her as I was when they allowed her to go alone. She had grabbed Izzo and dragged him along to the weapons locker, with Kelleher joining them along the way. Then Faith worked her magic and stabilized the bridge—though it had taken some time—and they came back for me. The rest is history.

She hadn't been down to visit me yet. They said the Chief Medical Officer wanted to check her over to make sure she was all right, and then she had to be debriefed, and after that they called her down to the lab to fine tune the bridge controls.

But I wasn't buying it. She didn't want to embarrass me; it was as simple as that. I made a fool of myself and had to be rescued by the very person I went to save. I figured I'd better get used to being the ship's resident laughingstock.

Having just shifted my ravaged leg into a less uncomfortable position and leaned back to rest, it came as somewhat of a surprise when Faith came breezing through the door, her smile lighting up the room.

"Hi, George!" She plopped down on the edge of my bed and gave me a quick hug. "How are you holding up?"

I shrugged. "Okay, I guess, considering the mess I made of things."

She looked at me as if I had three heads. "Are you kidding me? You're the talk of the ship!"

"I can only imagine," I grumbled.

She gave a sidewise glance and slowly shook her head. "No, I don't think you can. George, you're a hero."

I snorted. "Yeah, right. In case you missed it, you were the one who did the rescuing, not me."

Her shoulders slumped just a bit and a touch of sadness flickered across her features. She was clearly trying to make me feel better, and here I was acting like a jerk.

"In a way, maybe you did rescue me," she said, looking thoughtful. "You insisted—rather directly, according to Dr. Craighead—that they reopen the bridge right away, instead of waiting for Jacoby's team to arrive. If they had waited, if my end of the bridge had failed while I was still inside . . ." her voice trailed off.

She would have been gone. My mind didn't want to go there, not even hypothetically. Perhaps I had done some good, albeit inadvertently. "Maybe. I'm just glad you're safe."

And I was, more grateful than I could have imagined. Some of the tension drained away. I still felt like a dork, but Faith was safe and everything had worked out all right. It was time to stop grousing.

I decided to try a little levity. "Too bad no one recorded my escapades. Chasing shadows all over the landscape." I gave an exaggerated eye roll. "At least I proved a half-crippled storekeeper could track down a wild survival pack."

"Stop it! Just stop it!" Faith snapped, looking for all the world like a thundercloud getting ready to spit lightning at me. "You don't get it, do you?" A soft sigh escaped her lips. "You believed I was lost on that planet. Everyone believed I was lost. But you had the courage to come after me—and the skill to save me . . . if I had been there . . . you know what I mean."

She touched my hand, giving it a little caress. It was my numb one, but I didn't think this was the time to point that out. "You eluded the monster on the plateau. You climbed down a precipice and followed a trail you logically thought was mine." She pointed a warning finger at me when I started to cut in. "Shush. You confronted and killed a charging beast, physically battled a second one and scaled a cliff while being chased by a savage predator. If your gun hadn't jammed, you would have taken it out as well—even while it was mauling you."

Her eyes grew round and unfocused, her face turning white. I knew she was replaying that scene in her mind. I saw the same horror I felt when I thought she had been killed reflected in those beautiful eyes. Yet the same small hands that now trembled against mine had been steady and sure when she shot that creature off of me.

"Don't you see?" she said. "What you did down there, the rest of us could never have done." Sorrow clouded her features. "I should have let you go with me. No one could ask for a better protector. You're amazing."

To see yourself through someone else's eyes, the way they *really* see you . . . I didn't know what to say.

"George, you did things no one thought you could do, not even . . ." she hesitated, tears welling up in her eyes, "not even me." Her chin quivered. "I'm sorry, George. I'm so sorry."

I cupped her cheek in my hand; she hugged it to her. "I didn't think I could either. Until I had to." I smiled. "It's all right."

"No, it's not. You risked your life—you risked everything—to save me." She leaned closer. "You're *my* hero," she said, her voice barely above a whisper. A tear dripped from her lashes and splashed against my cheek.

Gently, I drew her face down to mine—and kissed her.

# *Shining Dagger*

## S. L. Rudder

Lieutenant Stafford had been standing at rigid attention before her Vlivlarian Captain's desk for the last ten minutes. The Captain was engrossed in something he was reading on his techpad, and appeared not to even notice her presence. As time went on, and the young lieutenant stood as if she were made from marble, a slight telltale flush could be seen near the Captain's ears. Outwardly, there was no indication that Stafford noticed. Inwardly, she was smiling with satisfaction.

Scuttlebutt had it that the captain liked to make the recruits from Earth sweat before he would inform them of why they had been called into his office. Like many Vlivlarians, he held a slight contempt for the upstart planet that had but only joined the Space League of Worlds less than thirty years ago. Normally, recruits from Earth were most impatient and, while not really prejudiced against any of his crew, seeing their distress seemed to give him pleasure.

The problem here was that Lieutenant Stafford was not a normal Earth recruit. While she listed Earth as her home, she was not human, she was Draknaroki. Even with the tentative trade agreement between the SLW and Draknaroke Prime, she was the only Draknaroki in the SLW. Her full name was Marlak'Muon Stafford, the adopted daughter of Colton and Marie Stafford. While on a scientific/exploration mission to a destroyed Draknaroki outpost, the couple had discovered her in a hidden stasis unit behind a concealed door inside a nearly demolished building, the only survivor of a mysterious attack on an agricultural research and development base. They were thrilled when they were allowed to adopt her, and they raised and loved her as their own child. Marie, a linguistic/cultural specialist, named her Marlak'Muon, which is Draknaroki for "small abandoned one." While applicable at the time it was given, the name did not seem to fit now.

Marlak'Muon stood six foot five inches tall, and possessed the athletic, muscular build of the Draknaroki. She was quite stunning with her dusky lavender/pink skin tone and her long, flowing violet/blue curls. Her "cat-eyes" were a rich amber with golden flecks around the slit pupil. The three rows of ridges that flowed from her nose back to her hairline just above her ears did not detract from her natural beauty, if her male classmates at the university were anything to judge by.

While she had been raised on Earth, genetics will tell. Marlak'Muon had the patience and discipline typical of her warrior race. The Captain could have kept her standing there for ten hours and she still would not have shown the least discomfort.

Seemingly, the Captain came to this conclusion as he laid the techpad on the desk and raised his eyes to meet those of the young lieutenant towering above him.

"Lieutenant Stafford," he addressed her, "I have here before me two reports pertaining to you. The first is from the chief medical officer. It is a request that you be reprimanded and possibly stripped of your rank. I am told that she has three current patients in her sick ward. All of whom are there because of injuries you caused."

The Captain paused for several seconds to see if perhaps this statement would bring some kind of a reaction from the young officer before him. Having this fail completely, he continued. "This is the third such report I have received from the chief medical officer during the two weeks since you joined the ship's crew!"

The Captain touched the techpad, changing the display. "This second report is from the head of security. It is a request to have you transferred from the Science Division to the Security Division. This too is the third such report I have received from this officer in this same amount of time." The Captain gave a slight shrug, the Vlivlarian equivalent of a human shaking his head in disbelief.

"I am told that the three patients the chief medical officer is so concerned about are all members of the security force, including the head of security, who requested you as a partner in training exercises. Please explain to me how you could injure and incapacitate three senior security officers not only all in the same day, but all during the same exercise."

Her eyes still locked with those of her Captain, Marlak'Muon answered, "I am sure the report is most complete. I participated in a hand-to-hand training exercise with the three security officers listed. Most unfortunately, all three were injured. If I have conducted myself in any way unbecoming to an officer of the Space League of Worlds, I am prepared to face my punishment."

The Vlivlarian Captain's eyes lit with approval at her reply. At least there was one recruit from Earth who could give a proper response.

"Be seated, Lieutenant Stafford." As she complied, he continued. "This report from the head of security states that he has approached you about changing your field of service on a number of occasions. His stated reasons are your excellence in hand-to-hand/melee fighting and also with any and all weapons that he has tested you with. Are you certain your choice to stay in the science/exploration division is sound based on these facts I have before me?"

"I am most certain, Captain. While I greatly enjoy the Security training, the field of Science is where my passion lies. Excelling in one area does not preclude ability in another."

"I quite agree. Both your scholastic records and service records bear out the fact that you are most qualified in your chosen field. I have reviewed your reports to your direct command officer. I have been most impressed with your work." Once again, the Captain changed the techpad display. "That is why the chief medical officer's report is so disturbing. She has suggested that a fitting punishment, if loss of rank is not to be considered, would be for me to cancel your solo mission to DOP001CE."

Marlak'Muon's jaw muscles gave a slight, uncontrollable twitch.

The Captain settled back into his chair, his face looking as pleased as possible for a Vlivlarian to have finally gained this small reaction.

"I see this mission is of some importance to you."

"Yes, Captain," was her only reply.

After a slight pause, as if waiting to see if he could obtain more of a reaction, the Captain leaned forward toward his junior officer. "You may rest assured that, based on the head of security's report and your service record to date, no reprimand or punishment will be meted out."

Marlak'Muon's jaws smoothed back to their standard appearance.

"In fact, we will reach DOP001CE in two hours' time. Return to your quarters, gather your equipment, and report to the shuttle loading area. Be prepared to launch at the prescribed time. Dismissed!"

The lieutenant rose gracefully from her chair, saluted, and left the office.

As the door slid silently closed, she leaned against the wall beside it and tried to slow her racing heart. If only her emotional responses were as easy to control as her physical ones. Taking a few deep, cleansing breaths, she made her way to her quarters to complete her preparations.

Marlak'Muon was in the loading area more than an hour before her departure time. Her two carrypacks and clothing module at her side, she kept her amber eyes glued to the techscreen waiting for the first view of DOP001CE.

DOP001CE stood for "Draknaroki Outpost 001 Completely Eradicated." This seemed like such a cold designation for the place one was born, but that was the

Vlivlarian system of naming for you. She often wondered what unknown titles she might have listed in her file other than the one she had worked so hard to earn. Speculation of this kind helped to pass the time when one had to deal with proper Vlivlarian scheduling. That, and doing mental inventories of her equipment and supplies. She knew this was also a futile waste. If there was one thing about the Vlivlarians that could be counted on it was their efficiency. The only way something would not be included was if she had forgotten it herself and she had triple-checked each of her lists—at least twice.

She had visited the Outpost with her parents many times while growing up. They made sure that even though she was raised on Earth, she knew who and what she was. This visit would be different though. At twenty-five, this would be the first time she was going by herself.

Having a cultural specialist for a mother had come in very handy for Marlak'Muon. She knew nearly as much about Draknaroki customs and practices as she would have if she had been born and raised on Draknaroke Prime. Now that she was twenty-five, she was ready for her KorBen'draok: Her coming of age ceremony. Tradition held this ceremony was to be completed on the planet of one's birth. In her case, this meant the *planetoid* of one's birth. She was going to perform her KorBen'draok during her two-week stay.

Not that anyone watching would notice, but Marlak'Muon was both eager and anxious to depart on her adventure. It was all that she could do not to jump and squeal with delight like a small child at the first sight of the rocky, teal planetoid. Her eyes did seem to glow more golden as she took in its moonlike appearance.

Despite seeming desolate and barren to so many, the small planetoid had always filled her with a warm and safe feeling. Not only was it the place of her birth, it was also where she gained the two most loving and caring parents any child of any race could ever want. It was through their encouragement that she requested this mission.

None of her fellow crew members understood why this mission meant so much to her, even though the two or three who could be counted as close friends offered to accompany her. Since her KorBen'draok was very personal and must be kept secret, she could not share with them the main reason for her excitement.

As with all their missions, the Vlivlarians had been very thorough on DOP001CE. Not only had they left a small security garrison in place, but every five years, follow-up scans had been made to see if anything new could be discovered that would point to the race that had destroyed the outpost. Nothing at all had been found since the initial mission when the infant Draknaroki had been rescued. The Staffords had accompanied each team sent to investigate, and Marlak'Muon had read every word written about the findings. It had been decided by the SLW that this, the twenty-fifth anniversary of the destruction, would be the final pass unless something of substance could be found. Lieutenant Stafford was nearly overwhelmed when her request to do a solo scan of the planetoid was granted.

Right on schedule, the shuttle delivered the Draknaroki officer to the security garrison. After checking in with Command and stowing her gear, Marlak'Muon took a slow hike around the perimeter of the destroyed base.

She had two weeks to scan and test anything she could find, as well as perform the KorBen'draok. Right now she just wanted to get reacquainted with the area in general. Each time she paused to gaze at the ruins around her, she could almost hear the explanations and stories that her parents told every time they had visited the outpost.

As she finished her hike back at the base, she thought to herself, "Today was just an overview. Tomorrow I will make a pilgrimage to the spot where I was found. Tonight . . ." she turned back toward the center of the destroyed outpost. Giving a wry smile and a small shake of her head, she headed to her quarters. "Tonight, I spend several useless hours attempting to get some sleep."

Much to her surprise, Marlak'Muon awoke when her alarm sounded shortly before "dawn." She had fallen asleep while once again going over Outpost reports. These were still streaming in a loop on her techpad. Turning the unit off, she quickly dressed and gathered up her hand-held techscan, techpad, and carrypacks and made her way outside the base and toward the center of the Outpost.

In all the years since the attack, nothing had changed. There was sparse vegetation growing outside the "burn zone" but nothing grew inside. The sight of the hydroponics buildings, flattened and barren, always caused her pain. The whole reason her biological parents had been stationed here, and why she had been born here, was because they were trying to find a way to grow food for the starving people of Draknaroke Prime. Upon making that discovery, the Vlivlarians, as head of the SLW, sent ambassadors with offers of relief to the suffering world.

Knowing the Draknaroki Code of Honor and their war-like tendencies, the delegation was pleasantly surprised to be received in a more or less friendly manner. Trade relations had improved a great deal since that first meeting, but the Draknaroki still refused to join the League. According to their honor code, to join would be a show of weakness. The trade of weapons and technology for food was profit. The one side benefit was the fact that much more information about the Draknaroki was available than had been before the destruction of the Outpost. As a result, Marlak'Muon knew much more about the race she was born into, including their language and customs, than her Earth parents ever dreamed possible.

When Marlak'Muon came within sight of the three-meter high standing corner of the ruins she was rescued from, she stopped to silently thank both sets of parents for preserving her life, then moved forward, eagerly anticipating the chance to explore it to her heart's content.

Everything was just as it was when the Staffords left it twenty-five years ago. Even though it had been repeatedly scanned over the years, nothing had changed.

The lieutenant smiled as she remembered her parents' accounts of that day. They differed in many points when told out of hearing of each other, but nevertheless, the ending was the same. She was saved, and they were a family.

She could see her father dashing across the broken floor, eager to get at the data bank they had discovered. Her mother calling to him to be careful, but not surprised when he did not listen. She could almost hear his grumbling voice as he talked to his equipment, trying to get it to interface with the strange Draknaroki technology, then her mother's triumph at being able to decipher some of the markings.

In her mind, she followed her mother down the half-hidden staircase to the basement below, and watched as she discovered the secret door and the hidden stasis chamber within. Knowing both parents well, she could replay the "discussions" they had on how to proceed upon finding her alive and well and waiting to be taken care of.

Coming out of her musing, Marlak'Muon made her way carefully down the crumbling staircase, through the "secret" door now standing open, and up to the side of the stasis unit. Her mother could never come to this place without getting emotional. She was not surprised to feel a tear make its way down her own cheek as she ran her hand over the open unit. For her, this was a testament to the unfailing love of not one but two mothers.

She took a seat on the floor facing the foot of the unit.

"Little bit, this is where we found you," spoke her father in her mind. "Right here, just waiting for us."

"That's right," her mother always agreed with a watery smile. "And if it wasn't for me, Little Bit would have been your name." Her parents would look at each other and laugh, shaking their heads. This was one point of her story that they always disagreed on. Each assured her that they were the one who determined that she should have a "real" name. Not that it really mattered that much what they had named her. They both still called her Little Bit more often than they called her Marlak'Muon.

Drifting back to the present, she reached for her carrypack and retrieved her techpad. Calling up the correct file, she turned her back to the stasis unit and leaned against it. Long ago her mother, Marie, had improved the program she used to translate the message they found in her bedding, and Marlak'Muon could speak Draknaroki as well as if she had been born on Draknaroke Prime. Nevertheless, they had always listened to the original translation on their visits here, and today she would do the same. Closing her eyes, she started the playback.

*"If you have find this talk, I dead. Care for small one I leave. My love/mate killed day past. Know not who. Fly over here. Beyond sight length. Take not small one to Draknaroke Prime. I give no name. Parents fail, small one be kill too. I place in . . . to save.*

*Please love her, as do I."*

Marlak'Muon ended the playback. She had not expected that hearing her mother's message here alone would affect her as it did. Hugging the techpad to her chest, she turned sideways and rested her tear-soaked cheek against the control panel on the foot of the unit.

"Dre'Ven!" she quietly sobbed out the Draknaroki word for mother.

There was a muffled click, then the control panel that Marlak'Muon was touching began to glow. The emotional lieutenant drew back away from the unit in surprise. She swiped at her eyes with the back of her hand, trying to clear away the tears and improve her vision. As she watched, a seemingly solid section to the right of the lighted panel opened and a lens extended from the hidden opening. There was a soft, internal whir and then a holographic figure appeared before her. The life-size image of a Draknaroki female did not move or speak. It appeared to be paused there, waiting for something, with a slight smile on her face.

48

Slowly, Marlak'Muon rose to her feet. She stared in disbelief at the image. How many times in the last twenty-five years had this chamber been probed and scanned? No hidden tech or moving parts had ever even been suspected. Yet, here before her was a holographic image being projected from the small stasis unit that had saved her life so long ago.

The clarity of the image was remarkable. Never had she seen a hologram whose quality even approached that of this image. It was so clear she almost felt like she could have reached out and touched it. Marlak'Muon stepped closer and examined the Draknaroki face before her. The skin tone was slightly darker than her own and the hair color more of a greyed violet, but for these two differences she could have been looking at an image of herself. There was one other difference. The face before her had only one row of ridges on each cheek. After years of study, Marie Stafford had discovered that the Draknaroki cheek ridges were genetically passed on to children from the father, not the mother. She had also found that the fewer in number, the higher an individual was in the genetic Draknaroki hierarchy. This was a female of the highest class of nobility on Draknaroke Prime.

Her eyes growing larger, Marlak'Muon realized there was only one explanation for this high Draknaroki female to have been here in the first place.

"Dre'Ven?" she whispered.

At the sound of her voice, the image before her came to life. Her heart seemed to swell within her as she heard the voice of her mother speaking to her in Draknaroki. With trembling hands, she started her techscan recording.

*"Small One. It is with great pride and sadness that I leave you this message. I do not know if you will ever even see this, but it comforts me here at the end to think of you listening to my final thoughts.*

*"These preservation units were brought here for just such an emergency as we are now facing. This is our third attempt at growing the food Draknaroke Prime needs so desperately. Each attempt has ended in the same manner, with ships traveling beyond the distance of our technology to detect bombarding us day after day until nothing is left.*

*"It had been hoped that our new protective field system would save us. It will not! To prepare for this circumstance, our commander, your Par'Ven [father], ordered these preservation units to be installed upon our arrival for the protection of the small ones. He had yours placed here in the main protective field system control tower in the hope that you will be safer than anywhere else in the compound. He sent us both here for our protection, but he returned to the command of our defenses. Your Par'Ven was killed this past morning defending our people with his life. I will soon leave you to lend what little help I can in our final defeat. How I hope he was correct, and you will be safe here hidden under this tower."*

Tears began running down the face of her mother's image, and Marlak'Muon's own tears began to flow once more.

*"This life-imager is programed to remain dormant and undetectable until twenty-five years after your birth. At that time, it can only be activated by a genetic sensor in the control plate reading your genetic code. Only your touch, proving you yet live, can bring me to your*

*sight. Only you speaking 'Dre'Ven,' showing that you have been raised Draknaroki, can bring me to 'life' before you. This was done to ensure that no one but you, my small one, could receive this, and then not until you are grown and ready to face your KorBen'draok.*

*"On the day of your birth, your Par'Ven prepared for your KorBen'draok just as he would have if we were on Draknaroki Prime. He was so filled with pride as he thought of you grown and beautiful following the path he laid. Here we have no mountains to scale or forests to conquer, but there are many craters scattered across this small rock. Some of these are nearly inaccessible. You will find a few of these differ in color from the surrounding soil. The cause of this is not important now. I mention it only to start you on the correct path to your KorBen'draok. Search for the one of deepest blue. It is here your Par'Ven prepared your path.*

A look of deep sorrow passed across the holographic face.

*"I long to speak your name, small one, and that of myself and my love/mate, your Par'Ven, but I dare not. Your identity must not be known until after your KorBen'draok is complete. When you have followed your path to the end, then you will be a full-fledged Draknaroki warrior and you can no longer be killed for the failings of your parents. This reason only could keep me from naming you now.*

*"When your KorBen'draok is complete, you will know all. Take great care my small one. The path before you will be hard, as is fitting a Draknaroki warrior. You will become a great warrior, and bring much pride to both myself and your Par'Ven. Through you, we will be vindicated and our failings will be no more.*

*"Good bye, my small one. Please know how much you are loved and cherished both now and into the Great Halls of our next meeting."*

Marlak'Muon forced a smile through her tears in answer to the sad smile on her mother's face. The image before her slowly faded from sight, and the young lieutenant switched off her techscan and took a few moments to pull herself together. Never in her wildest dreams had she imagined finding another message from her Dre'Ven. She hugged her techscan to her chest and sat in wonder, attempting to take in all she had learned.

From the time Marlak'Muon learned of the KorBen'draok from her mother Marie, she believed she would have to find her own path, as if her Par'Ven had died before her birth. Her heart swelled to learn that her Par'Ven had been there to prepare her path for her.

That evening in her quarters, Marlak'Muon rechecked her smaller carrypack to make sure she had all the things she would need for her KorBen'draok and nothing else. Since the KorBen'draok was a test of survival as much as a coming of age ceremony, the items she would include were few. There was no wildlife on the planetoid, so running into hostile animals was not a concern, therefore she would not need an energy weapon of any kind, even if it had been allowed, which it was not. She would carry the Draknaroki dagger that her father Colton gave her for her tenth birthday, just as her Par'Ven would have. Her mother had been sure she would kill herself with it, or at least cut off a finger or two, but she was happy to be proven wrong. Aside from a few slight cuts here and there, mainly from when she forgot the training she had gotten along with the dagger, were all she had received. Now she was an expert with its use, both as a weapon and as a tool. Also included was a small packet of Draknaroki "warrior" rations, two small bottles of water, and a mini techpad/compass. The last item in her carrypack was a poncho-type covering which could also be used as a blanket or tarp as needed. These few items were all that the KorBen'draok allowed a participant—no rope or climbing gear of any kind, no other weapons. As for clothing, a close-fitting jumpsuit, soft-soled shoes, and thin leather gloves completed her wardrobe for the upcoming  adventure. Marie had implored her to take an emergency medical kit, which was allowed but not encouraged, but she had refused. Even though she hated going against her mother's wishes, she wanted her experience to be as authentic as possible. The mini techpad had an emergency beacon, and she had promised her mother that she would keep it on the full emergency setting so that if she were unable to put in the correct code every six hours, it would automatically activate, signaling the garrison to come to her rescue. She was confident that she would not need it, but sometimes mothers needed reassurance.

After finishing her preparations, she went over all the charts and scans of the terrain that she had in her database. There were many blue craters, their depth and the changing strata seemed to be the main reason for this, but there was only one that was a truly deep blue. The surface scan indicated nothing there, but she knew that hidden in a crevasse or cave somewhere near the deepest point she would find her Par'Ven's KorBen'draok pack waiting for her. She gave up trying to plan out the best route, deciding she could not know anything for sure until she was on the ground and on her way. She knew the general direction she must move in, and had programed the coordinates and other essential data into the techpad/ compass. This device could not lead her to her ultimate goal, but it could tell her when she reached the most like- ly area and make sure that she did not stray too far off course.

Waking early the next morning, in spite of getting very little sleep, Marlak'Muon was outfitted and ready to go before first light. Dressed in her jumpsuit, her violet/ blue locks braided and tied out of her way, and her carry- pack securely on her back, she started out toward the cra- ter that was her final destination. Even though she knew it would most likely take her several days of walking and hard climbing to reach her goal, she had trouble keeping her pace down. In spite of the hard work she knew lay before her, she felt like a school kid on Christmas morn- ing when they saw the pony they had been asking for tied in the front lawn. Her excitement knew no bounds, and she had to call upon all of her training to stay at a reasonable speed.

After reaching the edge of the burn zone, this be- came less of a problem. The going became much more rocky and the strange vegetation more annoying. Noth- ing that grew on the planetoid was very tall, but all of it appeared to be very clingy. It seemed like some strange plant or another was constantly wrapping itself around the legs and lower torso of the young lieutenant. Each plant was stiff yet pliable, and most had thorns or barbs of some kind. The material of her jumpsuit was made to withstand almost anything, but unfortunately her skin was not. By the time she stopped for a midday break, she was already suffering from several nasty scratches. These caused more of an itch than any pain, but they were quite annoying, especially when her perspiration got into them. After eating a ration bar and taking a small drink, she checked her direction on the compass and was off again.

After an hour's time, she gained the first crater she would need to cross. The outer rim was like a micro mountain range, but caused her little trouble, seeing as it was only six or seven meters high. The inside of *this* crater was shallow and the walls sloped gradually down to the dish-like bottom. Marlak'Muon tried to keep from getting too encouraged by this fact. The bottom of this crater was no darker than the teal surface surrounding it. The deeper, bluer craters had all likelihood of being much tougher to descend and cross.

The rest of the day took Marlak'Muon through several similar craters and, much to her delight, fewer clumps of vegetation. Darkness was just falling as she decided to make camp for the night.

She was extremely glad for her poncho as the temperature dropped considerably as the evening lengthened. After finishing her ration bar, she worked her way into a sheltered depression, drawing her legs up and tucking the poncho securely around her. Surprisingly, she fell asleep quickly and woke refreshed and ready to go the next morning.

For two more days and nights the lieutenant faced much the same. Some craters increased in both color and depth, some were no worse than the first one she crossed. Other than having a hard bed at night and fighting the small patches of briar-like plants, she had not faced anything that caused her much difficulty at all.

The fourth day all that changed.

Checking her techpad/compass as she made ready to head out, she was surprised to find that she was farther off course than she had thought the night before.

"Skirting those smaller craters evidently turned me out of my way more than I thought," she said to herself. This problem would have to be corrected or she would miss the crater she was searching for entirely. Taking a reading once more, she clipped the techpad to the strap of her carrypack and started out.

Coming up out of the deepest crater she had crossed to this point, Marlak'Muon was happy to see that there was a large, flat area free of craters before her. She could see that the vegetation was much thicker here, but there appeared to be no way around it. She pulled out her dagger to help her clear a path. This worked very well, actually much better than expected. Where before she felt like the plants were trying to wrap around her as she moved, here they almost seemed to pull away as she cut off the larger branches that blocked her path. She gave a little shrug at this thought, then made her way forward toward her goal.

Midday found her only about halfway across the crater-free area. As she had gazed on the landscape that morning, she had planned on being well out of the plant growth before this. Having nowhere to sit in the close growing plants, she took what rest she could while standing to eat her ration bar.

Looking down at the bar in her hand with much less relish than the first day, she turned her eyes to the surrounding plants.

"Why couldn't these briars have raspberries on

them?" she mused aloud as she finished her last bite. "Guess with nothing here needing to be fed, it makes sense that there is no food growing anywhere. I sure would love some nice sweet berries right about now though."

Marlak'Muon barely noticed the fact that the ground was rising slightly as she made her way forward. The plant growth was taller here, and the need to cut her way through kept her eyes focused downward. She nearly stumbled as she finally broke through the last of the stubborn plants into a small, raised clearing atop a ridge just as the light was fading from the sky.

Before her, over the far edge of the ridge, stretched another band of plants more forbidding looking that the one she had just passed through, but not half as broad.

"Well at least I can lie down here," she thought as she looked around. "Not much in the way of cover. Lucky for me it seldom rains here."

No sooner had those words left her lips than she felt a drop of moisture hit her face. Looking upward, she could see the stars disappearing behind the growing cloud cover.

"Me and my big mouth!"

As the rain began falling faster and harder, Marlak'Muon struggled out of her carrypack and dug out her poncho, wishing all the time that she had packed a pop-up habitation like her mother had suggested.

"Stupid 'do it by the book' mentality," she said with a wry smile as she replaced the carrypack on her back and settled the poncho over her head, the wind and rain increasing every moment. "Who would even have known that I cheated anyway? Oh well, too late now."

Lightning shot with pink flashed across the sky overhead. Ice particles mixed in with the rain falling harder and harder.

"I am not even going to think that things can't get any worse," she thought just before the wind went roaring down the ridge she was on, nearly sweeping her off her feet.

"This is not the place to be right now." She made a futile search for cover. The only thing that offered any protection from the elements at all was the plant growth on either side of the ridge. Thinking that it is better the monster you know, she sat down in the opening she had just made in the plants behind her, and huddled down under the poncho to cover as much of herself as possible.

After a long, cold, sleepless night being buffeted by the storm, Marlak'Muon was glad to see the clouds breaking up as the sky grew brighter the next morning. The rain and wind died down as quickly as it had arisen the night before, and she crawled out of her burrow in the briars and stretched her tired, aching muscles. She carefully removed her dripping poncho and spread it over the low plants she had sought shelter underneath before carefully checking the rest of her equipment. She breathed an audible sigh of relief at finding everything intact and the techpad/compass in working order.

After going hungry the night before, she ate her morning ration bar with a renewed and more appreciative appetite.

"Funny how much better these things taste when you are really hungry," she grinned to herself as she took a reading in preparation for her day's trek.

"The great blue crater should be just past this next

band of plants," she said, pleased at the thought. "I *should* make it at least to the rim today." After checking the emergency setting on the techpad as she had each day before starting out, she clipped it back to her carrypack. "Here's hoping," she muttered, and crossed the ridge to take a closer look at the vegetation before her.

The plants here were in some ways similar to those she had encountered before, yet also strikingly different. This section of vegetation was nearly shoulder high, whereas none of the plants she had encountered before had even reached her waist. The thorns and barbs were also longer which corresponded with the plant's greater size, but the main difference was the coloring. She had come across vegetation of many varied colors on this quest, but all had been somewhat muted in shade. The plants before her were a vivid scarlet and appeared to almost glow in the growing light of dawn.

"Well," she thought, "as some ancient Earth warriors used to say, 'nothing to it, but to do it.'" And with a grim smile, she unsheathed her dagger and made ready to cut her way through the brush and undergrowth before her.

She did not have to use her knife for the first thirty meters or so, nearly halfway across the growth, much to her relief. The stems of these larger plants seemed to grow further apart than their smaller counterparts. Marlak'Muon reveled in this fact as she proceeded, not having to fall back onto using her dagger at all. A little bit of shifting and squeezing seemed to be all that was needed to make it through the red mass. Unfortunately, that ended after the first thirty meters.

She paused there to reset the six-hour alarm on her techpad, and as she started to move forward, the pseudo-path she had been following seemed to just close up in front of her.

"That's odd. Maybe I can retrace my steps a bit and see if I can find an easier way through."

She turned back only to find that there was no opening behind her either. In fact, as she looked around herself, she found that the only place with room to place her feet was exactly where she was standing.

"What is going on?" she questioned in disbelief as a glowing red briar jumped toward her like a striking reptile of some kind. She swiped at the plant with her dagger, trying to deflect it. There was no pulling away from her here as she had experienced with the plants in the earlier part of her adventure. As her blade struck the first one, a second vine-like briar leaped forward and grabbed her knife hand, the barbs deeply penetrating the skin where glove and jumpsuit did not quite meet. The lieutenant gasped in pain as she fought to free her wrist with her other hand. She finally succeeded, but with some very serious scratches and a few embedded thorns to show for it, nearly dropping her dagger in the process. As she stood there, cradling her injured wrist near her chest, she could hear a faint rustling noise coming from the scarlet plants surrounding her. Her vision was slightly blurred from the pain in her wrist and the perspiration running into her eyes, but it appeared as if the vegetation was closing in around her more tightly all the time.

The Draknaroki officer cast her eyes about in disbelief. None of the previous scans of the planetoid had indicated any sentient life-forms of any kind, but these plants were definitely reacting to her and her actions.

She raised her throbbing arm to try and alleviate its

swelling as she fumbled to slide her techscan out of the pocket on her carrypack.

"Focus, girl," she hissed between her clenched teeth as she started the device running a scan on the quivering mass of briars and thorns that surrounded her on all sides. Her eyes shifted back and forth from the reading on the screen to the plants around her. Since she had stopped moving and was no longer using her dagger on them, they seemed perfectly happy to just bide their time surrounding her.

Marlak'Muon took a deep breath and drew herself up to her full height just as the readings finished scrolling by.

"Okay," she murmured to the scarlet mass surrounding her, "so you aren't sentient. You just like my company and don't want me to leave." There was a slight, tentative smile on her face as she checked the compass readings to get her bearing. "Hate to disappoint you, but I don't like your company nearly as much as you seem to like mine. Let's see what I can do about that."

Returning both techscan and compass to their respective places, she faced the direction she needed to proceed, and attempted to move forward, keeping the hand holding her dagger well above her head. With difficulty she made it a few feet farther, then the plants began crowding in even closer, the barbs doing their best to hook into her jumpsuit. This slowed her progress, but unless forced to do so, she was not stopping or even pausing again until she reached the edge of this plant growth and freedom.

Each step became a fight to move forward. The vines wrapped around her legs and waist, pulling at her until she used nearly all her strength just trying to make a little headway.

After what seemed like days to the struggling lieutenant, she could finally see the edge of the clearing. She renewed her efforts, but so did the briars. Groups of the clinging, thorn-covered vines joined to wrap around her body, pulling her backwards toward the center of the growth. In desperation, she resorted to her dagger once more, using all of her failing strength to cut her way clear and break free. In a fury, the plants attacked her knife hand over and over until they had ripped through the material of her jumpsuit and nearly sliced her exposed arm to ribbons.

With a last desperate lunge forward, and a slicing cut at the briars wrapped around her lower body, Marlak'Muon broke free and rolled clear of the plants. She worked her way forward, crawling and pulling herself along with her uninjured arm, to put more distance between her and the trap she had just escaped. Finally, reaching the end of her limited strength, she collapsed onto the teal landscape and lay there gasping. Using her dagger, she cut the tattered sleeve off of her jumpsuit and using the sharp point was able to remove the few embedded thorns from her arm, but the pain was nearly blinding by then. The warning beep on her six-hour alarm sounded, causing her to jerk her drooping eyes open, and unable to think clearly, she switched it off just as she lost consciousness.

For two days, the Draknaroki lieutenant lay in a feverish stupor, never fully regaining her senses. She was fortunate that there were no life-forms on DOP001CE, as she would have been completely helpless and at their mercy.

As night fell on the second day, bringing a chill to

the air, Marlak'Muon roused to full wakefulness. She sat up and looked around in confusion. The fog cleared from her mind in an instant as her eyes fell on the dimly glowing edge of the scarlet band behind her. The battle she had fought to break free flashed through her memory and she scrambled backwards, further away from it, until she bumped into a large boulder in the growing darkness. Seeing this as a bulwark against the plants, she slipped around the far edge of it, never taking her eyes off the glowing red mass before her.

Unfortunately, this hoped for protection rested on the rim of the blue crater that she had been struggling for days to reach. The ground crumbled beneath her, and she slid and bounced down the near vertical drop toward the bottom of the deep basin. Luckily for her, the sides of the crater were crumbly and sand-like. After approximately nine and a half meters, it began to slope more outward and slowed her fall just before she reached a rock ledge protruding out from the wall. The Draknaroki caught herself as her legs and lower torso slid over the edge. After a few long, slow breaths, she pulled herself forward to what little security the ledge provided. She carefully gained a seated position with her back securely against the wall. Down inside of the crater, the darkness was more complete than up above. In the rapidly fading light, about all she could make out was that the area of the ledge she had landed on was big enough for her to safely rest there and wait for morning. Carefully, she braced herself against the wall, reclining as best she could. She passed a long and chilly night broken up by a few short catnaps as she anticipated the coming dawn, anxious to be able to get a look at what she was facing next.

As dawn broke over the rim of the crater, Marlak'Muon caught her breath at the sight before her eyes. The beauty of her surroundings almost made up for the bumps and bruises she had added to her scrapes and scratches. Her ledge was located about half way down the side of the crater and was crystal like in appearance. As she gazed across to the far side, she could make out the layers of the planetoid's strata. The changing colors were gradual yet vivid as the wall beyond her shaded from the light teal of the surface to a deep, rich cobalt blue of the depression's floor. All the way around the crater she could see other crystalline ledges and outcroppings. Each of these corresponded in color to the rock layer it was in. The increasing light brought the whole crater to life with sparkles and reflections from these crystals bouncing back and forth. As the sun slowly cleared the rim, there was a flash of light that was nearly unbearable. The young lieutenant covered her eyes with her arm and turned toward the wall behind her as she tried to shield her sight.

When she could sense the light decreasing, she turned back toward the depression. Blinking her watering eyes to try and clear away the purple blobs the preceding flash had left behind, she drew in a deep breath.

"Magnificent!" she murmured, awestruck by the sight.

The sun was shining through one of the crystalline ledges near the rim of the crater and being refracted from it to another one, beaming from crystal to crystal all around the perimeter and downward until the scintillating beam reached the very bottom, just a few meters from dead center, filling the crater with rainbow streams.

It took a few moments for her to fully take in the sight. She stared, nearly dumbfounded, then the scientist in her came alive. Pulling out her techscan she began quickly taking readings before the sun's position changed and the light show disappeared. While her equipment was working, Marlak'Muon simply gazed on in wonder, her eyes following the "rainbow" path. As her gaze reached the end of this beautiful pathway, she realized that the light was not being refracted or reflected in any way from the last crystal it had reached, embedded in the floor of the crater. Here the beam simply stopped.

Intrigued, she edged her way as close to the lip of her platform as was safe and leaned down to try and get a better look at the odd crystal that seemed to just drink in the beam. From her vantage point, it appeared to be the same as all the others, but the distance was much too great for her to trust her own sight.

Her techscan gave a soft beep, signaling that its work was complete. She moved back against the wall to study the readings just as the light pathways before her disappeared, as if a power switch had been cut as the sun continued to climb higher into the sky.

"Huh," she grunted, as she fumbled in her carrypack with her free hand and withdrew a ration bar. "Show's over." Her eyes dropped back to the scrolling screen as she absent-mindedly chewed on her breakfast, mumbling incoherent comments to herself as she made her way through the findings.

When she neared the end of the readings, she unconsciously leaned closer to the screen, anticipating the answer to why the last crystal in the pathway reacted differently.

"*Inconclusive data.*"

"Great! So what you are telling me is, your sensors are no better than my eyes." Marlak'Muon leaned back with an amused smile. "Guess I have spent too much time working with Dad. I talk to my equipment almost as much as he does."

The Draknaroki lieutenant ran through all of the data once more, just to double check the findings and see if there were some clue that would lead her on toward her KorBen'draok.

"Wait a minute!" She paused the data stream and brought the techscan unit closer to her face. "I was wrong. The rainbow path doesn't hit every crystal."

She scrambled to her feet, holding the unit to the side where she could compare the frozen image with the landscape in front of her.

"The refractions of light are not random."

The eager young officer transferred the selected data to her techpad/compass. She then boosted the techscan to its highest settings and took readings on two of the ledges closest to her, one that had refracted the light, and one that had not.

Her excitement grew as she compared the findings. The crystalline ledge that had refracted the light had been artificially altered. No difference could be seen by the naked eye, and her standard, preliminary scan had not picked anything up either. However, the high-intensity scan she had just run did show a difference. It appeared that the refractor crystal had been polished in some way to bend the light beam and direct it to the next crystal in the path.

There were two more of the refractor crystals within the

range of the high intensity scan. Marlak'Muon quickly ran checks on them with the same results.

"Looks like my 'rainbow path' truly is a path."

Quivering with expectation, she stowed her gear and replaced the carrypack on her back. Still holding the techpad up where she could see the display, she mentally traced the path down into the crater to its end on the mysterious crystalline boulder at the bottom.

"He really did prepare my path. Lucky thing that rock climbing has always been a passion of mine." Clipping the techpad to the strap after setting the compass to follow the rainbow path downward, she tossed a quick smile upward, into the morning sky. "Thank you, Par'Ven. May I be worthy of following the path you laid out for me."

Following the path seemed pretty daunting as she had viewed it in its entirety, but taking it one ledge at a time, while still strenuous and dangerous, was doable. Marlak'Muon carefully descended from ledge to ledge, searching to find toe- and finger-holds as she went. If a crevice was too thin to insert her fingers, she resorted to her dagger, either chipping away to make a better place to grasp, or inserting it and using it as a pivot to swing around to the next toe-hold or waiting ledge. None of this could be done quickly, and she had a few close calls as she worked her way downward toward the bottom of the crater, taking what rest she could on a few of the larger ledges.

Daylight was quickly fading and the Draknaroki feared she would have to spend another night clinging to a ledge. Shadows were growing deeper and deeper when she finally reached the floor of the crater. The light lasted longest in the center of the great depression, and it allowed her to stumble her way across the uneven bottom and find the "dark" crystal that was the final point on her "rainbow path" before complete darkness settled in.

Marlak'Muon looked up high above her to the darkening night sky. "Guess I will have to wait for morning to get a good look around down here," she said pulling out her techscan again. "But I don't need light to run a few data tests on you." She gave the "dark" crystal a smile, then started up the handheld unit.

Within minutes the "scan complete" beep sounded.

"*Inconclusive data.*"

"You have got to be kidding me!"

She checked the settings on her techscan and started it up again. Three times she tried this, and each time received the same message.

"*Inconclusive data.*"

Discouraged, she flopped down beside the boulder. "Morning it is then," she grumbled as she pulled out her poncho, threw it around her shoulders, and tried to get some sleep.

After a fitful night of constantly waking up and checking both the chronometer on her techpad and the skyline of the crater—not to mention trying to find a comfortable position to lie in—Marlak'Muon finally gave up about an hour before sunrise. She checked her equipment, making sure the techscan was ready to take readings when the "rainbow path" made its appearance. She wanted to compare the readings she had taken from the top with what she could get here at the bottom. She knew she should try and eat something, but anticipation sapped her appetite. Today was the day she should get some answers and complete her KorBen'draok. At least she hoped it would be.

At last her searching eyes were rewarded with the first blush of dawn. Once again, Marlak'Muon rechecked the techscan to make sure all of the settings were correct while she waited. Outwardly, she stood near the boulder patiently waiting for the rainbow path to make its appearance. Inwardly, she was pacing back and forth as if she was back on the drill squad at the University. Time had never passed this slowly for her in her lifetime, and the lieutenant was about ready to jump out of her skin.

Finally, the crystalline ledges started their sparkling light-show as the sun cleared the rim. Well remembering the blinding flash of the past morning, Marlak'Muon held the techscan up with one hand and used her arm to once again protect her tightly closed eyes. Even at that, the explosion of light caused her to see spots when she opened them. She blinked rapidly, glancing at the screen in her hand and then following the rainbow path as it made its way downward from ledge to ledge.

When it reached the boulder she was standing next to, it again seemed just to stop, but from her current position, she could see that the boulder was somehow soaking up the light beams that touched it.

"No, the light isn't touching it." She leaned down for a closer look just moments before the path was once more shut off. "The light was traveling around the boulder, but not touching the surface."

She placed her techscan on the ground next to her carrypack, hardly noticing the fact that it had signaled the end of its scan. Kneeling down and placing her face almost level with the ground, she took a closer look at the crystal. As she stared at it, she noted a disruption field of some kind mere millimeters above the surface of the boulder and what appeared to be a slight surge of some kind passing through it. She maintained her position long enough to notice this fluctuation happen twice more, at regular intervals, then fade out almost completely. She would have never noticed the field at all if she had not been staring at it so intently.

Returning to an upright position, she continued to gaze at the strange crystal a short time longer.

"Huh," she said, tipping her head to the side. "That's different."

She retrieved her techscan unit. "Let's see what you have to say about it now."

The fact that her legs were falling asleep from kneeling there so long barely registered as she studied the data before her. Most of the facts and figures matched up with the scan she had taken the previous morning. There were some details missing on this scan concerning the upper portion of the crater that had been included in the first. This was to be expected with the small size and limited range of the unit. On the other hand, the data for the lower section was much more complete, right up until it reached her "dark" crystal boulder.

*"Inconclusive data."*

"Yes, yes, you said that before, remember?" Her eyes returned to the puzzling crystal before her. Because of the anticipation of her KorBen'draok, she had put off doing a series of in-depth analysis scans on the stasis unit to find how the holo-emitter had remained undetected for so many years until her return. Now she wished she had completed those scans before starting out! If she had, she might have some data that would help her now.

"The warriors of the Draknaroki never look back," she quoted from one of the texts her mother, Marie, had found for her to study so many years ago. "Guess that means I start from where I am now. If modern technology can't find sufficient data to work with, looks like I am back to physical experimentation and examination."

From all outward appearances, her "dark" crystal was just the same as the many others that littered the floor of the crater. The young science officer took some readings on several of these, and the data corresponded to the reading she had taken on the ledges above. Except for the difference in color corresponding to their positions and the artificial polishing of those that were part of the path, every ledge and boulder she had scanned read the same. So why did her instruments come up with inconclusive and insufficient data when trying to read this one? She was determined to find out!

The visible top of the crystalline boulder was roughly the size of a small end table. It was oblong in shape, but the edges were far from being smooth and even. All this she discovered as she slowly walked around the perimeter, looking closely at it from every angle. The techscan was able to give her a reading on the size of the crystal, but the dimensions on the screen of the unit seemed to be slightly greater than she expected.

"Must be measuring that distortion field, whatever it is." She shut down the instrument, and returned it to her carrypack. "Guess it is time for a little 'hands-on' now."

This crystal appeared to be the end of her path, and

therefore should be safe for her to study, but she still took all standard precautions. Since her right-hand glove was in pretty bad shape, first from her battle through the briars and then the rock climbing that followed, she pulled on the left one.

Gingerly, she lowered her hand toward the surface, extending her index finger like a probe. When her finger reached the surface, from above it appeared to make contact with the crystal itself, but once again leaning down even with the top, she could see that her finger was actually several millimeters above the rock. She opened her hand, laying it flat on the crystal, and applied slight pressure. The texture she felt through her glove following this action was consistent to the object before her, but her palm was not in contact with it at all.

Fascinated, she looked around for something else to use as a probe. There was no plant-life here on the floor of the crater, and climbing up and facing that scarlet briar patch was not high on her list of wishes, so a stick of some kind was out of the question.

Marlak'Muon shifted her position to sit cross-legged and absent-mindedly tapped on her thigh. This action brought her hand in contact with the hilt of her dagger.

"Yes! This will do nicely!"

She drew the weapon and slowly poked the surface of the crystal with its point. It felt like the dagger was hitting the solid surface, but upon close inspection, she could see that it was not. She then struck the top of the boulder with the flat of the blade. The tone thus caused seemed much more muted than she had expected it to be. Leaning to the side, she struck one of the other close-by crystals. The tone from it was much louder and clearer.

The young scientist experimented on many of the nearby crystals, comparing the tones to the dark one's. While the size and shape of the boulders caused minute differences, they all had similar qualities, and none of them sounded like her mystery rock.

Next she struck the surface of the "normal" crystals with the dagger's edge. This move was rewarded with a shower of blue sparks. Repeating the same action on the "dark" crystal gained her nothing. The action felt the same when she struck the surface, but no sparks showed. Her cat-like pupils dilated in her excitement over each small finding.

The Draknaroki returned the dagger to its place and stripped off the glove she still wore on her left hand. Absent-mindedly pushing the remaining sleeve of her jumpsuit up to her elbow, she leaned forward and carefully reached toward the surface with her bare hand. It felt like all the other crystals she had touched right down to all the bumps and pointed edges. Slowly, she ran both hands back and forth over the boulder's surface, then in circles. The feel was correct, but close examination proved that she was still not touching the surface itself.

Rising up on her knees, she pressed down on the crystal leaning into it with the weight of her upper body. This action was rewarded with a minuscule tingle, much like static electricity, covering the palms of her hands.

"Aha!" she exclaimed as she jerked her hands away. "So there is some kind of power there. Not that I really doubted it. It is the only explanation possible."

She again laid her hands on the surface. Just as before, she felt nothing except the apparent surface of the boulder. By gently adding downward pressure the tingle returned. Deciding that she needed a closer look, she lay her cheek against the ground putting her line of sight even with the top edge and repeated the maneuver. From this vantage point she was able to detect a disturbance to the field and five hairlike lines that appeared to emanate somehow from inside the crystalline rock. These five "anchor-lines" were located roughly on the four corners and in the middle of the exposed surface of the crystal.

"Yes! Now we are getting somewhere." The lieutenant retrieved her techpad and entered her finding. The field and the five points that were seemingly its source resembled the set up of the protection field that had been in operation over the Outpost before its destruction. This fact reinforced the knowledge that she was dealing with technology her Par'Ven had put in place.

"All right, time to see if I can find out just how big you really are there, Rocky." Marlak'Muon shook her head with a lopsided smile. "I am sure doing Dad proud today. Guess I don't have to worry too much unless the objects start talking back."

Carefully, the young science officer began removing the soil around the outer edge of the exposed section of crystal. As she uncovered the entire upper surface she could see that the distortion field continued on down the sides and was actually holding the dirt away from the boulder. Intrigued by this discovery, she carefully enlarged the hole around the crystal to find that the boulder was only about a fourth as thick as the area of its exposed surface.

Inspection of the bottom of the crystal called for lifting it up from its resting place. She proceeded to do this with extreme caution, not knowing how the field would react to the added pressure. Once again the static tingle enveloped her hands, this time spreading up to her wrists causing the lacerations on the right one to burn slightly. Nothing else happened as she eased the boulder up and over the edge of the hole it had been embedded in.

The weight of the crystal surprised Marlak'Muon. As near as she could tell, it only weighed around twenty kilograms which was approximately a third less than any of the similarly- sized boulders she had scanned. Gently, she raised the near edge higher, tilting it slightly to enable her to get a look at the underside. This action brought another rush of excitement as she spotted what appeared to be a small metal plate located near the center.

She tipped the boulder up on edge and close scrutiny revealed another five-point anchor-line arrangement on the bottom that corresponded exactly to that of the upper surface. The metal plate appeared to be resting on the top of the field. Cautiously, she turned the boulder completely over, exposing the underside and the metal plate, and laid it down gently.

Relieved that this caused no untoward reactions, Marlak'Muon sat back on her heels and wiped previously unnoticed sweat from her brow with the back of her arm.

"Guess I am a little bit more tense than I thought," she said, rising to her feet. Slowly stretching out her cramped muscles, she looked skyward to verify the location of the sun. Surprised to find that it was midday, she retrieved both food and drink from her carrypack, and reclined against a nearby crystal to refresh herself.

Having finished her repast, she stared almost hypnotically at the smooth metal plate resting there on the exposed underside of the "dark" crystal. As time passed by, she let one theory follow another through her mind. She sat up with a start as she realized she had let her focus falter. She had allowed it to center on the boulder itself and its protective field to the point of nearly forgetting what it was a part of. This was the end of the path her Par'Ven had laid out for her KorBen'draok!

With renewed anticipation, the Draknaroki once again knelt next to the crystalline boulder. With thoughts of the genetic sensor in the stasis unit, she nearly held her breath as she placed her hand on the metal plate. With the slightest click, the crystal appeared to draw its surrounding field down into itself and the plate came to rest against the actual surface of the boulder.

Marlak'Muon gave a barely audible gasp as a section of the crystal opened up like the lid on a chest exposing what was hidden inside. There she found two items nestled in formed compartments. One was very familiar to her. It was a Draknaroki tech device almost identical to the one that had been in her bedding all those years ago. This unit was slightly thicker and, if her recollections were correct, slightly heavier. The other object was long and thin, wrapped in a cloth of some kind, concealing its identity.

With great care, the Draknaroki officer lifted the tech device out of its resting place and placed it on the flat top of a nearby boulder. Next she gingerly removed the other object. One corner of the protective cloth came loose as she was moving it to the boulder and peaked her curiosity. Gently she unwound the cloth to reveal what appeared to be a carrying harness and a weapon fashioned from Draknaroki blue-steel. The middle section of this was a leather wrapped, two-hand grip with about ten centimeters of exposed metal on each side. Both ends had blade points extending from them, one approximately thirty centimeters long and the opposite one about half that. Both blades were double-edged and extremely sharp.

Marlak'Muon turned the weapon carefully in her hands examining it, then placed it and the harness next to the tech device. Taking a moment to calm herself, she then reached forward and placed her hand on the recessed panel at one end of the tech device.

There was a slight click, the control panel began to glow, a solid section to the right of it opened, a lense extended, and with a minuscule internal whir, a holographic figure appeared before her eyes.

The lieutenant's anticipation was rewarded as the figure that appeared before her this time was a male Draknaroki warrior. The warrior's face was strong with chiseled features and a proud, yet caring mein. Marlak'Muon raised her finger and traced the three rows of ridges through the air from the nose to the hairline of the face before her, exactly like her own just as she knew they would be. The warrior before her stood close to seven feet tall with broad shoulders, a deep chest, and strong, muscular arms and legs. His coloring was very close to her own, with his skin a shade or two darker and his hair slightly lighter. His bearing was exactly what she had expected, knowing that every Draknaroki officer was a warrior first and foremost, no matter what their chosen field might be. Being the Commander of the base would have only reinforced this fact.

After several minutes of just gazing on this image

of her father, Marlak'Muon reached for her techscan unit, keyed it on to record, then spoke one word.

"Par'Ven!"

The image before her came to life and with lopsided smile and pride in his eyes, her Par'Ven began to speak.

*"Parak'Kravor, my small one, today I am filled with pride, for I have completed the path that will someday conclude your KorBen'draok."*

Parak'Kravor, shining dagger, her real name after all these years.

*"It is most fitting that your path is the first of the many to be prepared here. The small one of Commander Kravor'terak* [Dagger's edge] *and Botanist Chief Parak'Muon* [Shining one] *should by rights be the first to complete her KorBen'draok on this small world.*

*"It is a time of great pride for your Dre'Ven and myself, this time of your birth, but it is also a time of sadness, especially for my love/mate Parak'Muon. She had always dreamed of the birth of our small ones taking place in the Fortress on Draknaroke Prime, like all your ancestors before you. But sadly, this was not to be.*

*"The Par'Ven of your Dre'Ven was the Extreme Commander of all Draknaroke, but his early, and un-explained, death left his younger brother in control as acting Extreme Commander. Your Dre'Ven could not reign as Extreme Commander until after she finished her KorBen'draok, we had been joined as love/mates, and had returned to the Fortress following our "love/mate wanderings" as Draknaroki law decreed. The acting Extreme Commander would hold power only until this was accomplished. We returned to find that her power had been wrested from her during the time that we were*

*away. The Draknaroki have a law which states that a female heir may not reign in her Par'Ven's stead if she marries a member of any but the highest class. The exception to this is if the Extreme Commander puts forth a proclamation raising the chosen love/mate of lower class to the highest level and thus declaring their joining to be his desire and to have his blessing. Parak'Muon knew her Par'Ven had readied such a proclamation, but he departed to the Great Halls before he could make the formal announcement in the War Hall on Draknaroki Prime before the Council of Warriors. The acting Extreme Commander was to have made this proclamation to the Council in his stead during our time of mourning and grief. We had been led to believe that he had done this and after that period had ended, we were joined.*

*"He had not! We had been deceived!*

*"The members of the Council of Warriors were aghast when this was brought to light. Nothing could be done to right this wrong since our joining had already been accomplished without the proclamation, short of declaring war against the Extreme Commander himself. This step would have pitted those on the Council who had all sworn their oaths to protect the Extreme Commander against those who had not yet taken their oaths and were still sworn to protect your Dre'Ven's house. Ultimately, the entire Draknaroki Empire would have been torn in two, and unless we were victorious we would have been labeled as traitors and both of our houses totally destroyed.*

*"Well I wanted to fight for my love/mate and restore to her her rightful place."*

Sadness crossed the face before her, but was replaced with a look of resigned contentment.

*"Your Dre'Ven is far wiser than I. Choosing not to cause added turmoil to her people who were already in a battle for their lives and facing near starvation, Parak'Muon went before the Council and renounced her claim to the throne on promise that the new Extreme Commander would do all in his power to provide for the people. This he did gladly.*

*"In spite of how he took the throne, he has proven himself a good leader and has never ceased striving to protect and sustain the Draknaroki. It was in fulfillment of his promise that I was appointed Commander of this the third attempt at saving our people. It is our greatest hope that we succeed and that soon all of the Draknaroki people will be well fed and thrive."*

The holo-image before her paused slightly and gave a small shake of his head as if clearing away past regrets, then began to speak to her once more.

*"But now to complete your KorBen'draok, my Parak'Kravor. The weapon before you is your trakon'Draok [warrior's sword]. By traditions each Par'Ven fashions the trakon'Draok for his small one according to his wishes and abilities. Because of this, individual trakons vary greatly. It is your great fortune to have an Engineer Chief for your Par'Ven. Never before has a Warrior possessed a trakon'Draok such as the one you have now earned the right to bear.*

The lop-sided smile of pride again lit the face before her.

*"Pick up your trakon'Draok and hold it out before you, longer blade pointing upwards, and right hand above the left. Now give it a hard twist to the right."*

The holo-image before her demonstrated this exercise

then paused long enough for her to accomplish it. There was a solid click and the sound of sliding metal as both blade points instantly extended to twice their beginning length.

*"Now, twist in the opposite direction."*

She again copied his movements, and with a nearly inaudible hum, a deep blue field quickly rippled down each blade, then became nearly undetectable, just as the field on the crystalline boulder had been.

*"What you now hold in your hand is* MY *version of the trakon'Draok. The field that encases the blades adds to their strength immeasurably while not interfering with the cutting edges in the least. Your trakon'Draok is nearly indestructible and the most powerful of its kind. To disengage the field and retract the blades simply slide your hands to the metal shaft past the wrappings. The genetic code readers will deactivate the mechanism so that this can not be done accidentally."*

Marlak'Muon did this, and the field shut down and the blades retracted back to their starting position.

*"Your trakon'Draok may be used in battle in any of the three stages. The harness is fashioned to allow a quick release so that the trakon will be ready to hand at a moment's notice.*

*"Now, my small one, to complete the ceremony which will make you a full Warrior of the Draknaroki. Return your trakon to its harness, watch and do as I do."*

The image of her Par'Ven turned to face the location of Draknaroke Prime in space. Solemnly, he saluted his home world by forcefully crossing his clenched fist across his chest and bowing his head. Next, he removed his own trakon'Draok from its place on his back, raising it with his right hand and extending it toward Draknaroke Prime with the larger blade upward. He then carefully and slowly made a thin cut across his left palm with the upper blade. Next, he transferred the weapon to his left hand, reversing it to have the smaller blade on top and repeated his actions this time cutting his right palm with the shorter blade. He again reversed the weapon, and held it out before himself in a two-handed battle grip.

Marlak'Muon followed her Par'Ven through each step of the ceremony in total silence. She then repeated the ancient *Pledge of the Warrior* along with him at its conclusion.

*"By the blood on my hands and the blood on my sword I will defend my people from every danger, whether from without or within, until the blood in my heart is spent."*

Both Draknaroki, father and daughter, bowed their heads in a moment of respectful silence. Then for the first time a full-blown smile lit the face of the holo-image before her.

*"I am filled with such pride to know that you have now completed your KorBen'draok, Parak'Kravor. Parak'Muon and I welcomed you to this world on the day of your birth with more happiness than you can know until you have a small one of your own. Now you are a full Warrior of the mightiest race of Warriors. Please know that your Dre'Ven and I will be watching over you and guiding you as you follow your path to the end of time, whether it be by your side or from the Great Halls of our next meeting.*

*"Parak'Kravor, you have completed your KorBen'draok, but both now and forever we will love you, and you will remain my Small One."*

Tears were forming in the proud eyes of Kravor'terak as the holo-image froze at the end of the recorded message.

Marlak'Muon hugged her trakon'Draok to her chest as she slowly sank at the feet of her Par'Ven, tears streaming down her face unheeded.

Just then the six hour alarm sounded on her techpad. The lieutenant reached for the unit and reset it with a watery smile on her face. Here she sat between two reminders of the fact that she was loved by two very different sets of parents. Both of which had always done everything within their power to care for her.

"Well," she spoke her thoughts once more. "Marlak'Muon Stafford or Parak'Kravor daughter of Kravor'terak, Little Bit or Small One, scientist or warrior, I will always be caught between two very different worlds. It is certainly good to know that I am loved enough to get me through both."

## Children of the Stars

C. K. Deatherage

**P**eter! I sit up, shaking, sweat soaking my clothes. My stomach roils, and I swallow the bitter juices in my mouth. I quickly survey the bunkroom, desperately hoping I had not spoken out loud in my sleep. No one stirs. I lie down again, willing myself to forget. To wipe the memory from my mind as I was commanded to do. As we all were commanded.

But the images keep coming, the memories. Peter, my friend and fellow Apprentice. Like me, he too was training to be a Preserver. Like me, he too was fascinated by our heritage, how our Community came to be, why we are who we are—our history, our customs, our laws. And like me, he too felt there must be something *more*. Something *beyond* what we are and what we have been. We loved our past, but we hoped for our future. Peter had hoped a little too much. He had *Invented*.

It was a small thing. A model of a machine, just the

size of a loaf of bread, that could harvest wheat and other grains much faster than hands could pick or scythes could cut. It was beautiful, made of bits of scrap metal he had scavenged from the smithy. Miniature bars and gears and blades, all polished and crafted to work in harmony, turned by a tiny handcrank. A working version would have been as large as an ox. Maybe larger. Peter's model was just a toy, really. A wish. A proposal. But the Elders had not seen it that way. To them it was poison, a contradiction to our laws. It was Technology, the bane of humanity.

I try to stop the images, but they play on. Tears tingle against my eyelids and my throat tightens as once again I hear the Judgment. Peter was Banished. His name would be stricken from the Records, never to be spoken again. His life would be forgotten. He would become as one who was never born. His parents wept at the Judgment, the last time they would be allowed to weep for their lost son.

I turn over on my bunk, pulling my woolen blanket up to my ears, willing myself just to forget and sleep. But Peter's pale face keeps floating before my eyes. He had accepted his Judgment quietly. The Elders asked which he chose—the Wood or the Arrow. Only one man in my 17 years had ever chosen the Wood for Banishment. That was Samuel Crabtree. He was a wild man, mean to his family and a scourge on the town. He had been Warned three times to change his behavior, but he merely laughed. In a fit of anger, he burned his neighbor's cornfield, and he was sentenced to Banishment. He chose the Wood, so they branded his forehead as a warning to other Communities not to accept him. Then a group of Hunters led him blindfolded and bound into the Wood and left him there, without knife, axe, bow, or provisions. He never returned, but rumor has it that Samuel Crabtree (though his name is never spoken) runs naked with the wulver and eats his prey raw.

I shudder. Peter, gentle blond-haired, green-eyed Peter, was nothing like Samuel Crabtree. We all knew he would never survive in the Woods. He knew it too. He chose the Arrow. I twist the blanket in my fists. I don't want to remember. I'm not supposed to remember, but the memories come: the hood fitted over Peter's pale face; the five Hunters, lined in a row, black bands tied to each arm, each carefully fitting a black arrow to his bow, the tips of which were made of finely polished metal, honed to the sharpest point and edge. The arrows are designed to kill quickly and mercifully. I had closed my eyes. I couldn't bear to watch my friend die, but I heard the twang of the strings and the thunk as each arrow found its mark. I heard his body fall to the ground. Then the Chief Elder spoke.

"This was Peter Thrushollow. He is no more. He never was."

My voice was hoarse as I and all the Community echoed the words.

The Chief Elder continued. "Never again shall the name Peter Thrushollow be spoken or thought. He is no more. He never was."

"He is no more. He never was," the Community responded. We all turned our backs on the scene of execution and trudged back to the village. The Hunters, we knew, would gather up Peter's body and carry it into the Woods for it to be devoured by wulver and scavengers.

All of his meager possessions were burnt. Peter is no more. He never was.

Except in my mind. Peter was Banished over two months ago, yet he invades my dreams almost nightly. I wonder if anyone else in the Community suffers as I do. If they do, they do not speak of it. To do so would mean Banishment. So I keep my thoughts and dreams to myself and pray I do not speak Peter's name aloud in my sleep.

The morning light finally shines through the unshuttered windows, and memories of Peter fade as the day begins. Dust motes dance in the beams as we each fling off our blankets and don our Apprentice uniforms. Mine, the uniform of a Senior Apprentice Preserver, is dark blue edged in silver. When I become a full guild member, the silver will change to gold. The air fairly pulses with our excitement, for today we will receive our assignments for the Great Centennial. As I step through the rough-hewn doorframe of our bunkhouse, the smell of fresh-cut wood, smoke fires, meat sizzling, porridge bubbling, and tea brewing pleasantly overwhelms my sense of smell. But it is the glorious pageant filling my vision that takes my breath away as it has done for nearly three weeks.

Nestled everywhere in our small valley, between cabins and barns, in the town square, between the newly built Delegate bunkhouses and the Grand Hall, even on the greensward of the Community Courthouse, are tents and pavilions of all hues and colors, shapes and sizes and patterns. Delegates from Communities all over the world, some traveling for two or three years by ship and horse and on foot, have gathered for the Great Centennial. One hundred years ago at the last Centennial, the Northwestern Continent was chosen for the next Site. Then lots were drawn from the Northwestern Regions for the privilege of hosting the event. Our Region won, and among the Communities, our village was the largest, so we became the Center for the Centennial.

I shake my head, marveling at the complexity and beauty of it all. Three years ago, we began clearing land and felling trees to build the Delegate Bunkhouses, Grand Hall, and the barns and corrals for the travel and pack animals. Then in this past year alone, volunteers from all across the Northwestern Continent arrived in batches to help with the construction, to hunt and cure extra game, and to supply more grains and fruit and vegetables than our valley alone could produce. The Delegates who arrived in our Community would need to be fed not only for the days of their stay, but to be supplied for their long trips home. Others brought cloth and gifts for foreign dignitaries. It was hard labor but the honor to our Continent, our Region, and our Community is great. I take in every detail of it, every aroma, every sound, every sight, that I might preserve it in our oral Records. Our great-grandchildren will still be speaking of it when the next Centennial occurs.

"Thomas! Thomas Longbough—hurry! The Elders are almost ready to give us our Assignments!" Almar, the Senior Woodsmith Apprentice, waves at me from the bottom of our bunkhouse hill. I nod and wave back, jogging down the hill to join him in worming between bodies and lodgings to reach the Community Courthouse. Though it had been planned for 100 years, I still find the transformation of our small village of 2,500 to a Center for over 10,000 Delegates and their officers a marvel.

When the Delegates began arriving three weeks ago, I had never seen our village in such an excited tizzy. Now that everyone is here, the excitement hangs above the valley like a cloud bouncing on a joyous wind.

Almar and I take our seats with the other Senior Apprentices toward the front of the hall. I find myself clenching my fists, waiting for the meeting to begin. Only for a moment does a shadow cross my thoughts as I wish Peter could have been here to share it all. I immediately push the idea from my mind and focus on Chief Elder Applethwaite. He's nearly 92, almost old enough to have seen the previous Centennial. He rises slowly, and we stand in respect. His hair is white, his eyes a rheumy blue, his hands shake as he raises them, but his voice is as firm as a thirty-year-old's.

"Apprentices of Pinebrook, welcome! You have been indispensable to the efforts of this Great Centennial celebration. Tomorrow will begin the official festivities, Presentations of the Regions and Communities, and the Ordinances by the Delegates. There are over 80 Regions and 3,102 Communities represented here. I want you to mingle with the Delegates and their parties, offering your services where needed. Make everyone welcome. Now, Elder Thornburne will give you your Assignments."

There are over 40 of us, and the Elder begins with the lowest-ranking Apprentices, who receive more menial duties, such as keeping the grounds free of trash and animal refuse. Next come the Junior Apprentices. They are assigned the honor of running messages between various Elders and Delegates. Finally, we Senior Apprentices are called. I find myself holding my breath as my fellows are one by one given their Assignments. Most of us are to act as personal pages for the highest-ranking Delegates. I say *most of us*—my breath gives out long before my Assignment is named. That's because it never is. I am left standing alone as the Apprentices file out of the Courthouse. Almar throws me a concerned look as he sidles out of the row of benches and walks slowly down the long aisle to the open double doors. Since Peter's Banishment, Almar has become my best friend.

Elder Thornburne remains behind the podium, his dark eyes made darker by the huge bushy black brows above them. I swallow and try to breathe calmly, but my mind is racing, trying to think of anything I had done wrong to deserve Exclusion—or worse. Had I whispered Peter's name in my sleep? I shudder and look down at the rough wooden bench in front of me. Then he speaks.

"Apprentice Thomas Longbough."

"Yes, Elder." I flinch as my voice cracks.

"You may not have heard, but Preserver Wordsmith injured himself yesterday rather badly." I must have looked startled, for Elder Thornburne waves one hand. "The Healer has assured us that he will recover, but that leaves you as the Senior Apprentice to deliver the Remembrance two days hence. Do you think you can do this?"

I blink. "I—me?"

"You are the Senior Apprentice, are you not? In a few years, you will become a Village Preserver. You must be ready to stand in when needed, and you are needed now. Can you do this?"

My hands shake, so I clasp them behind my back. I nod, finding my voice. "Yes, Elder Thornburne, I can do this."

The Elder smiles and nods. His rugged, black-bearded

features look almost friendly. "I knew you could. We've had our eye on you, young Longbough. Preserver Wordsmith believes you will make an excellent Preserver. This is a great honor. Treasure it well."

He walks away, still smiling, and I stand a few moments letting his words sink in. My knees are quivering, my stomach in knots. I am both ecstatic and terrified. Me, Thomas Martin Longbough, an orphan and fosterling and nobody of particular standing—*I* am to deliver the Remembrance for the Great Centennial! I will be the first Senior Apprentice ever to do so. My thoughts still dazed, I meander out of the Courthouse and down into the maze of tents and pavilions.

Almar leaps at me from behind a bright red and gold canopy. "Well? What happened? Are you all right?"

I lick my lips. Then I reckon my face nearly splits in half with the grin I give him. "Preserver Wordsmith is unable to give the Remembrance, so as the Senior Apprentice, I am to do so."

"No! You? Woohee!" He slaps me on the shoulder. "Man, wait till the others hear this! Has an Apprentice ever given the Remembrance before?"

I shake my head. "None are mentioned in the oral Records of the past 1000 years."

"You scared?"

"*Terrified* doesn't quite do it justice."

Almar grins. "You're the best Apprentice Preserver in the Region. I heard Elder Hinckleberry say so. You've got almost all the oral Records memorized, and—what did he say? Oh yeah, your *presentation skills are impressive*. You'll do great. People will be talking about it for the next 100 years!"

"Only 100?"

Almar cuffs my head. I duck, but his fingers skim through my hair. We both stand there grinning. He shrugs. "Well, I have to find Delegate Shemar from the Middle Eastern Regions. I'm his page." He turns to leave, then gives me a teasing glare over his shoulder. "Don't get a swelled head over this. You're still only an Apprentice, you know."

I let my eyes follow Almar's brown, silver-trimmed Woodsmith's uniform as he dashes between tents and tarps, almost being spit on by a camel–a tell-tale sign he was nearing the Middle Eastern Region's campsite. As I turn, planning to visit Preserver Wordsmith in the infirmary, a flash of gray catches my attention. Apprentice Johnny Brackenridge dashes up to me, his blond hair tousled by his run, his face flushed, his smoky gray Scout uniform, two sizes too large, all askew. His blue eyes fairly bulge with excitement as he grabs my arm and says, "Thomas, have you heard?"

"Heard what?" I could think of nothing more exciting than my own Assignment.

Johnny takes a few deep breaths before spurting out, "Delegates from a Lost Community have arrived!"

I blink, stunned. Rumors have always abounded of Lost Communities, separated and hidden in the furthest reaches of the world–but to have a Delegation from one actually show up at the Great Centennial—well, there is no record of it having *ever* occurred! Lost Communities are fairytales, stories to tell at Hunting camps while lying out beneath the stars. Or so I had thought. So we all had thought.

"What . . . what do they look like?"

Johnny waves his hands as he speaks. "They are tall and of various Races. One, who seems to be their Elder, has red hair with white streaks. He is pale-skinned like us, and his eyes are blue. But another is dark with short, tight, curly hair—like the Delegates from the Middle Continent. A third has reddish-brown skin, black hair, and brown eyes like those from the Southwestern Continent. And a fourth has the yellowish skin and black hair with the narrowed eyes of those from the Far Eastern Regions. Yet they all wear the same uniform—a silky black jumpsuit with silver-white trim. Their boots and belts are black and polished. How can one Community contain so many Races?"

I am worried. "I don't know, Johnny, but did you see . . . did they have any . . ." I pause, hardly daring to say the word. "Technology?"

The young Apprentice Scout shakes his head. "Not that I could see. They carry bows and knives. The dark one has a spear. The arrow tips and spearhead are of some blue-black metal, but that's the only metal I saw on them. Well—except for their belt buckles. They are shaped like silver circles with shaded patterns in them, almost like tiny sculptures of the moon."

I relax a little. The Ordinances for making and carrying forbidden weapons are severe--though I wonder if grace would be extended to a Lost Community unfamiliar with the Ordinances passed each Centennial. Thankfully, this group of Delegates doesn't seem to have anything forbidden. Then I shake my head and grin, clapping one hand on Johnny's shoulder. "Your Scouting skills are quite good, Brackenridge. You'll be moving up to Junior rank quite soon, I bet."

Johnny grins. "I gotta tell the others. See you at the bunkhouse, Thomas!" He turns and dashes into the mulling crowd.

I continue on to the infirmary, my thoughts whirling with the honor and responsibility of my own Assignment and the wonder of Delegates from a Lost Community. It is almost too much for my mind to handle.

I swallow when I see Preserver Wordsmith lying in the infirmary bed. His pale face is covered in scratches, and his left arm is bandaged heavily, but it is his right leg that looks the worst. Wooden splints run along either side, and strips of cloth hold the splints in place. His bare toes look blue. I feel my stomach clench at his pain. The Preserver is my mentor and the closest thing to a father to me since I was orphaned at five.

"Preserver?" My voice is scarcely above a whisper as I near his bed.

He opens his eyes and holds out his right hand, which I clasp in both of mine. "Ah, Longbough! How refreshing it is to see you!" His voice is raspy, but his eyes are bright. He waves his left hand toward his leg. "As you can see, I took a rather nasty tumble from the roof of a stable we were finishing up. I landed in a pile of broken lumber–which did not set well with my body, I'm afraid." He cocks his head and smiles. "Are you ready to give the Remembrance?"

"I—yes," I answer. "I know the stories. You are a good teacher."

"Good, good." He closes his eyes for a moment.

And I clear my voice. "Preserver, do you know anything about Lost Communities?"

His eyes pop open, startled. "Why do you ask?"

"Delegates from a Lost Community have arrived today." I repeat Johnny's description word-for-word, a skill necessary to be a Preserver.

Preserver Wordsmith closes his eyes again and is silent for a long time. I begin to think he has fallen asleep. Then he opens his eyes and points to a chair opposite his bed. His blue, gold-trimmed uniform lies draped over it. "Take my uniform and put it on."

I blink, but do as he says, first stripping off my Senior Apprentice clothes, then pulling on his outfit. It is a little big, the legs bunching around my ankles and the sleeves coming down to the middle of my hands. I look at him as he nods approvingly. "Now stand by me and place your right hand over your heart."

My heart begins to pound and my hands tremble as I obey. The Preserver raises his own right hand and fixes me with a steady gaze. "Do you, Thomas Longbough, swear to abide by the code of the Preserver, uphold the histories of our Community, Region, Continent, and to the best of your knowledge, of other World Communities?"

I lick my lips and whisper, "I do."

He nods. "Then by the authority of the Preservation Guild, I, Donald Riken Wordsmith, do admit with full rank and privileges one Thomas Martin Longbough to the position of Village Preserver." He smiles. "Welcome, Preserver."

"I-I don't understand, sir." My initiation into the Guild was not supposed to be for two more years.

"What I am about to tell you is Hidden Knowledge, Thomas. Only those of the Preservation Guild hold this knowledge, and it is to be revealed to the people only in extreme necessity." He pauses as if pondering his decision. Then faintly, almost too low to hear, he says, "These strangers have been here before."

My mouth goes dry, and I feel a strange weakness pass through my body. I don't know if it's fear or excitement–or both. The Preserver continues.

"Each Centennial, for the past 900 years, they have come, offering to share their knowledge, their help, and, yes, their Technology with us." He sighs, then adds, "And each Centennial, the Elders and Delegates have Banished them, erasing even the memory of their visit from the history and minds of the people."

The Preserver's eyes seem distant as he pauses, staring past me to something only he can see. Then with a sudden sharpness, he fixes his gaze on me. "At the last Centennial it was decided by the leaders of the Preservation Guild that should the strangers appear once again at the Great Centennial, the 1000-year celebration of our recorded history, the Remembrancer would tell their story. Things must be different this time. It fell to me to tell their story, but now . . ." He waves at his leg and grimaces. "Now, it's up to you, Preserver Longbough."

My legs tremble and I sit down quickly on the edge of his bed. "Me? But I don't know their story. Who are they? Where do they come from? Are they friend or foe?"

Preserver Wordsmith smiles then shakes his head. "I will tell you their story, as we have preserved it from their own lips from their previous visits. But first you must know the possible consequences of revealing it."

I breathe deeply, knowing already what he would say.

"If the Elders and Delegates choose to Banish the strangers once again, you would be Banished with them, and a rift would open between the Elders and the Preservers, for they would know that we do not forget what is commanded to be forgotten. This is a consequence I and the Guild are willing to pay. But you are young and lack the experience of a Village Preserver. It is much to ask of you. If you wish, I can appoint a Village Preserver from another Community to give the Remembrance and tell the strangers' story."

I lick my lips and meet his gaze. "You do not forget what is commanded to be forgotten?" I ask, my voice sounding hoarse to my ears.

"We do not. We are Preservers. Nothing—and no one—should be forgotten."

"Not even those Banished?"

"Not even those Banished," he replies softly.

My insides reel with elation and terror and rebellion all rolled into one. I feel my lips twist into what I can only imagine is a grim smile as I lean forward and answer, "Then for Peter Thrushollow's sake, I will do it."

\* \* \* \*

My hands tremble as I clasp them tightly in my lap, awaiting the opening of the Assembly for the Great Centennial. The Grand Hall is filled beyond capacity. People stand in the aisles and squeeze themselves along the walls. Every Delegate is present along with the Elders of Pinebrook. I sit on the front platform between Elder Applethwaite and Elder Thornburne and feel the sweat run down my back, dampening my new Village Preserver's uniform. There had been a stir when the Elders first learned of my promotion two days' prior, but Preserver Wordsmith had assured them that I was ready and that it was necessary to promote me early as it was not appropriate for a Senior Apprentice to deliver the Remembrance. They had agreed. They would not break with tradition at such an important event.

Almar's eyes had bugged when he saw me in my gold-trimmed blue uniform. He congratulated me–though it was awkward. Now he has to call me *Preserver*, and I had to move my meager possessions from the Apprentice bunkhouse to the Guildhouse. There, the Preservers from various Communities, near and far, welcomed me. None spoke of the task I was given, but I could feel their support in each handshake, shoulder-clasp, and glance.

I can feel it now–the hope, the determination for things to change. I breathe deeply and exhale. I must not fail. I glance to the left front row where the strangers had been given the seat of honor among the Delegates. They would introduce their Community and give their Presentation after the Remembrance. A Remembrance such as had never been heard for 1000 years, and, if I fail, may never be heard again.

Elder Applethwaite rises unsteadily to his feet and shuffles over to the speaker's podium. He raises his blue-veined hands and the murmurings grow still. "Welcome, Delegates all, to the Great Centennial. We are honored at your presence and treasure your wisdom. These past two days, you have been presented with five new Ideas and their Inventions: Sky Flowers from the Far Eastern Region, with which we could signal brief messages using different colors and patterns; two new horse breeds from the Old Continent, one for increased speed, the other for hard labor; one new healing herb from the Southwestern Continent that reduces fevers and infections; and . . ." He pauses, and I feel a sense of justice and satisfaction at his discomfiture. Then he continues. "And a harvesting machine designed to swathe, harvest, and bundle hay and straw more quickly than can be done by hand. This is from the Northwestern Continent."

My mind races to Peter's *Invention*. The two machines had similar designs and purposes. But the Elders of the other Inventor had deemed the new machine worthy for consideration. Peter's Elders, *my* Elders, had considered Peter's machine dangerous—and Peter too, for thinking of it. I blink away the sight of Peter's arrow-ridden body and breathe in hope. Never before had so many Ideas and Inventions been proposed at a Centennial. Maybe things are about to change. Maybe the strangers' story will be just the nudge everyone needs. Maybe.

"As is tradition, once we have voted on new matters, we will review the Laws and Ordinances to decide if any changes should be made," Applethwaite's voice broke in on my thoughts. "But now, I have the honor to present our newest Village Preserver, Thomas Martin Longbough, who will give the Remembrance. After which, we will hear from the Delegates of the New Earth Community."

My heart pounds as I stand, bow to the High Elder, and walk to the speaker's podium. I cannot help but glance in the direction of the strangers, the Delegates from New Earth. They study me with calm, and I think, expectant eyes. Do they know? Did the Preservers speak to them of this Centennial's unusual Remembrance? My hands are shaking, so I place them on either side of the podium and take a deep breath. I close my eyes and begin the story of Remembrance.

"Over 2,500 years ago, the world was ruled by giant

nations. Many of the people of these nations lived in huge cities. They possessed great knowledge, which they preserved by placing it in things called 'books' or recording it on objects known as 'computers' and 'CDs' and 'drives.' They used this knowledge to build Technology. And with Technology came weapons. Terrible weapons. These nations began to envy each other's power and to seek more power, more control, more land, and more powerful weapons. Wars came and went. And with the wars came famine and disease. Finally came the Wars of Destruction when the greatest of weapons was unleashed, nation against nation, Continent against Continent. Billions of humans and animals died. The Earth itself was poisoned. The cities fell to ruin. The nations vanished. And so, it seemed, did humanity.

"But we survived. Humans lived in small villages and Communities. It took 1000 years to rebuild our scattered pockets of civilization. Then the Age of Exploration began. We discovered each other and charted the Regions and the Continents. One thousand years ago, the Elders of each Region and Continent sent Delegates to the Community of Ancients in the Old Continent. There they formed the Ordinances that would govern each Continent, each Region, and each Community for the next 100 years. This was the First Centennial. At this Centennial, all Technology was banned. Books that had been written since the Wars of Destruction were burned, and writing was forbidden lest the poison of our progenitors infect our civilization as well. For 1000 years we have lived in peace. For 1000 years our Communities have prospered. For 1000 years we have remained *unchanged.*"

There is a rustle in the crowd of Delegates. I had

altered the Remembrance. My grip tightens on the podium, and from somewhere deep within, I feel determination and a strength that surges through my voice as I continue.

"To this day, we uphold the Ordinances established at the First Centennial, and though we review them every 100 years, we have never altered them. They make us feel safe. They give us security. They prevent, we believe, the old ways of our progenitors from re-emerging and destroying us. As long as every Community on every Continent follows the same Ordinances, the evil of the ancient nations can never return. No more wars, no more squabbling over land or vying for power. No more dangerous, war-mongering Technology. And so we trust in our founders for their wisdom. For their way has worked, worked for 1000 years."

I pause and then in a low but powerful voice, I say, "But we are not alone. Others, too, have survived the Wars of Destruction, and their Elders found other ways to rebuild humanity. Ways like, yet unlike ours. They too have experienced peace and prosperity—but they have done so without erasing the past or forbidding knowledge and Technology. They are the Children of the Stars."

This time a loud murmuring surges through the Grand Hall, and many fling fearful and suspecting glances at the strangers seated in the front row. Soon, someone would step up to stop me, but for the moment the old tradition about respecting and listening to the Preserver would prevail—but not for long. I plunge on, my voice rising above the murmurs.

"Before the Wars of Destruction began, a few Elders scattered among the nations realized the doom of humanity was eminent. They gathered together children and young adults from each nation and built a ship to take the children to safety. This ship would not sail the seas—for where on this Earth could there be safety? This ship sailed among the stars, leading the children, who slept for 723 years in suspension, to a new planet. One they called New Earth. There they awoke and studied the records given to them by their Elders. They rebuilt their civilization avoiding the evils of their progenitors, and in time, they sailed the stars again, looking for the planet from which their forbears came. And they found us. They have returned each Centennial, hoping to re-unite the two branches of humanity once again, hoping to learn from us the wisdom of our survival and to share with us the wisdom of theirs. Yet, each time, they have been Banished and forgotten. Let this Great Centennial be different. It is time to listen. It is time, however little, to *change.*"

Silence greets my final words. Deep. Serious. Fright-ening. No one moves. Then suddenly, the red-haired Delegate from New Earth stands and mounts the plat-form. He moves up beside me at the speaker's podium and places one hand upon my shoulder. "My name is Dale Everest," he says, his voice a rich and commanding baritone. "I am the—let's call me the 'Elder' of the Star-ship *Ambassador Ten*. What Preserver Longbough has spoken is true. We, my shipmates and I, are descendants of the Children of the Stars—your brothers, survivors of the Wars of Destruction. Like you, our forbears devised a Code to guide and protect us, to prevent the evils of Old Earth from happening again. Unlike you, our Code does not forbid the use of Technology or writing or even remembering certain knowledge brought from the Old World, knowledge that helps us grow crops and prevent diseases or work more efficiently. Knowledge that lets us travel the stars."

He pauses, and again silence prevails, but I can sense a subtle change. There is an air of curiosity—and of fear. Elder Everest holds up his right hand and turns it to and fro as if studying it. "This hand has no will of its own. It is commanded by my heart. If my heart is evil, my hand will do evil. If my heart is good, my hand will do good. We believe it is the same with Technology and science and other knowledge. In themselves, there is neither good nor evil. It is the heart of those who wield them that decides how they should be used. Set the heart right, and the hand will follow—so our Code says."

At last a voice speaks up, somewhere in the back— accented as if from the Middle Continent. "Tell us of this Code."

The man from New Earth pauses and closes his eyes, much like a Preserver before telling a story. "On board the starship that carried our forbears to New Earth was a boy. His father had been a-a . . ." he paused, searching for the correct word, "a shepherd. A shepherd of people. He taught his son the Code. It came from an ancient book, long preserved. The boy, who became our first Overseer by election, taught the first Council the Code. And the Council has preserved it ever since. It is the standard to which we all apply. Here is the Second Law of the Code: 'Love others as much as you love yourself.' 'Do this," our first Overseer said, 'and you will never know war nor poverty nor injustice nor tyranny.' We have kept the Code. And found the Overseer's promise is true."

Again, there is silence, but his time Elder Applethwaite speaks from behind us on the platform. "And what is the First Law of your Code? And are there more Laws? And of what nature are they?"

Everest turns so that his face is shared by both Applethwaite and the audience. "There is so much more," he says softly. "So much of our Code and our knowledge and our Technology we would share with you–if the Council of Delegates will permit it."

This time Elder Thornburne, sitting beside Applethwaite, growls out, "If you possess Technology like that before the Wars of Destruction, how do we know you won't use it against us?"

Elder Everest points to his officers. "You have seen us in the camp. Though we possess weapons of defense and hunting far superior to what you use, we have honored your Ordinances and brought only what is allowed." He sighed. "We do not want to conquer you. We want to . . . share with you and you with us. There is much we can learn from each other. We are brothers."

Elder Applethwaite stands to his feet and moves toward the podium. Elder Everest and I step aside. "Delegates, it is time to decide, to vote on the Ideas and Inventions shared today and to review Ordinances, and . . . to ponder the request of the Delegates of New Earth. Let all who are not voting Delegates leave." He turns slowly towards Elder Everest. "I ask that you and your officers remain in your tents until matters are decided." Everest nods, and taking my elbow, turns to leave. His grip is firm though not threatening, and I accompany him without resisting.

Their tent is huge, black, edged with silver. The

entrance opens into a large central room with smaller rooms partitioned off by cloth dividers. There are soft rugs on the floor and silky cushions scattered around the extinguished fire pit. Against one set of cushions lies a wooden lyre. I hesitate just inside the tent, not knowing what they want with me or where to sit. Elder Everest lays his hand on my shoulder.

"You are welcome, Preserver Longbough. Please sit where you wish as we await the decision of the Delegates," he says.

I move to a set of red cushions across the firepit and facing the entrance. "Why did you bring me here?" I ask as I sit down. Elder Everest sits next to me. The others spread out in the open room, with the man who looks as if he came from the Far Eastern Regions standing guard by the entrance.

Everest sighs. "To keep you safe. At the First Centennial, our ambassadors—or Delegates, as you call them—were met with fear and violence. Nine attended the Centennial, but only two returned to the ship. Since then, we have always scouted first, pretending to be from other Communities, in order to learn the Ordinances passed by previous Centennials and to appear non-threatening, leaving behind our technology and anything forbidden. Always, our ambassadors have been banished, but never again with violence. This time may be different."

I stare down at my hands and swallow. "You mean, I-we, the Preservers, shouldn't have revealed your story? We should have let you tell it your own way?"

Everest shakes his head and smiles. "No, you did well. Things are changing. I sense the desire growing to move on and explore and to try new things. Never before have there been so many ideas and inventions proposed at a Centennial. But with this desire to learn and advance will come a backlash of fear. And fear often produces violence. It's best to be cautious until we see what happens."

He leans back against his blue cushions, resting on one elbow as he studies me. "You must have many questions about us, where we come from, what we believe. Ask whatever you wish to know. If we are banished again, you will have to decide whether or not to come with us."

"Go with you?" The thought buzzes in my head. "To the stars? To New Earth?"

Everest waves one hand. "If you are banished too, would you rather face the Woods or the Arrow—or come with us? This is what you must decide."

The image of Peter's pale, dead face fills my mind. My hands clench. Peter—whose only crime was thinking of an *Invention* in a village whose Elders were terrified of anything remotely technological. I exhale slowly. I know what Peter would have chosen.

"If it comes to that, I will go with you." I glance over at Everest's face. His blue eyes seem to light up.

"You would be the first," he says with a smile.

I give a shaky grin. "It seems I'm the first in a lot of things recently—the first Senior Apprentice chosen to give the Remembrance, the first Senior Apprentice given an early promotion, the first Preserver to tell your story. And possibly the first Preserver to be Banished." I shrug my shoulders. "What's one more new thing to experience?"

"Fair enough. What would you like to know about us?"

My mind races. Where should I begin? I've been taught our heritage, always looking to our past. How does one look to the future? I study the other New Earth Delegates scattered around the tent. They return my gaze with steady eyes. Most of them smile. "Let's start with your names," I say.

\*    \*    \*    \*

It takes three days for the Council of Delegates to settle matters, the longest vote since the First Centennial, which had taken a week. When a messenger arrives at the tent to summon us to the Grand Hall, it is not a Junior Apprentice, but Elder Thornburne himself—along with a patrol of twelve Hunters in full gear. It does not bode well. In spite of myself, I feel my legs tremble as we are escorted to the building, down the long center aisle, and up onto the platform. There Elder Applethwaite faces us. His face is pale and grim.

"It is the will of the Council that the Delegates of New Earth, otherwise known as the Children of the Stars, be Banished. Their names and stories stricken from the Records, never to be seen or heard of again." Applethwaite's voice quavers ever so slightly. He stares hard at Everest (whom I now know is called *Commander* rather than *Elder*). "Having spoken with various Preservers, who, against the ruling of the Elders and Delegates of previous centuries, have preserved your story, I take it you have means of transporting yourself away from here without the need of further Judgment."

The Commander nods. "We have. We will leave quietly. There is no need for you to do more."

Applethwaite turns his foggy blue-eyed gaze to me and speaks more softly. "As for you, Preserver Longbough, you are young and inexperienced in the ways of deception. We feel you have been ill-used by rebellious Preservers and are not accountable for your actions. If you swear never to speak of this again and to remember no more of things that are forbidden or those who are Banished, you may remain as our new Village Preserver."

I breathe deeply. If I am the new Village Preserver, that does not bode well for Preserver Wordsmith. I wonder if he's been Banished—along with all the rest of the so-called "rebellious Preservers." The room remains silent, awaiting my reply. I straighten my shoulders and return the Elder's gaze with a steady one of my own. "I am a Preserver," I say, my voice strong and passionate. "We do not forget anything—or any*one*. How can we learn from our past if we refuse to remember it? And if we forget our past, how can we face the future? I cannot accept the terms. I will be Banished with the Delegates of New Earth."

Applethwaite stands stunned. The silence of the Grand Hall is broken by a young man's cry: "Farewell, Thomas Longbough, my friend. Remember us, though we are forbidden to remember you." I search the crowd of faces and find Almar waving, tears streaming down his face. Several other Apprentices wave as well. I notice other faces, some compassionate, some angry, some frightened—and some reflecting the passion I feel. I nod and smile. There's a definite shift in the mood of the Grand Hall. Things are beginning to change. Then Elder Thornburne steps up, his dark eyes flashing.

"You, who hail yourself as the Children of the Stars, leave this world and never return," he roars. Then he looks at me and snarls, "And take this rebel with you."

Commander Everest nods. "We will leave you now, and we will take our brother with us, but as for never returning, that I cannot promise."

Thornburne sneers. "We will be ready for you next time."

The Commander gazes out over the crowded hall. Many Delegates look away, but a surprising number meet his gaze. "Yes," he says softly, "I believe you will." He nods to the crowd. "Farewell, my reluctant brothers. Keep the heart right, and the hand will follow."

I brace myself. That is the signal the Commander had given for our departure. There is a bright flash and my body tingles. My brain swirls as the flash turns to darkness and silence. Then I hear a dull murmur and my vision slowly comes into focus. Commander Everest and Lieutenant Shakar are holding me up. I try to stiffen my trembling legs.

"First transport is difficult, but with training and practice, you'll get used to it," the Commander says.

Lt. Shakar nods and grins. "Hey, you did better than my first transport—I threw up all over the lead officer!"

I try to grin back, but I'm not so sure my stomach will behave any better. I swallow. "Where are we?"

"You are onboard the Starship *Ambassador Ten*," the Commander says waving his free hand to take in the area.

We are standing in a hall. Before us is a large glass viewport. I feel my eyes widen. Outside is a living blackness speckled with more stars than I can count. But in the center of it all is a large blue-green ball. My mouth goes dry. "Is that . . . ?"

"Yep, that's Earth—Old Earth to us. We're in a tight orbit." Lt. Shakar gazes at my home planet with me. The three of us stand there for an uncountable passage of time, silent, thoughtful. My thoughts are jumbled as I study the planet on which I have lived all of my life. I think of what is happening at the Great Centennial right now—how Elder Applethwaite is telling the people that Thomas Martin Longbough is no more and never was. I hear their reply—some with hoarse and broken voices. Tears fill my eyes, and Commander Everest lays one hand on my shoulder.

I shift my gaze to his face. "We'll return someday, right?"

"In 100 years, Preserver, and next time, I think things will be different." He squeezes my shoulder. "You've started something that all of our previous visits never accomplished." He smiles. "And if I'm not entirely mistaken, I think there'll be some who'll remember the young Preserver who sailed the stars."

Almar's face flashes across my mind, and I nod. Yes, some will remember and pass the Forbidden Knowledge on to their children and children's children. Stories will be told in low tones around hunting fires of Thomas Martin Longbough, Village Preserver—and a Child of the Stars.

## *Love at First Sight*

C.S. Marks

Do you believe in "love at first sight?" That a man can look into the eyes of his future partner and know—just *know* somehow—that they are destined to be together? It's a romantic notion, to be sure, treasured and dreamt about by young men and wistful girls alike, though most would not admit it. It is also, in my experience, utter nonsense.

I met my future partner under less than ideal circumstances, I'll admit. After all, I didn't have much of a selection, and I needed a horse. That's right—a horse. You no doubt thought I have been referring to men and women, and I suppose it's fine if you did, as I don't believe in love at first sight in that case, either. At any rate, there I stood surveying the sorriest selection I'd seen on four legs. Spavined, cow-hocked, ewe-necked, underfed things they were. In the dealer's defense, I didn't have a lot of money to spend, so he had kept the better stock hidden away, but I'm a ranger, and a ranger can't range very far without a horse. I would have to buy something, and he knew it.

Just as I was about to settle for the least terrible of the lot, my eyes lit upon a youngish fellow, not geld-ed, and I thought my luck had changed. Rather Nor-dic-looking but taller than most, shaggy, sturdy, and well made, he sauntered over to the end of the line. "Is he there by mistake?" I asked the horse dealer, tipping my hand at once. I have never been known for shrewd business dealings.

"No, he's part of the group," said the dealer. "He is, of course, the highest-priced animal, but he can be had for what you can pay."

I approached the tall, sandy-colored dun horse, who regarded me with a friendly, curious expression. "What's wrong with him?"

"I am a dealer in horses, sir. It is not my place to point out his faults; they are yours to discover, if you can find any."

"Fair enough," I said, remembering the protocol. I could ask direct questions, and the dealer would be ex-pected to answer them honestly, but he was quite right in that it was up to me to know which questions to ask. "Has he ever been lame?"

"Not to my knowledge."

"Can he be ridden?"

"Oh, most certainly."

"Is he swift?"

"He is young, and we have yet to really test him, but I would foresee strong and steady rather than swift."

I nodded. It seemed an honest answer, one I would

have given myself. I approached the horse and stroked his neck, his winter hair coming off in my hand. He would be quite pretty in summer coat, as the hair beneath was golden rather than sandy. His dark muzzle was like velvet, his eyes brown and soft. I have always loved a good dun—I know it makes little sense, but somehow they always seem tougher than other horses. "Well," I said, "he has good feet." I stroked his back and legs, feeling for signs of old injuries, and found none. Young, sound, sturdy…what would stop me?

"May I try him?"

"Did you bring your own gear? I have neither saddle nor bridle to lend. And the last time I allowed anyone to try a horse without paying for it first, I saw neither horse nor man again."

I did not have a saddle. Mine had run off with my last horse, who had been liberated from our picket line by a notorious thief. I shook my head.

"Well, then you will need to ride him without either if you wish to try him here, and I wouldn't suggest that. He is young and inexperienced, after all," said the dealer. "But you are a strapping fellow yourself, with obvious ability. I'm sure you will be just fine."

"Do you have a saddle for sale?" I asked, though I really didn't have money to buy one and the horse as well. The dealer shook his head. I would soon learn that when a horse dealer tells you he does not have a saddle to sell, he's probably lying. I would also learn that it is most unwise to buy a horse, no matter how wonderful he looks, without trying him first.

\* \* \* \*

I bought the dun horse; in my mind I had little alternative.

Besides that, I have always been swayed by a long, thick forelock, and this fellow had a fine one. He shook it at me as I approached with head-collar in hand, and allowed me to put it on his noble, intelligent head. I thought I had made the bargain of my life as I led my new partner away with a farewell wave at the dealer, who smiled broadly— perhaps too broadly—and waved back.

I rejoined my fellow rangers at our encampment, having walked all day and well into the evening. One of them would have a saddle I could borrow. I would try the horse in the morning. They were quite appreciative, looking my purchase up and down in admiration, as I stood back with my thumbs hooked into my sword-belt, my reputation as a judge of horse-flesh assured. "How did you ever afford this?" they asked. When I told them what I had paid, and who I had paid it to, they got very quiet.

"Now all I need is to borrow a saddle so that I can try him out," I said.

"What…you mean you haven't *ridden* him?"

"Not yet, but I was assured he can be ridden. Besides…look how strong he is!"

My friends were shaking their heads, a few were chuckling. "Oh, dear…" said one, trying not to look directly at me.

"Don't worry," I said. "Horse dealers put their reputations on the line each time they sell an animal. I'm sure he's fine. I asked all the right questions."

"This one has a reputation, all right," said another of the rangers. "We'll see tomorrow, won't we?" For some reason, I didn't sleep especially well that night.

\* \* \* \*

In the morning I borrowed a saddle from one of my companions. They had all gathered to watch, as a new horse sometimes provided entertainment the first time it was ridden. I bridled the tall dun…easy enough for me, as I am very tall myself. Then I saddled him. He stood willingly, grunting a little as I cinched him up. I walked him around until he relaxed, then snugged the saddle up again. One of my companions held my offside stirrup, and I swung carefully aboard—in short, I did everything right.

I gently urged the young horse forward, and he stepped out willingly. I rode him in a large circle at a nice, long-striding walk, to the disappointment of my friends, who were not getting the show they had expected. I smiled and patted my horse's neck. "Good man. There's a brave fellow." Then I squeezed him into a trot.

I remember flying through the air, and then sitting on the ground in a billowing cloud of dust, but nothing else. My horse approached me with a quizzical expression. *What are you doing on the ground?* I looked around for my friends. When I saw them, their eyes were round and their jaws had dropped open. I was nearly fifty feet from where I had been, and every bone in my body had been jarred. I swallowed blood, having bitten my tongue on landing. The horse flipped his long forelock up and down, which, I would come to learn, was his way of laughing. *No worries,* I thought. *Something startled him, is all.* I got slowly to my feet and brushed the dust from my breeches, then walked calmly over to my new horse and patted him. "There, now, let's try again, shall we?"

I mounted again, and the horse stood perfectly, as if almost apologetic. When I asked him to move forward, he did so as before. I walked, trotted, even cantered a little. He was quite a nice animal to ride—soft, easy movement that never jolted or jarred—and I relaxed in the saddle, having now decided my fears were groundless. The next thing I remember was lying flat on my back, looking up at the morning sun slanting through the trees, as my captain walked over and extended his hand. "Let me help you up."

When I had regained my feet, the captain brushed the leaves and dirt from my shoulders. "That horse has an unfortunate sense of humor, and he appears to be smarter than you are. I'm afraid you're most likely doomed." He walked away, chuckling. My face burned with humiliation, but I can be a stubborn man, and I resolved that, somehow, I would prove the captain wrong. My horse stood before me, flipping his forelock up and down. "We'll see, won't we?" I muttered. "We'll see which of us is laughing in the end."

Thus began a rather difficult period in my life. I rode the young horse every day, and sometimes he allowed me to stay in the saddle. When he did, I was delighted, as he truly was a wonderful ride. When he didn't, I could count on a new assortment of bodily insults, and I was soon covered with bruises in various stages of healing. I learned that he was much more likely to cooperate when I was in a humble, respectful mood. If I got complacent or prideful, or if, heaven forbid, I grew impatient or lost my temper, he would deal with me accordingly. "You had better start wearing a battle-helmet when you ride him," my friends would say. "He'll rattle your brain!"

*I'd say it's rattled already, or I'd just sell him and be done with it,* I thought. But there was something about him that wouldn't let me do that. He was special, and I meant to make him mine . . . I just hoped it wouldn't be the death of me. I named him after the gentle river Eros, as when he was being a good horse he flowed like soft waters over the ground. I could ride him all day, when I could ride him, though I sometimes worried that my companions might butcher him for meat. He liked to untie himself from the picket lines, which was bad enough, and he liked to untie the other horses as well. He enjoyed rummaging in our gear, searching specifically for treats like dried apples and honey. He was actually quite stealthy in his nightly raids. Once caught, he would pretend to be quite the compliant lamb for a while until we let our guard down again. As the captain had said, he was smarter than I am. Things got more peaceful once we finally discovered a knot Eros could not untie.

In a way, we were like one of those couples who always seem to be fighting and making up. They love one another—it's plain to see—but they constantly test and try and argue. Sometimes you wonder why they stay together, or what brought them together in the first place. Then you realize the truth of it: when they work together, it is a thing of beauty.

\* \* \* \*

One dark and rainy night we would be tested, when a band of thieves approached our encampment. Their leader, a wily sutherling buzzard whose name, translated, meant "Scorpion," absolutely hated northerners, especially ones who felt it necessary to interfere with his pillaging of defenseless northern settlements. He was also one of the most accomplished horse thieves in the western lands—it was said that you would not own a horse for long after he set his eyes on it.

Scorpion had stolen my last horse, a fine bay that I thought was the best horse I had ever had, or could ever have. He was a tall, swift animal with a very willing and cooperative temperament; we were so much alike that he seemed to sense everything I wanted of him before I did. He came to me with the rather unimaginative name of Walnut, which he answered to, so I did not change it.

Unfortunately, his cooperative disposition had allowed him to be taken easily, and he went willingly with Scorpion, who had stolen into our encampment in broad daylight without alerting anyone. In fact, we didn't even notice Walnut had gone missing until we went to feed the animals that evening. Don't think I didn't hear about *that* for a while; my fellows teased me without mercy until they realized how truly despondent I was. They even took up a collection to replace Walnut, sending me to the market with enough to buy a horse, if not a very fine one. I knew I would never find another horse as wonderful as my tall bay, and I vowed that Scorpion would never take one of my animals again.

\* \* \* \*

That night the rain made it difficult to hear the bandits' approach, and, of course, there was no moonlight. I had been sleeping somewhat fitfully, as I have never had much luck sleeping in the wet, and I had a lot to worry about. I was actually wondering whether Eros and I would ever be able to work together, when I heard the horses nickering and stirring restively. I looked over at the picket line; Eros was trying to untie himself again, but that was nothing unusual.

*Something's wrong . . . Eros fiddling with his picket line doesn't explain why they're upset. . . .*

Then I noticed the dark-feathered arrow protruding from the neck of the man set to keep watch, and I knew I had to rouse the camp at once. Someone obviously intended to attack us unawares, and I wondered whether Scorpion had returned for a second try. *If so, he is in a less benevolent mood than last time, as he has killed one man already. Well, if I have anything to say about it he will kill no more men tonight—and he will not have Eros!* Slowly and carefully, I gently prodded my neighbors awake, admonishing them to keep still, but be ready for imminent attack.

I still had not laid eyes on the bandits, but Eros, by now, was squealing in frustration. *He either sees them or smells them, apparently. I'd better go to him before they silence him with an arrow in the eye.* With as casual an attitude as I could muster, I made my way over to where he was tethered, ostensibly to calm him down. "There, now," I said, patting him gently. Then I whispered, "If you have ever wanted to prove your worth, let it be now!" I could just make out the sound of several men creeping toward the picket line. I glanced over my shoulder at the other rangers, who stared back at me with half-lidded eyes, still feigning sleep. I could see their hands on their sword-hilts.

Tonight it would be bareback and bridle-less, at least for me. I snicked my blade carefully through Eros' tether, and then led him down the line, pretending to calm the other horses. We knew we would not be able to fight the bandits—they had too great an advantage—but we hoped to escape with our lives and at least some of our horses, and it would fall to me to create the diversion we needed. I looked over at the captain and nodded. *Now, Eros, let's see what you're made of.*

I swung aboard my unreliable mount with a fierce yell and charged into the brush where Scorpion's men were hiding. Eros did not hesitate. He snorted and plunged through the tangle of undergrowth, bearing down right on top of them, startling them so badly that they could not draw their weapons. My friends ran to their horses, taking advantage of the bandits being occupied with Eros and me.

We moved like a single creature, leaping and ducking and swerving through the difficult going; my horsemanship skills were put to the test as never before. I caught an arrow in the meat of my left arm, but hardly felt it. Then, as we emerged into the clear, I saw at least fifteen of Scorpion's men standing with drawn blades, looking toward me in surprise. Here came a wild-eyed man, riding an equally wild-eyed horse, the man yell-ing and waving a sword as the horse leaped straight for them. One of them was holding a fine bay horse, one that I recognized, and I ground my teeth.

As far as I knew, this was the first battle Eros had encountered, and he handled it like a veteran. Most horses must be trained to ride down an enemy—it is the nature of a horse to avoid trampling a man if he can—but he did not hesitate. He hurtled toward the bandits with a will, and, as large as he was, they lost their nerve, parting like tall grass in the wind. He bowled into the man holding Walnut, who then turned and galloped off beside us. I reached out and snagged one dangling rein, hoping the animal wouldn't decide to swerve or stop abruptly, as that would have probably unhorsed me. Now all I had to do was escape…

Eros, apparently, had been far more observant that I knew. He had studied me in the past weeks, learning the way my body moved. All I had to do was think of where I wanted to go, and he went there. *Like Walnut… only better!* I was too exhilarated to be terrified. *I'll have myself a real battle-mount if we can manage to get out of this.*

They chased us with arrows, but they were not inclined to pursue the raving ranger and his crazed, formidable beast through the now-driving rain. It was too dark, they were too disorganized, and we made too small of a target for them to bother with…at least that's what I hoped as I urged Eros through the wild night, his great hooves splashing and churning beneath me. I made a wide circle, as I did not wish to get too far away from my companions, finally taking shelter beneath an overhang of rock beside the riverbank.

Once I was sure there would be no pursuit, I looked to my horse. He had been grazed twice on the hind-quarters, but his hide was tough. I dressed the shallow wounds with pine resin before looking to the unpleasant task of removing the arrow from the meat of my arm. Eros was still panting and blowing, steam rising from his soaking wet body, and I shrugged out of my oilcloth coat, covering him with it. "You earned that, my friend." I patted him and offered him a handful of dried apples. We both stayed alert and watchful until the sun rose in the morning.

I heard the captain's horn at first light—a gathering-call—and decided to make for it. The bandits would most likely still be in the area, and the captain wanted to make a hasty retreat. As it turned out, my comrades had escaped for the most part, though two had been killed and two others wounded. But my stampede through the bandits' ranks had certainly prevented a far greater loss, and my companions were both thankful and impressed. We had lost no horses, and I had reclaimed one, which was probably a matter of some personal disgrace for Scorpion. I had the feeling he would avoid us in the future.

I sat tall on my damp-and-steaming golden battle-mount as the captain approached me. He looked appreciatively at Walnut. "At least you now have a serviceable saddle again. And you can go back to riding your reliable mount if you wish." He paused for a moment, regarding Eros. "I still think that horse is smarter than you are, but he proved his worth last night. Apparently you weren't as doomed as I first thought."

I drew myself up tall, patting Eros with a confident hand. "Indeed not," I said. "I may have chosen wisely after all. I think I'll give Walnut to Brodda—he has always admired him, and it seems his horse's back is always sore."

Eros, apparently sensing that I was being just a little too self-congratulatory, took the opportunity to shake his entire body like a wet hound dog, spilling my bareback-riding self onto the muddy ground. "Fine," I muttered. "I do *so* enjoy mud-caked breeches." I looked up at Eros, who was, predictably, waving his long forelock up and down. I decided to laugh along with him. I might have temporarily lost my dignity, but I had found my partner at last.

## *A Change of Shoes*

C. K. Deatherage

"I need to change my shoes, Willy boy," Auntie Mae said sadly. "There's more needy youngsters out there than these old, worn shoes can fit. Just yesterday, the sheriff from Burlington stopped by to ask if I could take three more children—two boys and one girl. Their parents died of the pox not too long ago. But where's the room?"

Willy shrugged and shook his head. Already each bed held two children, and the toddlers often came three to a bed. Being the oldest at nearly fifteen, Willy had a bunk to himself. He was willing to share, but only one more could fit. That left two children without beds. They were plum full, that's for sure. Seventeen kids in all, eight of them under five. They were a handful, and sometimes the food stock got a little small, but they had managed.

The old woman sighed. "Back some twenty-seven years ago, when I was more spry, I found these old cast-off shoes. Ogre by the look and size of them. They took awhile to air out, and I had to patch a few places and polish the leather till my arms nearly dropped off, but when cleaned up, they made a fine home for myself and the few children in my care. But now . . ." She just shook her head.

"I could find some work. Maybe Farmer MacDonald could use another field hand," Willy offered. "Then maybe we could afford to build a real house."

"Ah, Willy boy, you do this old heart good, you do, but it would take years to save up enough for a large house. And I'm afraid these old shoes won't last that long. There's a hole over the big toe of the right shoe where a patch has pulled away. The leather's cracked and worn in many places. And don't tell me you young ones don't feel the chill despite the fireplace in the heel of each shoe. I need to find new footwear or . . ." Her words trailed off, but Willy knew her thoughts.

*Or she'll have to farm us out to different home,* he thought. He shuddered. All the kids who lived in the shoes were either foundlings or outright orphans, as he was. They had become a family. He couldn't imagine losing any of his brothers or sisters. They were poor. Clothes were passed down from child to child until too threadbare to wear. They depended on donations and the food they raised. But they never went to bed hungry— despite the ugly rumors that sometimes spread about old Widow Langley and the children who lived in the shoes. He couldn't let his family be separated. He had to do something! Then he remembered something—or rather *someone* who might be able to help.

"Auntie Mae," he said, "I think I know someone who

could help us. I've heard stories about his adventures. He might just have what we need. He only lives a few towns away. Let me go to him."

The old woman looked interested. "Is this fellow of a decent sort?"

Willy nodded. "He's always the hero in the stories I hear told."

"And have you ever laid eyes on the man, Willy? Does he really exist or is he just a tale sung in the taverns?"

Willy licked his lips. "Well, *I've* never seen him, Auntie Mae, but Alan Johnson, the miller's son met him in person and told me all about him."

"And do you have a name for this hero, Willy boy?"

Willy took a deep breath and let it out slowly. "It's Jack the Giant-Slayer."

"Jack." The old woman said the name softly, a smile toying with her lips. Then she sighed and shook her head. "Jack has done some wonderful deeds, to be sure, but they come at a price. We have nothing to offer him, Willy boy. I doubt you'd find him overly eager to help an old widow and two shoes-full of orphans. Besides, he's nearly as old as I am. His adventuring days are long over."

Willy straightened his shoulders, a sure sign of a stubborn streak coming on. "But we don't know for certain he wouldn't help us. Maybe he has an old shoe or two he's kept from his giant-slaying days he could give us. Please, Auntie Mae, let me try."

The old woman pursed her lips, her brow furrowed, her gray eyes squinted in deep thought. Finally, she nodded and said, "I'll fix you a travel sack with some bread and cheese. And a little gift to give to Jack. It might just do the trick." She paused, again a faint smile on her lips. "Yes, this could work."

Early the next morning, before the toddlers were out of bed and scampering through the kitchen, Willy shouldered his travel sack, shaking hands with the older children who were helping with breakfast.

"You're really going to see Jack the Giant-Slayer?" asked Jeffrey.

"Yep."

"Do you think he'll help us?" Mary queried.

"Well, he's a hero, isn't he? Heroes help people."

Before the others could bombard him with more questions, Auntie Mae hurried him out the wooden door in the side of Shoe One. "Here," she said, thrusting a small, brown-wrapped parcel in his hand. It fit in his palm. "Give Jack this, and tell him Mae Warren sends her regards."

"Warren?"

"My maiden name. He'll know. Go on with you now, and beware of scallywags and scoundrels!" The Widow squeezed his shoulder then gave him a gentle push to set him on the path.

By late afternoon, Willy found himself in the town of Chesterton, standing outside a huge wrought-iron gate set in an equally huge stone fence. Behind the fence, Willy saw trees and grass and a large two-story manor. He swallowed. This was where Jack the Giant-Slayer lived—or so the village folks had said. Slowly he pushed open the gate and jogged up the long sidewalk to the house. Above his head, on the dark wood door was a large door-knocker in the shape of a snarling lion's head.

It looked as if it could have belonged to a giant. It took both of his hands to lift the knocker and let it fall with a clang.

Within moments, the heavy door was pulled back, and a man dressed in a fine blue velvet jacket, a red velvet vest, blue knickers, white socks, and a blue hat with a red feather stepped out onto the spacious marble porch. "Come for a tour, have we?" The man paused and seemed to size up Willy's patched clothing. "Hmmm, the free-to-the-public tour is next Tuesday. Come back then." He turned to leave.

"Wait, sir, Mr. Giant-Slayer," Willy piped up. "I haven't come for a tour, though that would be grand. I've come for your help."

"I'm honored, I'm sure," the gentleman said, "but I've retired and my hero days are over. You might try Robin Hood over in Nottingham, though if there's no gold in it, he might be rather reluctant."

Willy felt the salt sting behind his eyes and his throat go tight with discouragement, but he refused to cry. He hung his head and murmured, "Auntie Mae will be so disappointed."

The man paused in the doorway. "Auntie who?"

Willy remembered the small package Auntie Mae had given him. He reached in his pocket and pulled out the parcel, handing it to the fancy-dressed man. "Here, Mae Warren sends her regards."

The man unwrapped the package and opened a tiny red box. Inside nestled a simple silver ring. "Mae," he breathed. He stared a long time at the ring. Then he cleared his throat. "Well, this changes things. Come in, lad, come in. We've things to discuss."

The man (Willy had a hard time thinking of him as "Jack the Giant-Slayer") called for some tea and sandwiches and led Willy to a beautiful sitting room, complete with two white-flowered sofas and two matching chairs with footstools. Light came in from the large bay windows.

"Well, my boy, first your name, then how you're related to Mae, and finally, tell me what Mae needs."

The man did not sit though he motioned for Willy to take a chair. Instead he paced back and forth, hands clasped behind his back as Willy told him the whole story between bites of cucumber sandwiches and sips of hot tea—which were not quite as satisfying as good old barley bread and goat's cheese. The man continued to pace in silence for a few minutes while Willy ate and observed him. Willy didn't think Jack looked anything like the tales said. He envisioned Jack to be taller, with more hair, and less around the midriff. He also thought the Jack of the tales would dress in things a little more sturdy and hero-like than blue and red velvet.

"I'm afraid I'm fresh out of giant's shoes," Jack said at last. "Once had a pair, taken from an Arabian genie, but they were more like slippers and would do you no good, not in this climate." He paced some more, then stopped as if struck by the very genie whose slippers he had taken. "But I do know a giant who has excellent tastes in footwear. In fact, he was in town just last week, trading a basketful of vegetables for three horses and ten goats."

"He got all that for just a basketful of vegetables?" Willy asked.

Jack laughed. "It was a *giant's* basketful—enough

veggies to keep the town fed for the coming winter."

"And you're going to kill him and take his shoes?"

"Oh my, no. Killing is such nasty business. I only slew one giant in my lifetime, an ugly brute in both features and manners. Took to stealing livestock and endangering villagers." Jack shook his head. "No, I am more of a barterer. In fact, a more apt name for me would be Jack the Giant-Reaper. Most of the things you see in my manor are from the storehouses of giants, traded, bartered, and tricked out of the treasures of my large friends."

"Tricked?" Willy furrowed his brow.

"Yes, tricked," Jack answered. "You see, rather than slay giants, I learned their customs, laws, and codes. And with this knowledge, I could get almost anything I needed or wanted from them. For instance, a giant will never just *give* anything away. He will sell and barter, but only if he thinks he's gotten the better deal. You must make him think he's gotten the better of you and he'll fork over whatever you ask for. Another thing about giants is that they love pranks."

"Pranks?" Willy sat stunned. He had thought of giants as only ugly huge creatures that liked to grind human bones for bread, but Jack made them seem almost human—very *large* humans, to be sure.

Jack rubbed his hands together gleefully. "Yes, pranks. They love to trick each other and even to be tricked. They honor those who can turn out the best pranks. And that, my lad, is how we will get you—and Mae—your boots."

"Boots?"

Jack shook his head. "Can you only speak in monosyllables, boy? Yes, this giant wears an excellent pair of boots, enough to house fifty children, I should think. And I have a plan that might just work. Used it once on a self-styled emperor—a small king of a petty kingdom, in fact. But he was as vain as a peacock and dressed in the latest fashion. Those were back in my tailoring days, when my skill with loom and needle and thread were unequalled in the region. I and a few other tailors conspired to . . ."

"About the boots," Willy interrupted, fearing a rather long story about the emperor and his new clothes.

"Ah yes, well, fortunately for you, I've also had some experience in the craft of shoe-making. Come with me." Willy stood up, reluctantly leaving the remainder of the tea and cucumber sandwiches, to trail behind Jack into a back room filled with leather and shoe nails. Jack motioned him over to stand near a table upon which sat a cobbler's kit. "We will use this to trick our giant friend," Jack said, reaching inside the black leather bag to pull out—nothing. Jack held out this nothing between two outstretched hands, fingers clasping empty air.

"But, there's nothing there," Willy pointed out.

Jack lowered one hand and smacked his forehead with the other. "No, no, you don't give away the punchline so soon!" Then he reached down and picked up nothing and held it out, shaking it a little. "*This* is the finest of dragon hide, imported directly from China. It shimmers with iridescence, light as the dew, soft as spider's silk, yet as tough as woven steel. What's more its magical properties weed out those of lower thinking and tastes, for they are unable even to see it. Only those of higher intellect and culture can perceive its beauty and charm."

And that is what Jack, dressed richly in yellow and

orange, told the giant Rumblestoffer as Willy found himself, clothed as a page, standing and rubbing at the collar around his neck while trying not to gape at the huge man seated on the equally huge wooden chair across from him. He especially tried not to stare at the giant's boots, which were of light brown, highly polished leather with two large brass buckles. Each boot could contain at least thirty bunk beds, a play room, a kitchen, a large hearth, and maybe even an indoor toilet! The giant nodded as Jack took out a piece of dragon hide and let the light shine upon its nothingness. Rumblestoffer looked worried, but kept nodding as Jack praised the qualities of the Chinese dragon skin, turning it this way and that and tugging on it to show its toughness.

"As I have a large quantity of such hide, and—as you can imagine—not many of your intellect and taste who live nearby, I am willing to give you a discount on a pair of boots, made to order. I will charge only thirty gold crowns plus the boots you are wearing instead of my usual sixty-five crowns," Jack finished, folding the invisible leather and placing it back into the cobbler's satchel.

"And why do you need my boots?" demanded Rumblestoffer.

"I have a use for them, to be sure," Jack said, "but if you'd rather not, I'll take my business to Giant Steinsfelder, who is reputed to be a giant of impeccable taste. I'm sure *he* would have some fine boots to trade."

"Steinsfelder!" Rumblestoffer exclaimed, standing to his feet. Willy swallowed and gazed up nearly twenty-seven feet to see the giant's face. "Why, he has no more taste than a hog in its wallow! Of course, I want a pair! When can you have them ready?"

Jack smiled. "In three days' time. The dragon hide is quite easy to work with. Please let my apprentice and me measure your feet. Then in three days, bring your boots and your gold to the Elephant's Back about eighteen miles south of here. Do you know where that is?"

Rumblestoffer nodded. "I will be there. Just have my boots ready—or else."

Jack bowed, then took out a large length of rope, which he and Willy used to measure the giant's feet. "In three days," Jack said, bowing again and beckoning for Willy to do the same. Then they left.

"Auntie Mae and us kids live near the Elephant's Back," Willy said as they rode in Jack's horse-drawn wagon back to the hero's manor. "Do we really want a giant that close to our home?"

"You do if you want him to set his boots down nearby so you can move right in—well, after they've aired a bit."

Willy sat thoughtfully as the wagon jounced down the dirt road. "Won't Rumblestoffer be angry when he learns he's been tricked?"

Jack grinned. "Terribly angry, but only for a moment. Then he will see the humor in the prank, and, in a giant's own peculiar way, he will feel honored—I hope."

"Hope?" Willy's voice squeaked.

"Most giants I've met would feel honored. I don't know Rumblestoffer that well. But if he holds to the giant's code, all should be well."

"And if he doesn't?"

Jack pursed his lips. "Then I hope you've got a knack for giant slaying. I'm getting a little too old for the job."

"Great," Willy muttered.

Jack shook his head. "There you go—speaking in monosyllables again. If you're going to be a hero, you need to expand your vocabulary."

*　*　*　*

Three days later, Willy stood next to Jack near the large white humped boulder, nearly the size of a house, that folks called Elephant's Back. He was holding the front of a long sapling that they had cut down, de-barked, smoothed, and shaped into a large needle-looking thing, complete with a carved "eye." With this they were putting the finishing touches on the dragon's hide boots just as Rumblestoffer strode up.

"Well?" he demanded, looking around.

"Well, indeed!" Jack shouted up at him. "Just feast your eyes upon this masterpiece. Never have I cobbled a pair of boots out of material so grand! They shine with all the colors of a mermaid's tail. And the touch! Smooth as a polished pearl."

The giant looked in the direction Jack pointed near the large boulder. Again, he seemed disconcerted, even a little fearful. Willy caught Jack's wink as the older man shouted again, "You do like them, don't you? I used the latest fashion with overlapping cuffs."

"Yes—yes, they are quite acceptable." Rumblestoffer reached down to touch them.

"Oh no, let my apprentice and me have the honor of placing these boots upon your feet. Just take off those common boots and set them over there by that old pair of ogre shoes. Watch out for the children. Those shoes are infested with them and they're terrible to clean out if squished between your toes."

The giant did as he was told, walking carefully so as

not to step on anybody. Fortunately, Willy had told Auntie Mae to keep everyone inside as soon as the giant came into view, so no children were in danger of being squished.

"And now, kindly take a seat on the Elephant's Back," Jack instructed. Rumblestoffer obeyed.

"William, please do the honors," Jack instructed. Willy took a deep breath then clambered up the giant's right leg with a rope. Once seated upon the knee, he lowered the rope, which Jack pretended to attach to the boot cuff. "Kindly lift your foot just a little," Jack told the giant, who obliged, still with a worried look on his face. Jack then heaved and slipped the invisible boot cuff over the foot. "Okay, William, hoist it up!"

Willy hoisted until Jack yelled, "That's good. Now for the other one." They followed the same procedure; then with great relief, Willy climbed down the now booted left leg.

"Well, what did I say?" Jack hollered up to the giant. "Try walking in them. Light as goose down, they are, and they breathe like the finest cotton." Rumblestoffer took a few hesitant steps in his bare feet. Jack continued his description, now addressing Willy. "Look William, how they gleam in the sunlight! They blaze like the fiery chariot of Apollos! I have outdone myself! Well, Rumblestoffer, what do you think?"

The giant hesitated, then said, "They are all you said and more. Here is your money." He carefully lowered a tiny bag—tiny in his hand anyway—to Jack. "Count it if you wish."

"I trust you," Jack said, stuffing the bag in a pocket. "Enjoy your new boots. A pleasure doing business with one of such fine company."

Willy watched as Rumblestoffer ambled north across the countryside in his bare feet. A mile away, he stubbed his foot into a small hill and let out a yowl. Then the yowl became a roar as the giant turned and strode angrily back to where he and Jack stood waiting.

Towering over them, Rumblestoffer bent low so they could see the scowl on his black-bearded face.

"You tricked me!" he growled.

"Yes, yes we did," Jack admitted. Willy said nothing, trying to will himself as invisible as the giant's new boots. "We tricked you fair and square, right down to the last stitch. It was a prank worthy of one of your rank and standing, a prank that only I, Jack the Barterer, could hope to pull successfully."

The giant stood up, silent a moment. Then the ground began to tremble as a deep, throaty chuckle erupted from his throat. He threw his head back and laughed so loud it sounded like thunder claps. Willy resisted covering his ears with his hands. Finally, the giant's guffaws ceased, as he wiped his eyes and blew his nose with a handkerchief as big as a carnival tent. "Well, well, so I've been tricked by the famous Jack the Barterer—or the Giant-Slayer as the wee folk like to say. I didn't know you were still in business, Jack."

"I wasn't until this lad here persuaded me to do one last trick, one worthy of both our reputations."

"Indeed, and why did this young one wish this?" The giant bent low, stroking his beard.

"He needed your boots," Jack explained, waving at the leather footwear off to one side.

"Aren't they a bit too large for him?" Rumblestoffer asked, eyeing a very uncomfortable Willy.

"Not if you add about fifty more of him, plus furniture," Jack answered.

"He's going to *live* in my boots?" Rumblestoffer blinked.

"I told you those old ogre shoes were infested with children," Jack said. "Well, they've run out of room, and I could think of no finer footwear to replace them than your excellently-crafted boots."

"True. I am honored that you chose my boots to steal." The giant stood to his full height. "I have a brother who lives a few days' walk from here. If you're up to it, I'd like to hire you to pull the same prank on him. It is a fine trick, a fine one indeed!"

"The honor is all mine," Jack shouted up at him. "May I bring my apprentice?"

The giant nodded. "I'll send for you both when I'm ready." Then off he strode, in his bare feet. They watched until his tall frame became tiny on the horizon. Willy turned to Jack. "Did you mean that—about my being your apprentice?"

"I did indeed, lad. I'll give you a ten percent cut of the profits." Jack winked.

"I'd like twenty-five, as I figure I'll be climbing most of the giants' legs." Willy stood with arms crossed.

Jack grinned. "Already you're learning. Twenty-five it is. And now," he turned to face the ogre shoes, "now I have an old friend to visit." He looked back over his shoulder. "Coming, lad?"

Willy nodded. "You bet."

## *Footprints in the Dream*

### B. David Spicer

A melia's eyes snapped open, and she blinked in the bright morning sunshine. *Late* morning sunshine. She stared at her alarm clock, which blinked 12:00 over and over in glowing red numbers. Her phone rang again.

"No, no, no!" She picked up the phone, pressed it to her ear, and hissed through her teeth. "Hello?"

"Amelia?"

"Carmen? Oh thank goodness it's you! My alarm didn't go off, the power must have gone out again . . . ."

"Amelia, listen to me! Girl, you'd better get here right now! Howard Long, you know, the district manager who delights in loud, public firings? Well, he's on his way here now; some sort of surprise inspection. Today would not be a good day to call in sick. You know how Howard is..."

"Great. What about Neil?"

"Don't worry about him. I told him I sent you to the office supply store. He's too busy polishing his tie tack to notice that you're not here, but only if you get here *right now*!"

"Carmen, I just woke up. I can't be there in less than—"

"Girl, you'd better find a way! Oops, I gotta go!"

The line died and hummed in her ear. Amelia slammed down the phone and sat on the edge of her bed, rubbing her temples with her fingertips. "Great, just great!" She went to her bathroom and started the shower. As she disrobed, Bowser, her cat, rubbed his furry head against her legs.

"Not now, Bowser. I'm late." He meowed and kept up his rubbing, darting between her legs as she started to step into the shower. She lost her balance and snatched at the shower curtain in a desperate bid to avoid falling. The curtain held, but the rod did not, and down she went in a jumble of arms, legs, plastic, and splashing water.

She stared, blinking at the ceiling until Bowser licked her nose and rubbed his head against her cheek. She sat up, pressing her hand against her forehead and breathing heavily. She clambered into the shower, which had no hot water, despite the curtain resting in a sodden mess on the floor of the bathroom. She stood under the water, letting it wash over her body while her hands manically clutched at her head. She staggered to her bedroom, still dripping wet, and threw on the first clothes she set her hands on.

Bowser leapt onto the unmade bed and watched Amelia burrow through her purse. She pulled out a bottle of ibuprofen caplets and opened it. She shook the bottle, but nothing came out. "Wonderful! What else could go wrong today?" She threw the bottle at the wall and tried to hold her head together. She checked the time on her watch, and flew out the door.

The elevator at the end of the hall had a hand-lettered sign that said 'Out of Order' in childishly large red letters, so she took the stairs, stumbling her way down twelve flights. Stepping out of the dim stairwell into the bright sun made her wince and squint, but she managed to find her car in the parking lot. She unlocked the door and sat behind the wheel, then burrowed through her glove box for her sunglasses, which she couldn't find. "What *is* it to-day? Nothing is going right!" She backed out of her park-ing space and aimed her car toward Latimore Telecom, where her cheery cubicle sat empty, awaiting her arrival.

At the intersection of Market and Main, a garbage truck had collided with a truck hauling live chickens, which meant that the street teemed with wandering hens and smelled like a landfill. Traffic came to a standstill, and Amelia rested her head on her steering wheel, occasional-ly pounding the passenger seat with her clenched fist and muttering the words her mother said ladies never used. "Why is this happening?"

Eventually the tow trucks got the mess sorted out, and she was at last able to continue her way to work. She pulled into the parking lot just in time to see district man-ager Howard Long get out of his car, followed by the sy-cophants and hangers-on from corporate HQ. She bit her lip as she watched them pass through the glass doors and into the lobby. "Why did he have to come here today?" She frowned and rubbed her temples. "Why is he here anyway? It doesn't make any sense!"

She found the last available parking spot in the very last row, as far away from the building as one could get and still be in the parking lot. She heaved a great sigh and started toward the building. Halfway there she stepped in something that might have been Alpo the previous day, but was that day far more malodorous. She nearly retched as she tried to scrape it off on the asphalt. "Okay, Amelia, don't start crying. It's just a bad day, just one whopper of a bad day." She sniffed back her tears and strode toward the front door.

"Here she is now! One of our finest account analysts!" Her manager, Neil, sidled up next to her, taking her arm in his. "I knew she couldn't have gone far." His maniac smile couldn't be more contrived, and she could see the sweat on his brow.

Howard Long frowned and crossed his arms across his chest. "I hope you aren't just getting to work, Miss Follett."

Neil waved that away with a chuckle. "Of course not, Howard. Tell him where you've been, Amelia."

She cleared her throat and took a deep breath before answering. "Carmen, my section leader, sent me to the office supply store."

Howard's scowl deepened. "Really? What did you buy there? I don't see any shopping bags."

"There's a bad accident downtown. I, uh, I had to turn around and come back."

Howard grunted, but turned back to Neil. "About the report?"

Neil snapped his fingers and his phony grin became even phonier. "Howard is here to see the report on the McAdams account. It's ready for him to see, right?"

Amelia's brows furrowed. "No, you said it wasn't due until the 18th."

Howard spoke through clenched teeth. "Today *is* the 18th."

"Today is the 17th, I was going to finish it today. . . ."

"Amelia, Howard's right. Today is the 18th, I assure you." He found something interesting on the floor to stare at.

Howard threw up his hands. "I can't believe what I'm hearing! Do you tolerate this sort of incompetence, Neil?"

"No, sir, it was just a simple mistake. . . ."

Amelia winced and pressed her fists against the sides of her head; neither Howard nor Neil seemed to notice.

"A mistake, yes, I'd say it was a mistake—and a costly one at that!"

Her breath came in ragged gasps from between her teeth, and Amelia's body began to list to one side.

"Look, Howard, the report's almost done. I'm sure she can finish it up for you in an hour or so."

"I have to present her findings to the board of directors in a conference call in half an hour!" He turned to Amelia and jabbed a finger in her direction. "You get me what you have done, then you clean out your desk. There is no place for incompetence at Latimore Telecom!"

Amelia curled her fingers into her brown hair and felt her lungs swell, then she felt herself screaming. She saw Howard and Neil's mouths drop open in surprise, but she couldn't hear her own anguished cry. Instead a roaring sound, like the ocean during a hurricane, sounded in the space between her ears. The world seemed to ripple, then twist, as if reality were only a photograph that danced in the wind, flickering through the air on capricious currents. The edges of her vision darkened, but at the center a single bright dot burned like a supernova, which grew until she could seen nothing else.

*    *    *    *

Amelia opened her eyes and saw the sun, then turned her head and saw blue sky, billowy clouds and green leaves. The leaves danced in the gentle breeze and hosted birds with vividly-colored plumage. She blinked a few times and sat up, her breath catching in her throat. She sat in a little clearing surrounded by trees and daisies, with bees buzzing around her ears and birds singing cheerful chirping tunes. "Oh my gosh. Where am I?"

"You're on the ground, of course."

Amelia whipped her head around but didn't see anybody. "Who said that?"

A bird that looked like a raven except for his deep purple feathers landed on the ground next to her. "I did."

"Who are you?"

"I'm who I am." He shook his head and trotted around her, looking her up and down.

"Do you have a name?"

"Of course I have a name!"

She waited, but the bird seemed rather literal, and didn't offer his name. "What is your name?"

"Som."

"Som?"

The raven flapped his wings and hopped around her. "Yes, yes, yes. I just said that!"

"I'm sorry."

"Yes, so you are, so you are!" He paused and angled one of his eyes toward her. "What manner of thing are you?"

143

Amelia stared at him for a long moment. "Uh, I'm a person. A woman."

Som resumed his bobbing walk around her. "Yes, yes, yes, that's what I see, too. But what sort of thing are you?"

"I don't understand what you're asking me. What sort of thing are *you*?"

He squawked indignantly. "I'm an oneiropomp! One of the best, one of the best!"

"A what?" Her brows furrowed. "I don't know that word."

"We bring the dreamers to the dream." He gave her a dose of his eye. "Are you a dreamer?"

She held up her hands. "I don't know, but that would explain a whole lot. I mean, I must be dreaming, right?"

"Must you? Must you, must you. I cannot speak to that."

She bit her lower lip. "I was at work, then something happened, a bright light, then I was here. I must be dreaming."

Som nodded slowly, then resumed his pacing. "Must be in the dream. She says so, says she *must* be dreaming. But she isn't a dreamer, is she? *Must* she be dreaming?"

"What are you going on about?" She had to turn her body to see him, and when she did she saw that the grass that she'd been sitting on was gray and dead. She lifted her hands and found more of the same. "What the heck?"

Som hopped forward and peered intently at the ground. Then he flicked his wings and fluttered several feet away. "You *aren't* a dreamer! You said you *must* be a dreamer, but that's an untruth!"

She stood up and examined the ground where she'd

been sitting. The grass had withered away to nothing and even the soil had taken on a sickly gray appearance. "What's happening?"

"You're killing the dream!" The raven hopped and fluttered and squawked. The birds in the trees took up his cries and soon the air rang with chattering birdcalls. Finally, another bird, this one a jay with green and yellow feathers, landed beside Som.

"It isn't right, Som. None of us brought this one through the veil. It doesn't dream."

Som bobbed his head twice in quick succession. "Yes, yes, yes! She isn't a dreamer! How did she get here? How do we make her leave? She's killing the dream!"

The jay hopped forward and peered intently at the dead patch on the ground. "The dream dies."

"What do we do? We didn't carry her here; we can't carry her back! What do we do?"

"The Seer will know! The Seer must know!"

"Must he?" Som fluttered and squawked. "Yes, yes, yes! He must!" He took to the air and circled Amelia. "Follow me to the Seer!"

Amelia sighed. "Are we off to see the wizard?"

Som made a disgusted sound. "The Seer! I said the Seer!"

She smiled. "Right. The Seer." Som flew through the woods, and she followed him. The chattering birds became silent, and the sudden stillness caused her to look back. Each step she took left a gray patch of dead foliage behind her. "My dreams are so weird."

She walked for what seemed like a long time, but the sun seemed fixed in the same place in the sky, which gave the day an odd, timeless quality. Som soared ahead of her, circling back when she lagged too far behind. They left the woods behind them and entered a vast meadow. A tow-headed little boy, maybe six or seven years old, sat on a stone staring at a caterpillar that sat in his hand. Som landed in front of the boy and bowed awkwardly.

"Seer. . . ."

The boy held up a finger. "Wait." He stared at the caterpillar for another minute, then carefully placed it on the ground, where it wriggled away. The boy watched it for a moment before looking up at Amelia. "So, you're the one. Younger than I'd expected."

She grinned. "I could say the same."

"Are you a dreamer?"

"Seer, none of us brought her through the veil."

The boy nodded. "I know, Som. I just want to know why she thinks she's here."

Amelia bit her lip as she watched the boy. "I don't know why I'm here, or how I got here, or even where *here* is." She pointed to the growing gray patch on the ground. "If this isn't a dream, then I must have had a stroke or something. Am I dead?"

The Seer frowned, his pale blue eyes growing serious. "The dead can't enter the dream, so you aren't dead."

"Well, that's good."

"You are alive, but you aren't supposed to be here."

She sighed. "Do you know how I can get home?"

"Your world is gone."

"What?"

"Your world is gone."

Amelia flopped down onto the gray ground. "Where did it go?"

The Seer shook his head. "You tell me. You sent it away."

"What are you talking about? I did no such thing."

The boyish face looked sad. "Oh, but you did. You made a wish and pushed your world out of existence. Don't you remember?"

She rubbed her forehead with her fingertips. "I had such a terrible headache, and something bad happened. I lost my job."

"What were you thinking just then?"

Amelia closed her eyes and struggled to remember. "Everything had gone wrong all day. I was very unhappy. Very upset." She took a long shaky breath. "I just wanted everything to just go away."

The Seer held out his hand, and a bee landed on it. "And so it did."

"I never *really* wanted it to happen. I was just upset!"

"Your intent doesn't matter, you made a wish with your mind, and that wish was granted."

"Granted by what?" She held out her hands. "I couldn't have done it! I'm just a nobody!"

The boy shook his head. "Oh, you are a somebody, everybody is, but you are right when you say you couldn't have done this thing by yourself. Some power granted your wish."

"What power? What could destroy a world?" Her voice trembled and her eyes welled.

The boy stood up, and she saw that he had the lower body of a goat. "Look at the ground below you. What do you see?"

"Dead grass."

"Yes, your presence here wilts the dream, but it only

looks dead." He pointed behind her and she turned. The footprints that she'd left in the grass, the spots that were gray and lifeless were now covered with new shoots of bright green grass. "The nightmare clings to you."

"Nightmare? Is that a place?"

The Seer nodded. "As much as the dream is a place, the nightmare is also a place. It is there that you'll find your answers."

"Can I bring my world back?"

"Only you can know that."

"How do I find out?"

"You must find your wish to undo what you have done."

She stood up and dusted herself off. "Where do I have to go?"

"Hold out your hand." When she did, he coaxed the bee off of his finger and it hovered above her hand. "Follow the bee, and you'll find the nightmare.

She turned her body in either direction, but no matter how she moved, the bee stayed in place above her hand and pointed in the same direction. "It's like a compass."

"When you find the river, don't let a drop of it touch you. It's the River Oblivion, it unmakes everything it touches."

"I'm not in the mood for a swim." She aimed a smile at the Seer, but neither he nor Som were anywhere in sight. She heaved a great sigh and started walking. "Well, come on bee. Let's find the nightmare."

\* \* \* \*

She trudged through the meadow, and then over several steep hills, but surprisingly, no matter how steep the hills got, she never got fatigued or even winded while climbing them. Her footprints still scorched the grass, and she could see each footfall for miles behind her. Eventually, she heard the sound of flowing water and came to a brook. A stone bridge spanned the two banks.

She glanced at the bee, which still indicated that she was going in the right direction. "I guess I have to cross." As soon as she stepped onto the bridge, the bee buzzed once and fled in the direction from which she had come. "Goodbye, bee."

She peeked over the edge of the bridge and saw a gentle flow of water about three feet below her. "This is the River Oblivion? I'm a little disappointed." As she moved onto the center of the bridge she could hear a roar coming from below her, so she took another look over the side. The water had become a raging torrent a thousand feet below her and the stone beneath her feet trembled as if it might soon tumble into the surging water. She rushed across, her legs burning from the effort. It felt like she barely moved despite her adrenaline-fueled flight. The bridge stretched out before her, a hundred thousand feet long, and crumbling before her very eyes. She stopped running, closed her eyes and clenched her fists. She took three deep breaths and opened her eyes.

She saw her feet, and around them a spreading patch of cheery green grass with a few delicate spring flowers thrown in for color. She smiled and took another two steps without looking up, and just like that she found the end of the bridge and stood in the nightmare. She watched where she stepped, and sure enough, the grass and flowers sprouted. The sunless sky above her churned and roiled with the intensity of an approaching storm and rumbled with echoing thunder.

She wrapped her arms around her body as a raw wind blasted down the slopes of the jagged mountain peaks that towered above her. No matter where she looked, the only vegetation she saw was in her footprints, and even that didn't last long before curling up and turning gray. She strode into the nightmare, not knowing where she was going, but somehow knowing that she'd find what she was looking for.

From behind her a rhythmic crashing caught her attention, and before long she could make out a column of what looked like an army. She stood perfectly still as they approached, the grass spreading out from her in every direction. As the soldiers came closer, she could see them more clearly, twisted parodies of people, monstrosities worthy of living in the nightmare. The column stopped a few feet from the edge of her green carpet.

A gray-skinned creature in iron armor stepped forward and spoke in a raspy voice. "Are you her?"

"I suppose I am. Who else would I be?"

The creature blinked and bashed his fist into his helmet a few times. "You are coming with us."

"Am I?" She plucked a daisy that sprouted beside her foot and inhaled its aroma. "What if I don't want to?"

"You ain't got a choice."

"Don't I?" She tossed the daisy toward the grotesque soldier, and he clambered away from it until he crashed into the other soldiers. "I think I'm in charge here. Where do you want to take me?"

The creature stepped forward again. "To her."

"Who is that?"

The creature frowned. "Her is her."

Amelia took a deep breath and let it hiss through her teeth. "Fine, where is she?"

Instead of answering, the soldier simply extended one claw toward a towering fortress whose immensity made its reality difficult to grasp. Amelia tried to see the top of the thing but couldn't. "That wasn't there a minute ago!" She blinked when she realized that she could extend her arm and touch the iron-clad front gate. "I think this place cheats."

The gate swung inward with a metallic squeal, showing her a tall staircase that led up to an enormous doorway. She stepped through the gate, which crashed shut as soon as she passed it. The soldiers stomped away, and Amelia began climbing the stairs. Unlike the hills in the dream, the stairs in the nightmare seemed never-ending, and her legs and lungs burned from the effort by the time she reached the top. The door opened, and she stepped into the fortress.

She could hear the echoes of whispers carried on the dank drafts that wafted through the immense hallway, as well as the quick scurrying of tiny feet or flapping wings. Guttering torches hung in rusting sconces along the wall, barely illuminating the floor before her. She could smell the musty odor of mildew and the fetid aroma of decay. Even here in the dimness, fresh grass sprouted from her steps, and it glistened as if reflecting the light of a spring morning.

"I'm here."

The whispers became louder. "She's here! She's here!"

"Yes, I'm here. Now what?" She turned around to watch the grass wilting behind her.

"Welcome!"

Amelia spun around to find a young woman who looked much like herself, close enough to be a mirror reflection, assuming you were looking through a darkened mirror in the nightmare. The woman wore a billowing gown of gray and burgundy silk and had her hair up in a complicated mass of brown curls and red ribbons. She raised her arms and danced down the staircase at the end of the hall (that Amelia knew wasn't there a minute ago). "Welcome, Amelia!"

Amelia scowled. "Who are you?"

"I'm the nightmare."

"I thought the nightmare was a place, not a person."

"Well, let's just say it's both—I'm both." She turned and took the stairs by twos. "Come on up, Amelia. Dinner is on the table!"

"Dinner?" She plodded up the stairs, huffing and puffing from the effort. When she finally stepped through the door at the top, she found a long dining room table that could have easily seated a thousand people, and every square inch of the table was cover with food. Huge haunches of beef, racks of lamb, piles of baked potatoes, pastas, turkeys, corn on the cob, huge tureens of soup, and desserts of every description, pies, cakes, custards, puddings, and things that defied easy description. All of it was rotten, alive with vermin and teeming with wriggling things that gorged themselves on the rot.

The nightmare sat at the head of the table with an enormous wine goblet in her hands. "Please sit. Shall we have a toast? To Amelia, our honored guest."

Amelia peered into her wine glass but quickly looked away. "Thanks, but I'll pass."

The nightmare laughed, a dark parody of Amelia's own laughter. "As you will, sister dearest."

Amelia sat in the chair at her end of the table. "Okay, let's get down to business, shall we?"

A smile, if such a cheerful word could be applied to such a poisonous thing, spread across the nightmare's face. "Oh, yes, lets."

"Did you destroy my world?"

"Oh no, sister dearest! You did that yourself."

Amelia shook her head. "No, I'm just a regular person. I don't have the power to destroy a world."

The nightmare waggled a solitary finger back and forth, as if admonishing a naughty child. "You underestimate yourself, dear one. You *do* have that power, every one of your people does, just so long as you *really* want it to be so. All I did was give your wish reality. It was your desire that made it happen. I just showed you how to make it real."

"Why?"

The nightmare laughed again. "Why, for you, dear sister, I'd do anything."

Amelia laughed this time, which caused the nightmare to wince. "Cut the act, *dear sister*. I know baloney when I hear it."

The long table between them suddenly shrank and the nightmare scowled at her from across a tiny table that only had a single bowl of rotting fruit on it. "The truth, then."

"Yes, that'd be nice."

"I gave you what you wanted; your world can hurt you no more. Now, I want you to give me what I want."

Amelia leaned back in her chair. "Which is?"

"I want to leave this place."

"You mean the nightmare? I thought you *were* the nightmare?"

She waved her hand and began pacing back and forth. "Never mind that, I just want to leave."

"I don't blame you. What's stopping you though?"

"The nightmare is part of the dream and can't be separated from it. I'm trapped. Not trapped *in* a place, I'm trapped *as* a place!"

"So, what can I do?" Amelia watched the nightmare's hands curl into clawed fists.

"You can stay and be the nightmare."

Amelia's breath caught in her throat. "What?"

"I'm asking you to take my place as the nightmare." She flung herself on her knees just inches from the grass at Amelia's feet. "I'm begging you! You wanted your world to go away, and I gave you that! I'm begging you to take my world away from me! Please!"

She backed away from the nightmare. "I can't do that!"

"Yes, you can! Here, your life can be anything you want it to be. You're only limited by your whimsy!" She stood and clapped her hands twice, and suddenly they stood in an enormous ballroom filled with masked revelers all dancing and feasting in a riot of exuberant merrymaking. An orchestra had assembled on a dais and pounded out a lively tune that sounded vaguely familiar and discordant all at once.

Amelia whirled around, suddenly clad in a voluminous ball gown of lace and ribbon. The nightmare stood still in a tumultuous sea of dancers. "Do you see, Amelia? You can have anything you want in this place: wealth, power, friends . . . lovers?"

A muscular man with long, flowing blond tresses

strode up to Amelia with a single blood-red rose in his hand. "For you, my lady." He spoke in a rumbling baritone that carried with it just a hint of an accent. "A beautiful rose for a beautiful woman." He smiled, flashing a pair of dimples at her.

"It's not real..." Amelia knocked the rose out of the man's hand. "None of it's real!"

The nightmare clapped her hands again, and they stood alone in a throne room of crumbling majesty. "It's as real as you want it to be, Amelia. All of it. In this place, reality is what you deem it to be. Think about it. Here you'll never get sick, never grow old, and never die!"

Amelia turned away from her. "If it's so perfect, why do you want to leave?"

"Do you have any idea how long I've been here? I just want it to end, and one day you might as well, but that time is so far in the distance that a billion-billion lifetimes will pass before you stumble upon it. When you do, you'll understand what I'm asking you to do, and why." She plopped herself onto the ancient wooden throne.

Biting her lip again, Amelia turned to face her. "I'm really sorry for your situation, but I don't want your job. I just want to find my world and wish it back into existence so I can go home."

"So, you're declining my offer?"

"Yes, I am. I'm sorry, but I am."

"That is unfortunate."

Amelia licked her lips. "Is it?"

"Oh yes, most unfortunate." She reached into her bosom and pulled out a round blue gem that dangled from a golden chain. "Look at this, Amelia, dear sister."

She bent close and examined the stone. "Is that . . . ?"

"Yes, this is the wish that ended your world, but re-duced to a bauble on a chain. Most unfortunate."

"Why is it unfortunate?" Amelia stepped away from the nightmare's throne.

The nightmare laughed. "It's unfortunate because without me, your world will remain where it is forever. Only I can show you the way to wish it back into exis-tence, which I'll only do if you agree to take my place as the nightmare."

Amelia's jaw tightened. "So, you couldn't get what you wanted by persuasion, so now you're using force?"

"Oh no, Amelia. This is still persuasion. I can't force you to do anything." She smiled venomously. "It *must* be your choice, or the transfer won't work."

"Fine, what if I still say no?"

The nightmare held her hands palms up. "You are not supposed to be here, not in your physical form. What happened when you touched something in the dream?"

"It died."

"Exactly, and in the nightmare your presence causes the grass to grow. Do you see yet? Just by being here, you disrupt the very fabric of the dream itself. If you do nothing, eventually you'll unmake the dream completely, tear it apart, and the nightmare will go into oblivion with it. Everything you've seen here will shatter and fall to pieces, everything except you. Even when eternity swal-lows everything else, when trillions of lives are snuffed out, you'll still remain, all alone in the dark with only your guilt to keep you company. Forever. So you see, dear sister, one way or another, I will get what I want."

Amelia wiped tears off her cheeks. "You've caught me in quite a trap. Why me? Will you at least tell me that?"

The nightmare shrugged. "You wanted the world to go away. You wanted it more than anybody I'd ever seen, and believe me, I've been watching for a long time."

"I wasn't happy with my life."

"You hated it, Amelia. Especially your job."

"I didn't hate everything. I loved my cat."

The nightmare threw her head back and laughed, and suddenly Bowser lay purring on her lap. She stroked him as she watched Amelia. "That's not much of a life, if the only bright point is your cat. Why did you stay at a job you hated for all those years? You could have left."

She sniffed back more tears. "I don't know. I guess I was afraid. In a way, I was as trapped in my life as you are trapped in yours. We're both pathetic in our own ways."

"Take my place, Amelia, and I'll take yours."

Amelia frowned at the nightmare. "What do you mean you'll take my place?"

"Once we wish your world back into existence, I'll go there as Amelia Follett, and you'll stay here as the nightmare."

"You can't be me!"

The nightmare shrugged. "What did you think would happen to me once I passed through the veil into your world?"

She scowled at the nightmare. "I honestly hadn't given it much thought, but you can't be me! I'm me!"

"Come now, what are you? Just a collection of memories, prejudices, and programmed responses in a sack of meat and bone. I *will* be you once we complete the transfer of power. You'll have to get over it."

"I won't do it! I won't agree to anything you want!"

The nightmare waggled her finger again. "Tut, tut, tut. We both know you won't condemn all those countless people to unlife just to spite me."

Amelia clenched her fists and bared her teeth. "You don't know what I'll do!"

"And what about Bowser?" The cat sat up in the nightmare's lap watching Amelia intently.

"What about him?"

"Would you condemn him to eternal unlife as well?" She stroked his fur one last time, then his eyes widened and his flesh withered away, and his fur fell away from his body in clumps. When only his bones were left, they clattered to the floor and crumbled into dust.

"No! Stop it! I'll do it!"

The nightmare grinned. "Of course you will."

\* \* \* \*

"Okay, what do I have to do to become the new nightmare?" Amelia held out her hand and the nightmare dropped the blue gem into her palm.

"You just have to say the words."

"That's it?"

"If you'd prefer a complicated ritual with a thousand chanting cultists dancing around a bonfire, I can certainly make that happen." She smiled, the first genuine smile Amelia had seen on her face.

"No, I'd rather not make a big production out of it. Where do we have to do it?"

"Anywhere in the nightmare."

Amelia nodded. "Fine, let's go to the border with the dream. I'd like to be looking at it when I become part of it."

The nightmare clapped her hands, and Amelia found

herself standing a few feet from the raging torrent of the river. She could see the sunlit hills of the dream, only a stone's throw away.

"Can I go there, you know, after?"

The nightmare put on a disgusted face. "Yes, but only when they invite you to cross the bridge."

"Do they invite you often?"

"No." She almost looked embarrassed. "Almost never."

"Great." Amelia held up the blue gem and looked at the dream through its faceted face. "So how do I get my world back?" She spun the gem on its chain, watching the dream waver and whirl.

"You'll have to want your world to return as badly as you wanted it to go away before. I'll direct your desire to shatter the gem, and your world will be as it was before."

"How do I make myself want it that badly?"

The nightmare looked down, and there stood Bowser, rubbing his head against her leg. "Think of the things you loved, especially your cat. Feel how their loss twists in your soul; that is what it'll take to bring back your world."

"And then you'll take over my life, and you'll have the things that you want me to remember loving. For me, those things will be lost no matter what. I'll be here, living as nothing more than a nightmare. Is that right?"

The nightmare nodded. "Yes."

"I don't think so, sister!" Amelia flung the gem into the abyss.

"No!" The nightmare lunged to catch it, but it fell between her outstretched fingers and plopped into the black water of the River Oblivion. "What have you done!"

Amelia tried to speak, but no sound came out. She couldn't seem to draw breath into her lungs and a bright light seemed to burn its way into the center of her vision. She could hear the nightmare chanting one word over and over: "No!"

"No! No! No!"

\*   \*   \*   \*

Amelia rolled over and looked at her alarm clock: 6:55, a full five minutes before her alarm was set to go off. She sat up, fully awake and feeling as refreshed as she'd ever felt before. She turned off the alarm and headed for the shower. Bowser followed her, meowing sleepily. She knelt to pet him. "Good morning, Bowser!"

She stood under the warm water, trying to remember a dream and feeling like singing for some reason. She selected her clothes while she dried off, and then heated a bagel for breakfast and even gave Bowser a couple of extra treats as she was leaving her apartment. The elevator whisked her to the ground floor without stopping once, and she caught every green light on her way to work. "Must be my lucky day!"

Carmen caught up with her at the coffee pot. "Amelia! The district manager is coming today!"

Amelia sipped her coffee. "Good morning, Carmen. Coffee?"

"Girl, are your ears broken? I said Howard Long is coming today!"

Amelia shrugged. "That's nice. I do have something to tell him though."

"What about the McAdam's report? He'll want to see that right away!"

"I finished it yesterday, Carmen. Old news."

Carmen blinked and her mouth hung open. "You did?"

"I sure did. Now, if you'll excuse me, I'm gonna find Neil and get one of those doughnuts he always brings in when he wants to suck up to Howard."

Carmen watched her walk away, but it took a few minutes before she remembered to close her mouth. "What happened to her?"

Amelia burrowed into the warren of cubicles and found the one with her name on it. She sat her coffee on the desktop and pulled her chair back when she saw a little blue gem on the seat. Then it all came back: the dream, Som, the Seer, the nightmare. She clutched at her throat as the memories propagated through her mind.

The nightmare's voice whispered in her ear, a sibilant hiss of coiled rage. "You've won nothing, dear sister. What you've done once, you'll do again. Nothing's changed."

Amelia chuckled and threw the gem into her wastebasket. "Oh yeah? Keep watching."

She read over the McAdam's report and found not even a single typo. She grinned when she heard Neil's oily, pandering voice and Howard's deeper basso-profundo moving through the warren toward her.

"Uh, Amelia?"

She spun around in her chair. "Neil—and Howard—how nice. What can I do for you boys?" She sipped her coffee and threw them a carefree smile.

Howard's scowl didn't relent. "The McAdam's report. I need it now."

She handed the folder to him. "I think you'll be especially interested in their payments from October through

January. It's all in the summary, but I'd recommend pro-
ceeding with the lawsuit. It's clear they were committing
fraud, and any judge with half a brain will agree."

Howard scanned the summary page, his stony coun-
tenance slowly breaking into a hint of a smile. "This is
very good work, Miss Follett."

"Thanks. By the way, I quit." She gave Howard a
companionable punch on the biceps. "Don't worry; I can
show myself out." And she did.

She drove out of town, just to be moving, singing
along with the radio and loving her life.

# Treasure of the Thrushspire

S. L. Rudder

THUNK! Another quivering dagger joined the trio already pinning a rather messy piece of sheet music to the front of the cupboard.

"That's for making me learn the lute!"

THUD!

"And that's for making me compose a score for the lute!"

Just as the enraged young Dwarven female drew back another dagger to throw at the unfortunate page, the door of her chamber burst open. She spun around toward the portal with the dagger still in hand, a wave of auburn hair spread out like a cloak behind her. Her dark brown eyes were shooting sparks, and the look of rage on her lovely face would have quelled the sturdiest Dwarven warrior. Yet she was met with a cheerful giggle.

"Poor Master Kurek!" the new arrival said with a slight shake of her head. "What did he do this time?"

Thuria slammed the dagger she was holding down on the desk beside her while giving the newcomer one last glare before she plopped down on the stool behind her with a sigh.

"He is making me learn the lute," she said with a shake of her head. "Just when I had finally almost mastered the harp, he is forcing me to switch to the lute!" Both her voice and color raised slightly on the last line. "Bregna, you know how I hate playing the lute!"

Bregna attempted to hide another laugh behind her hand but to no avail.

"Stop laughing at me!"

This was met by a full storm of giggles and the young visitor dropped down into a nearby chair to wipe her watering eyes.

"I'm sorry, Thuria. Really I am." She tried her best to compose herself not wanting to further anger her friend.

She rose and made her way over to investigate the offending sheet of music, tracing her fingers over many blotches and crossed out sections.

"Looks like a battle was fought on here before the daggers entered the picture."

Thuria leapt off of her stool and wrenched the daggers free, tossing them to the top of the desk with one hand as she crushed the tattered composition with the other. Then, drawing a deep, shuddering breath to calm herself, she resumed her seat and flattened the crumpled sheet of music out before her.

"I just can't seem to get anything right with the lute, no matter how hard I try. And you haven't heard the worst part."

"Well, out with it. You know you will feel better if

you tell me. You always do." Bregna perched on the edge of her seat and leaned forward to place her hand on her friend's shoulder.

"You're right. I always do." She even managed to smile into the amber eyes looking at her so intently. "I went to Master Kurek and calmly told him that I wished to keep playing the harp at this time." Thuria greeted the skeptical look on her friend's face with a half-hearted glare. "Well, I started out calmly!"

Bregna raised an eyebrow at this, but did not comment as Thuria continued.

"Anyway, I told him that I wished to keep playing the harp, and that I had hoped to obtain a superior instrument so that I could advance even more quickly. He was furious and completely unreasonable! He wouldn't even listen to my argument!"

"Well, he IS the Master and you are just a lowly apprentice."

"It just isn't fair." Thuria pushed a stray auburn lock behind her small ear with a sniff. "As punishment, I must carry this LUTE with me at ALL times." She reached back behind her and pulled the instrument around thrusting it into Bregna's face for inspection. "If I am not sleeping or bathing, I must have my lute with me. On top of that, he won't allow me a new harp until after I have mastered the lute selection he assigned me and have composed a 'fitting' one of my own."

"I'm truly sorry, Thuria. I am afraid that is the type of thing we apprentices must put up with."

Sliding the lute back around behind her, Thuria cut in before Bregna could go further. "Yes, but you love to bake anything! No matter what your Mistress asks of you, you can't wait to try it."

"Yes," Bregna agreed with a smile. "My trouble isn't what I am forced to do but the things that I am not allowed to do. Take today for example." She settled back comfortably in her seat. "We have been commissioned to make a special cake for the supper being given in honor of the diplomatic envoy that just arrived from the Dwarf-holt of Kaesviharn all the way up in Ros. It is to be stupendous! And do you think that my Mistress would—"

Bregna jumped up out of her seat, looped braids the shade of young carrots swinging around her, her palm slapping against her forehead.

"Oh no! I can't believe it! I have totally forgotten why I came here in the first place. The diplomatic envoy and his party have just arrived! You are wanted in the Great Hall!" Grabbing Thuria's arm, she tried to pull her off the stool and toward the door.

Thuria yanked herself free, a look of disbelief on her face.

"What are you saying? Why, by King Rurik's beard, would the diplomatic envoy from Kaesviharn Dwarfholt wish to see me?"

"Oh no, not the envoy, silly," Bregna said with a laugh. "He is here to see King Rurik. As I was placing the fresh rolls I baked on the banquet table, I heard a young Dwarven scout asking where you could be found."

Thuria tried to break in, "Why would a scout from Kaesviharn wish to speak to me?"

Bregna continued as if she had not heard. "Wait until you see him! He is just about our age, can't be over seventy-five or eighty, and he has dusty black hair, I bet it shines in the moonlight, though his beard is a bit short for my taste. . . ."

"Why does he wish to speak to me?"

"And he had the dreamiest hazel eyes you ever saw in your life! I could have just stayed there and stared at him for hours. I even dropped my tray of rolls, but luckily it landed on the table and none fell to the floor or I don't know what my Mistress would have done."

Her face beginning to grow red, Thuria grabbed her friend by both shoulders and gave her a good hard shake. "WHY DOES HE WISH TO SPEAK TO ME?!"

Bregna covered her mouth with one small hand as a giggle slipped out. "Oh, didn't I tell you?"

"No, Bregna, you most certainly did not!" Thuria turned loose of her friend's arms and stepped back, grimacing as her lute bumped the desk beside her. She was trying to count to ten under her breath, the way Master Kurek had instructed her to in situations of this kind, but it seemed to be impossible at the moment. She could barely reach five.

Bregna was quaking with suppressed laughter by the time Thuria had herself somewhat back under control. She was even able to muster up a small smile, but Bregna realized she had best reach her point quickly.

"I didn't hear all that was said. As you might have guessed, I was a wee bit distracted by his appearance."

"Yes, I thought you might have been," Thuria said with a soft laugh of her own. She had a quick temper, but she also had a well-developed sense of humor, which at this particular moment was vying with her curiosity for supremacy.

Bregna giggled once again. "Very well then. I heard

him asking one of the Door Wardens where he might find a young Dwarf maiden by the name of 'Thuria.' Seems he has a message and a package of some sort for you. Since I was right there, as you know, and had already made my presence known by dropping a metal tray of rolls on the table, as you also know," Thuria smiled as her friend's face turned a lovely shade of pink. "I spoke up and said that I knew you well and that I would fetch you back to meet him right away. We must hurry!"

Thuria's deep, brown eyes held a look of confused wonder. She had not the faintest idea why a Dwarven scout all the way from Kaesviharn would be wanting to see her. The wonder and confusion were soon exchanged for a look of determination as she took Bregna's arm and began pulling her along toward the closed portal.

"Well, if we must, we must! Come along, I wish to see this fine young scout that has you in such a fluster, not to mention find out what in the Seven Dwarfholts kind of message he could have for me."

"Don't forget the package!" Bregna added as they nearly ran down the wide hall earning a few reproving looks from the older Dwarves they passed by.

"Oh no! We must not forget the package," Thuria returned with a laugh.

A short time later the two Dwarf maidens stopped just short of bursting into the Great Hall. They had remembered in the nick of time that King Rurik, the envoy, and his company were all at table there, and had stopped just outside of the wide double doors that were standing open in welcome to the travelers.

The two young maidens peered around the door frame to catch a glimpse of what was taking place within.

Bregna snickered and Thuria growled as the lute bumped between them. In the Great Hall the Dwarven lanterns burned brightly, showing the grandeur of the enormous chamber carved from the red granite of the mountain. The eight tall stone pillars supporting both the ceiling and the lamps were carved in the shapes of Dwarf warriors in full battle array. The highly polished surfaces of the pillars and the warm glow of the lamps seemed almost to give life to the warriors, and many a Dwarven youngster would have sworn that the warriors' eyes would follow them as they moved through the chamber. Of course, this belief was given some credence by more than one Dwarven matron hoping to instill proper etiquette and decorum in their small charges.

Thuria's eyes grew wide in awe at the size of the large banquet board before them. The table nearly filled the raised dais that comprised the front third of the Great Hall. Sitting at the head of this table was King Rurik. His sagely face was wreathed with smiles at something that the envoy, sitting to his right, had just said. Clearly this was a meeting of old friends as well as a diplomatic one. The two maidens barely noticed the dignitaries as they swept the faces of the other diners, searching for that of the scout.

"I don't see anyone who looks like your scout," Thuria whispered to her companion.

"I don't remember saying that he was *my* scout. After all, he came here looking for you. That would make him *your* scout," Bregna whispered back.

Both maidens drew back around the corner, out of sight, to battle a case of the giggles. Even the dour looks from the Door Warden did little to calm them. That is until he spoke to them.

"Is there something that you wish?" came his gruff inquiry.

The two friends quickly attempted to compose themselves, and Thuria was finally able to reply.

"My friend here," she said, gesturing to Bregna, "has informed me that my presence was requested by a member of the envoy's company. We are attempting to locate him."

The Warden's eyes sparkled at the regal mein Thuria had achieved by the end of this short speech. One could almost believe that being summoned to the Great Hall was a common occurrence for her. That is, if one had not just witnessed her giggling with her young companion or taken notice of the delightful rosy blush blooming on her round cheeks.

"Well, miss, both the easiest and the correct way to do this would be to ask a Door Warden."

The rose of Thuria's cheeks deepened to a more dusky shade. Bregna's fair complexion became a bright pink from her throat to her hairline.

"Yes, of course," they replied quietly in unison.

The Warden's face softened even more. These two reminded him of his own young daughter.

"If you would look to the left of the doorway, you will find the scout you seek waiting on a bench along the wall."

The two maidens peeked inside once again, and then turned to each other sharing a bright smile before Thuria again composed herself.

"Thank you, sir," she said, giving him a slight nod. "You have been most helpful."

The Door Warden allowed himself a full-blown

smile after the pair had passed through the portal. While the time spent might be enjoyable, he could not help but think that the youngster from Kaesviharn would have his hands full dealing with these two red-headed maidens.

The young scout smoothly came to his feet as Thuria and Bregna approached his resting place. Bregna rushed to introduce her companion.

"Here she is, this is Thuria. Thuria, this is . . . is . . ." her cheerful smile faded. "I am so sorry! I guess I didn't wait to learn your name."

"Not to worry, miss." The scout gave Thuria a deep bow. "I am Thogar, son of Thorgan. Pleased to be at your service. Now, if you would be so kind as to introduce me to your kind friend who fetched you for me."

Bregna burst into giggles and Thuria gave a knowing smile.

"Thogar, may I present Bregna. Bregna, meet Thogar, son of Thorgan."

The scout repeated his bow to the second maiden. "Thank you for your service, Bregna. I am pleased to be at your service as well."

After the formalities were finished, Thuria turned to Thogar with an expectant look. "Bregna tells me you have journeyed all the way from Kaesviharn to bring me a message."

"And a package!" spoke up Bregna helpfully.

"Thank you so for the reminder," Thuria acknowledged with a tight smile.

"No trouble at all." Sarcasm was often wasted on Bregna.

Thogar's hazel eyes took on a sparkle as he broke into a slow smile, causing Thuria to catch her breath. The scout seemed not to notice as he bowed the fair maidens to a seat on the bench he had just vacated. Thuria grimaced as her lute bumped into the stone edge as she took her seat. She strove to regain her dignity, but having Bregna poking her in the ribs and whispering I told you so's in her ear did not help in the least. She gave her annoying friend a good pinch when Thogar turned his back to retrieve both message and package from his bag.

While doing this, Thogar knocked his crossbow leaning against the bag to the floor with a loud clatter. This echoed through the enormous chamber and drew reproachful glances from those seated at the banquet table. It also gave proof to the fact that his hands were less than steady. Knowing this helped Thuria get her jangled nerves back under better control so that she was more ready to face him when he turned back around.

Thogar cleared his throat and pulled at the bottom of his jacket to straighten it before he addressed the expectant pair before him. Even through his discomfort, the maidens could see that he was taking his quest very seriously.

He stood at attention as he faced the Dwarven maidens. "The first course of action I must take is to ascertain if you are indeed the 'Thuria' I seek."

Bregna whispered, not altogether softly, in her friend's ear, "Of course you are the Thuria he seeks! There isn't another Thuria in the entire Dwarfholt! I told him that before I went to fetch you."

For once Thuria's patience came to the fore. She gave Bregna's hand a slight squeeze and hushed her before addressing the scout.

"As it seems my companion has pointed out to you, I

am the only Thuria currently living here in Drost. When I was born, my great-grandmother asked my parents to name me after her twin sister, Thuria," the maiden's eyes widened in understanding and surprise, "who she was parted from when Thuria wed a Dwarf from Kaesviharn and left Drost! It is tradition in our family to have a 'Thuria' every fourth generation. My great-grandmother asked that I be named Thuria to carry on this tradition. Her sister's husband was killed battling a snowbeast near the northern Ros border shortly after they were wed and before great-aunt Thuria was blessed with any offspring. My great-aunt Thuria, so I am told, could not bear to marry another after her husband's tragic death, and therefore had no children of her own. She chose to remain in Kaesviharn instead of returning here to Drost, the place of her birth. She claimed that she felt closer to her late husband there in the home they had shared for such a short time and could not leave it."

Thogar's stance eased as he gazed into the deep brown eyes before him.

"That is all the proof I needed, having heard the same story myself upon starting my journey," Thogar faltered slightly at the intense looks he was receiving from both maidens.

"Yes, well," he cleared his throat and once again drew himself up into a more rigid posture. "As I was saying, that is the same story I heard myself."

Thuria's smile grew brighter, and Bregna did her best to stifle her giggles.

"Yes, well," the scout's face above his short beard blushed slightly in confusion and embarrassment, and he pulled at his jacket once more. "Anyway, where was I?"

Thuria had trouble controlling a soft chuckle of her own. "I believe you had a message for me?" She smiled sweetly at the scout's predicament.

"And a package!" broke in Bregna, laughing aloud.

"Yes, yes, of course." Thogar looked down at the objects in his hands. Dealing with young Dwarf maidens was harder than tracking moostadons in a snowstorm!

"Your great-aunt Thuria has but recently passed on. This message and the accompanying package were found among her belongings along with the instructions that were given to me.

"I was instructed to give both message and package to the youngest 'Thuria' living in Drost. Since, as I have been told, you are the only 'Thuria' living in Drost at this time, you are the recipient."

He held the message out. "I was further instructed to have you read the message before I delivered the package into your keeping."

Thuria took the scroll before her with a nod and a smile. She was amused at the young scout's formality, but also impressed by his bearing and adherence to protocol. She gave Bregna a sharp poke in the ribs with her elbow as the young baker attempted once again to whisper something into her ear.

"Thank you, sir." She held the scroll for a moment before breaking the seal. It seemed strange to receive a message from a great-aunt for whom she was named but had never met.

"Well, what does it say, for goodness sakes?" Bregna spouted impatiently.

Thuria unrolled the scroll and scanned its contents before quietly reading it aloud.

"Long has it been since I walked the Halls of *Drost. The memories of my youth spent there are very dear to my heart. Leaving my home was at once the hardest thing I have ever done, outside of being forced to bid good-bye to my dear husband so soon, but also the easiest. While I hated to leave my family and all I had ever known behind me, I was more than happy to move here to Kaesviharn with my dear Darrig and start our life together. The home we built here is so full of the memories we shared, be they fleeting, that I have been most happy to remain here.*

"Of late, I have grown nos*talgic and have missed Drost very much. Alas, I have grown too old to make the return journey. I feel my time drawing ever closer to the end. This thought brings me no sorrow for I know that I will soon be reunited with my Darrig, so do not mourn my passing too greatly.*

"When sorting through some old trunks, I came upon this small chest. It is an heirloom that has been passed down in our family for nearly an age, going from one *Thuria to the next. Inside you will find the key to the Treasure of the Thrushspire. To my knowledge, no one has been able to discover this hidden treasure, but it is said to be of immeasurable worth! The key did not come to me until after I had left Drost, so I did not have the opportunity to search for the treasure myself.*

"My hope *is that now that the key has returned to its home, it will be able to lead you to the treasure. There is a warning that has been attached to the treasure, so heed it well. The warning is this:* 'The Treasure of the Thrushspire is immeasurable, but its greatest worth can only be obtained if it is shared.'

"May your search be rewarded and may you find treasure beyond your wildest dreams."

For once, Bregna was speechless and remained quiet as Thuria silently read through the message once more. She turned to her companion, her eyes filled with questions.

"I thought I knew Drost well, but I have never heard of this 'Thrushspire.'"

Bregna gave a small shrug. "Nor have I."

Thogar broke into their musing as he handed the package to Thuria. The young Dwarven maiden took it eagerly from his hands, hoping it would contain a clue to the mystery of the Thrushspire's location. She carefully untied the leather bindings and pulled the rough cloth wrappings free to reveal what was hidden inside.

The small chest the package contained, though it appeared quite old, was a beautiful piece of craftsmanship. It was square and flat with a slightly domed top, formed from highly polished steel. The chest was decorated with gold and silver vines twining about it. These vines were studded with flowers of multicolored gemstones all along their length.

"Oh my!" Bregna breathed at Thuria's shoulder as she reached a hand over to touch the polished surface. "That chest is a treasure in itself!"

Thuria nodded her head in agreement as she slowly and thoroughly examined the chest in her hands.

"Why, there doesn't seem to be any way to open it!" Bregna said with a shake of her head. "I don't see any hinge, clasp, or even a seam!"

Thuria paid her companion little mind as she continued studying the chest. After just a few moments, she discovered that some sections of vine and a few of the flowers would move when pressed in.

"It's a puzzle box!" she exclaimed, her eyes glowing in excitement. "Now I just have to figure out the puzzle."

Bregna crossed her arms and leaned back against the wall with a huff. "That will either take forever or be impossible!"

Thogar and Thuria shared an amused smile as the young maiden continued to experiment with the moving decorations. In just a few minutes, there was a soft click and the lid of the chest sprang open.

"You did it!" Bregna stated the obvious. "I didn't think you would ever be able to figure it out!"

Thuria gave her friend a cheeky grin. "All it takes is a little bit of thought and concentration— and less fussing over what can't be done. Some of us are just better at thinking than others."

Thogar did his best to turn a surprised laugh into a cough. Bregna turned slightly pink at this, then leaned in closer to get a look at what the chest held now that the puzzle was solved.

Nestled in a bed of deep red satin lay an exquisite gold necklace.

"Where is the key?" Bregna burst out. She snatched the scroll from beside Thuria on the bench and started scanning it frantically. "I thought there was supposed to be a key in there!"

Thuria paid little attention to her friend as she drew the necklace out of the box and held it up for a closer look. The necklace was formed by a simple, heavy gold chain holding a pendant that was the size of Thuria's small palm. The pendant itself was an intricately wrought combination of musical instruments. Thuria gave a rather unladylike snort as she realized that a lute was front and center while the harp was nearly hidden at the back.

"Seems I can't get away from the darn things anywhere," she mused as she readjusted the strap of her own lute. "I bet that Master Kurek had a hand in this somehow."

A slight look of confusion passed over Thogar's face and the two Dwarf maidens joined in peals of laughter, yet again drawing stern looks from those gathered at the banquet table.

Thogar gently grasped the arms of both maidens and pulled them from their seats.

"I do believe we should find a more private place to finish this discussion. If we don't, I am afraid that this might be my last task as well as my first."

Doing their best to stifle their amusement, the pair nodded in agreement and waited for Thogar to retrieve his belongings before exiting the Great Hall past the amused Door Warden.

The Dwarven maidens led Thogar through a short series of connected corridors to the bakery where Bregna was apprenticed. Bregna motioned her companions to seats at a small table and then obtained refreshments before joining them. Thuria took a small sip of her steaming tea, while Thogar took one look at the plate set before him and pulled it closer to start on the delicious-looking pastry it held. He had never seen the like! The dough of the pastry was rolled in a spiral, raised to an unbelievable height, and had the most tantalizing spicy fragrance he had ever smelled. It filled the small plate that held it and had a thick, sticky icing dripping down the sides.

Thuria placed her cup of tea back on the table and turned to Bregna with a knowing smile. "Tried making something new again, hey?"

She was answered with a nod and a smile.

Thogar missed this exchange as he cut off a large bite and popped it in his mouth. Both maidens dissolved into giggles as he quickly took a second, larger bite and slowly closed his eyes, a look of complete contentment on his face as he leaned back in his chair and savored it.

Thuria reached eagerly for her own pastry. "From the looks of our young scout's face, I think I will give this a try myself."

Beaming with pleasure, Bregna took a seat and started in on her own pastry. It felt extremely good to have one's work so appreciated.

After finishing her pastry, and as Thogar started on his third, Thuria returned to her study of the chest and its contents. Bregna scooted her stool over closer to her friend for a better look, and both girls rolled their eyes as she bumped into the lute hanging on Thuria's back.

Carefully, Thuria examined the puzzle box, searching for a second compartment where a key could be hidden. There was no other compartment; the space that contained the pendant and the satin it rested in filled the entire chest. She even removed the satin lining, which lifted out easily, but it concealed nothing either inside or underneath.

Finally, Thuria turned to the pendant itself. The chest was a puzzle; there was always the possibility that the pendant was also, that it held a hidden key in amongst the musical instruments.

"Nothing! It is formed from a solid piece of gold. Nothing twists or turns or opens in any way."

Bregna reached eagerly for the necklace. "Here, let me try." She too probed and examined the pendant. "The only thing I can find strange about this is the fact that the back has this raised diamond pattern. It seems odd to decorate the back of the pendant as well as the front. I mean, who will see the back? It will be hidden when the necklace is worn."

Thuria nodded in agreement as she placed the necklace back into the chest, closed it, and set it on the table. Both maidens sat silently staring at the chest, hoping for the answer to just come to them.

After a few moments, Thuria gave an unladylike snort of disgust. "This is getting us nowhere! Maybe we should stop worrying about the key for now and concentrate on discovering where this 'Thrushspire' is located."

"That sounds good. But how are we going to do that? Drost is a huge Dwarfholt! It would take us years to search the entire 'Holt looking for a lost spire that neither of us has even heard of before!"

The two friends discussed the problem forwards and back for quite some time without getting any closer to reaching a solution.

Thogar finished his pastry, looked longingly at the last one on the tray, placed his hand on his stomach, gave a shake of his head, and pushed his plate forward. "Why don't you just see if the Chief DelveCaptain has a map you could use?"

Both maidens turned toward the scout in surprise. They had been so busy discussing possibilities that they had nearly forgotten his presence.

"What did you say?" Thuria asked.

Thogar ran his hand over his short beard, checking for crumbs as he repeated his question. "I said, why don't you just see if the Chief DelveCaptain has a map you could use?"

Thogar's face began to color as the two red-headed maidens stared at him in wonder. "I just thought that would be what I would do." He moved nervously in his chair. "I mean, if I were wanting to find some place that I had never heard of."

"I hadn't thought of that!" Thuria declared.

"Me either!" chimed in Bregna.

Both young females placed their elbows on the table and leaned in closer toward the dwarf across from them.

"Do you have any more wonderful ideas?" Thuria asked.

The young scout looked at the two maidens before him. For just a moment all he could think of was how lovely they both were. Two sets of bright, sparkling eyes, one deep brown and the other golden amber. Two heads of long, shining hair, one dark auburn and wavy and the other carroty orange and in looping braids. Then with a shake of his head and a pull at his jacket, his face warming yet again, he got himself back on track and proceeded to give the benefit of his wisdom.

The trio spent the next several hours sharing ideas and making and discarding plans. Bregna kept their cups full of tea and plates full of treats. It was growing quite late when they realized that the three of them had somehow decided to go on this adventure together. After a few minutes of trying to figure out just how that happened, they decided the best thing to do was to retire for the night. Thogar needed to check in with his captain and discuss the possibility of his remaining in Drost long enough to join the quest. Bregna had to be at work long before dawn. The baked goods had to be ready for those who came to the shop looking for a morning treat. She had to see to that before she even thought of asking her Mistress for permission to miss work for a few days. Thuria was glad that she did not have to face Master Kurek for her next lesson for another week and a half, time enough to explain to him her lack of practice when she saw him. No need to face that adventure yet. The young Dwarves said their good nights after agreeing to meet back at the bakery early the next morning to start their adventure.

Bregna had just finished putting the last batch of baked goods out on the counter as Thuria and Thogar literally met at the door. They untangled his crossbow from her lute amid much laughter. After each had settled their packs once again, Thogar bowed Thuria inside and they made their way to the table Bregna had all set and waiting for them.

Thuria reached for her cup of tea in hopes of hiding her warming face behind it. Thogar did not seem to notice her discomfort as he tugged on his jacket and smoothed his beard before reaching for his own mug. Bregna did notice, but for once she simply smiled from behind her own steaming cup with her eyes shining at her friend. Thuria pretended she had not seen, but her round cheeks became even more dusky.

Bregna was the first to set aside her cup and get down to the business at hand. "I talked to my Mistress. She wasn't happy, but she said that I could have the rest of the week off. She assured me that I will be washing mixing bowls for the next month to make up for it."

"And I have obtained permission to remain in Drost," Thogar said eagerly in between bites. "In fact, I took my captain with me when I talked to the DelveCaptain about obtaining a map of the 'Holt. The two of them agreed to a trade of sorts. It seems that one of your scouts here at Drost had been wanting to journey to Kaesviharn and do some exploring of his own. I will be taking his place for the foreseeable future. Lucky for us, his squad just returned from a trade mission to Mansker and they are off duty for the next two weeks."

Thuria impulsively reached over and grasped his hand. "That's wonderful!" she said. She quickly released her hold when she realized what she had done and poured more tea into her nearly full cup. "I mean, it will be so nice to have you along."

Thogar stared down at his hand for a few seconds before replying. "Well, yes. Yes, it will be nice, won't it."

Bregna gave a small snort before she burst into giggles. She agreed that it would be nice to have Thogar along, but she wasn't sure that the hem of his jacket would make it.

Thuria turned a half-hearted glare on her friend. "I mean, it will be nice to have him along since he was able to get the map and all."

"Oh, I am sure that was your meaning," Bregna returned with a grin. "I am sure that neither you nor I would have been able to get the map ourselves or anything like that."

Thuria's glare was reaching a dangerous level, so Bregna chose that moment to refill both her cup and

Thogar's. As she passed behind Thogar's chair, she held up her hands and counted off to ten on her fingers. Thuria's eyes sparked over the rim of her cup as she took a sip of her tea, trying her best to not throw it at Bregna's head. The poor scout was somewhat flustered by the whole thing even though he had not caught half of what had passed between the two maidens.

As Bregna returned to her seat, Thogar pulled a tightly rolled scroll from his pack. He carefully spread it out on the table. Calling a truce, the two maidens pulled their stools over closer, one on each side, so as to see better.

"The only map that the DelveCaptain had showing the Thrushspire was very ancient. He said that he could not allow it to leave his quarters, but he did allow me to make a copy."

Bregna and Thuria leaned even closer to look at the map.

"You made this copy? Why, it is beautiful!" Thuria exclaimed.

Bregna was quick to agree. "There is so much detail! How did you do such a wonderful job so quickly?"

Thogar's face glowed a rosy red with their praise. He tugged on his jacket and cleared his throat before he was able to speak. "Well, I did work on it most all last night. And my uncle is a map-maker for the DelveCaptain in Kaesviharn. He has let me help him from time to time."

The young Dwarven maidens looked at each other in surprise, then turned back to the map, much to the scout's relief.

"Let's see." Thuria began tracing locations on the map. "Here is the Great Hall."

"Yes, and here is where we are." Bregna placed her own finger on the map.

"Right," Thogar agreed, "and here is the Thrushspire. I marked it in red."

The two friends simply nodded as they studied the map between where they were currently and where they hoped to end up.

"That is quite a long way from here," Thuria noted. "It will take us at least a day and a half just to travel that far through the 'Holt."

Thogar silently nodded in agreement. With both maidens leaning in so close to him, he could not have spoken right then if his beard had been on fire.

"What do these symbols here mean?" Bregna asked.

"Oh, I added those in myself," Thogar admitted with a slight smile, somewhat proud that he had not stuttered in the attempt. "That is a section where an earth tremor damaged the passageway. That is the only way to the Thrushspire and the reason that it has been forgotten for all these years."

"You mean that we are not going to be able to get there after all?" Thuria looked questioningly at Thogar, her eyes appearing even larger and darker than before.

"Well, no. That is not what I was saying," he assured her rather haltingly. "I spoke to the DelveCaptain about that very possibility and he assured me that the way was not totally blocked. We should still be able to make our way through the passage. As you can see, it is very high up inside the mountain and near the surface. The only place it leads to is the Thrushspire itself, which is located here in this high peak. Since no one seems to think there is anything of import up there, it has never been reopened. They simply closed off the passage with a large door." He gave a shy smile. "I saw no reason to change his opinion by sharing our knowledge with him."

Thuria took hold of his hand once more. "I totally agree," she said with a beaming smile. Bregna set her braids to dancing as she nodded her head in agreement. "I mean, why should we bother the DelveCaptain with what might well be useless information."

"Right," Bregna spoke up. "I am sure he is quite busy enough. Why bother him over a little thing like *lost treasure*."

"Well, I did have to give him a reason for needing the map." Thogar broke in. "I told him that I had met two young maidens who wanted to go exploring and that one of you had heard of the Thrushspire from an old family story. He seemed to think that was a good enough reason, for he asked me nothing more after that."

Bregna gave him a playful jab with her elbow. "Not too bad at thinking quickly when necessary, are you?"

"Like I keep telling you, all it takes is thought and concentration and less fussing about what can't be done," Thuria said with a playful smile of her own.

Bregna simply rolled her eyes and gathered up their dirty dishes. After leaving them in the kitchen, she returned to the table with her pack along with a basket of baked goods.

"Well then, no time like the present. Are you two ready to start on this adventure?"

Thuria looked up at Thogar. The young scout

shrugged his shoulders with a look that said, "Why not?" and rolled up the map, tying it with a narrow band of leather. He then stood and retrieved his pack and his crossbow. That was good enough for the young minstrel, and she picked up her own pack. With Bregna's help she finally got both it and her lute situated on her back.

"It might be best if the two of you left both the basket and the lute behind," Thogar suggested. "No need to have the added and cumbersome weight. It will make you tire more quickly and once we are climbing the 'Spire passageway, they will both be a nuisance."

Bregna spoke right up, "The basket will most likely be empty long before we reach the passageway. I thought that we might be able to use it to help us carry the treasure back." Her voice dropped as she spoke the last sentence.

"Oh! Good thinking!" Thuria said, rolling her eyes. "And as far as this blasted lute goes, I would most gladly leave it behind, but if Master Kurek found out that I had disobeyed a direct order, he would no longer agree to my apprenticeship. He may be demanding, but he is the greatest minstrel in all of Drost since Grand Master Drogi of old. No other master would be willing to take me after he had refused me, and I would be left washing dishes for Bregna the rest of my life."

Thogar and Bregna both burst out laughing at the comical grimace on Thuria's lovely face.

"It will be bad enough when I don't have the composition he required done by my next lesson. I am not about to take the chance of disobeying him besides."

"Well, all right then." Thogar settled his crossbow across his pack. "Did you pack everything we talked about last night?"

187

Two red heads nodded in unison, eyes sparkling.

"And I have our 'key' right here," Thuria whispered as she pulled the pendant out of its hiding place under the neck of her bodice then replaced it once more.

"Yes, well, ah, let's be going then shall we?" Thogar turned on his heel and proceeded out the door of the bakery, his face red over the snickers he was trying to ignore behind him.

As was to be expected, they had very little in the way of adventure as they made their way through the Dwarfholt. Bregna and Thuria took turns pointing out places of interest as they made the trek through Drost. Thogar was very impressed with the massive 'Holt and asked many questions about its history. The young maidens were able to answer many of these, but were surprised at how many they could not. They began to realize that they took their birthplace for granted and seeing it through the eyes of a stranger awoke their own wonder.

Bregna had been correct about her basket of baked goods. It was nearly empty by the time they reached the garrison outpost near the door to the Thrushspire passageway. That happened on the second evening of their journey. It was here that they hoped to sleep for the night before their real adventure began. Thogar had no trouble since he could just bed down in the barracks. Thuria and Bregna, on the other hand, were a different matter. After some embarrassment, and after tasting the cookies that Bregna offered him, the commander finally gave up his own room to the two young maidens.

The trio had to dodge a few curious inquiries before they retired. Even though the garrison was so close to the Thrushspire, few of the guards even knew of its existence. The commander knew of the 'Spire, but had no idea why anyone would want to take the effort to get there. From all reports it was simply an empty chamber at the end of a ruined passageway. No one had even passed through the door for over five hundred years. Though they were surrounded by doubt, the three young adventurers simply exchanged knowing looks and said nothing about their quest.

Early the next morning, the commander himself led them to the Thrushspire passage door. With some effort, he drew back the ancient bolt. Swinging the heavy door back on complaining hinges, he wished them a grand adventure with a bow.

The Dwarf lamps still burned brightly at the start of the passageway, but the garrison commander had assured them that would not be the case for long. Luckily for Thuria and Bregna, their scout had come prepared and had not only brought a Dwarven lantern for himself, but also one for each of them.

The lamps gave out at about the same point that the passageway became a jumble of fallen rock, and the trio had to resort to the lanterns. Most places early on were easy to negotiate in spite of the rocks blocking the path. That is, unless you had a basket or lute tied to your pack. There was much laughing, as well as fussing and fuming, as the three made their way further along the passageway and higher up inside the mountain. Thogar helped his companions out when he could. Bregna received help gladly, but he quickly learned to differentiate between when Thuria wanted help and when she did not.

Late in the day, they came to a section that was more open than most. After clearing a few large stones out of the way, as well as a small boulder or two, they had a decent campsite for the night. Bregna pulled the last loaf of bread from her basket. Even though it was nearly four days old, it was still soft and delicious inside the thick crust. They were so hungry from all their exertion that they would have eaten it even if it resembled the rocks they sat on.

Unlike most of the passage they had traversed that day, here there was a large, exposed piece of wall that was largely intact. As Bregna cleaned up from their meal, Thuria walked over for a closer look. There was a coat of dust over everything, but when she wiped it away a beautiful stone mosaic was revealed. When he noticed what she was doing, Thogar stepped over to join her.

"That is really lovely work," he said from near Thuria's shoulder.

Taken by surprise in the midst of her study of the wall, Thuria spun around to face him. She had once again forgotten the lute on her back, and the neck of the instrument poked the scout in the mid-section.

"Oh my! Thogar, are you hurt? I didn't mean to hit you with this awful thing. Bregna, come quick! I think I have injured Thogar!"

The scout in question had turned his back to the worried maiden and was bent over, hand against the wall, gasping for breath when Bregna reached the pair.

"What happened?" she asked.

"This stupid lute!" Thuria nearly shouted back. "I hit him with it, and I think I must have injured him somehow because it sounds as if he is having trouble breathing."

Thuria placed one hand on the scout's shoulder as she moved around in front of him. She held the lantern close as she leaned down to see his face better. What she saw caused her to give his shoulder a resounding smack. Thogar had tears streaming down his face and the gasps were from suppressed laughter.

"Oh! And to think that I was worried that I had done you harm!" The auburn-haired beauty spun on her heal, nearly striking the young Dwarf with the lute again as she stomped her way back to her bedroll. She removed the instrument and tossed it on her bed before she flopped down next to it. Every line of her body screamed indignation.

Bregna looked back and forth between the two, uncertain which one she should go to. Thogar, having finally caught his breath, waved her aside as he made his way to the fuming minstrel. Bregna thought that either he was the bravest or most foolish Dwarf she had ever met, but she turned to examine the mosaic herself, giving them all of the privacy she could in the limited space.

Thogar wiped the last tear from his eye as he stopped behind Thuria's shoulder.

"May I sit down?" he asked, trying to steady his voice so as not to add to her fury.

His inquiry was met with a huff as Thuria turned farther away from him. Since she had not verbally refused his request, he chose to take it as consent and, moving the lute, took a seat beside her.

The young Dwarf simply sat and gazed at the auburn waves cascading down the rigid back before him for a few minutes. It was nearly all he could do to keep from reaching up and stroking them to see if they were as satiny and soft as they looked. Realizing that this was neither the time nor place, he tried to bring his thoughts back to the problem at hand.

"I am sorry that I upset you."

Thuria flipped her hair back over her shoulder, but otherwise acted as if she had not heard him at all.

"It was not my intention to hurt your feelings. Nor was I trying to make you feel worse about what had happened than you already did."

The back before him relaxed slightly, and he could see that Thuria's hands were playing with a fold in her skirt, pleating it and then smoothing it out. A lopsided half-smile slowly grew on his face. It seemed like he was making headway.

"Won't you let me make this up to you? After all, even though it was an accident, I am the injured party."

After a few more moments, Thuria gave a small sigh, pushed her hair back behind her ear, and turned to face the Dwarf beside her without looking in his face.

"I know," she said quietly. "I didn't think I had hit you that hard to begin with, but you made me think you were really injured when you were leaning against the wall there." Her small graceful hand waved back behind them. She raised her eyes to meet his and he could see that her cheeks were still quite rosy, but whether from anger or embarrassment he was not sure. "Then, when I saw that you were laughing, I thought that you were making sport of me."

Behind them, Bregna cast a quick glance their way. She was worried that her friend was still upset, but the seated pair spoke softly and their voices did not carry to where she waited. She took that as a good sign. If

Thuria were still angry, Bregna would have been well able to hear it in the confined space.

As Thuria had done twice before, Thogar reached over and placed his hand on hers.

"I am truly sorry you thought I would make sport of you."

Thuria relaxed as she saw the truth in the hazel eyes before her. She glanced down at the hand he held with a shy smile.

"The fact of the matter is that it was one of those situations where it is either laugh or cry."

Thuria looked back up at him in confusion.

"You see, the problem was not the force of the impact." Thogar's face grew slightly pink as he continued. "The problem was the *location* of the impact."

Thuria's eyes grew wide with understanding. Her hand flew to her mouth as she burst out laughing.

"Oh my! No wonder you didn't speak up right away."

She gave Thogar's hand a squeeze. "In that case, I guess it truly is I who owes you an apology."

Thogar reached over with his other hand and gently cradled Thuria's smooth, round cheek. "Let's just count it even, shall we?"

Eyes glowing, and still laughing, Thuria nodded in agreement.

Sensing that a truce had been reached, Bregna made her way back to where the others were sitting. She stood and shook her head at the smiling faces looking up at her.

"Well, I take it all is forgiven?" Both nodded in agreement. "In that case, may I go to bed now? That crumbly wall is fascinating, but I have been walking and climbing all day, and we do want to get an early start tomorrow.

"Agreed," Thogar said as he stood up. "We should be only one more day from the Thrushspire. Getting a good night's rest sounds like the thing to do." He moved across the campsite to his own bedroll. "I will see you both bright and early."

All three closed their lanterns until just the least amount of light shone forth, casting the campsite into nearly total darkness.

"Well," the two maidens could hear the smile in his voice, "early at least."

His comment was met by a chorus of giggles. They all swiftly fell asleep on that happy note.

A few hours later, before mid of night, Bregna's terrified scream woke her companions. Thogar, short sword in hand, threw his lantern's covering wide open flooding the dark chamber with light. The bright beam revealed Bregna attempting to pull one of her braids away from a slimy, green monstrosity. The young baker was beating at the multi-legged creature with her basket. The basket had little affect on the hard carapace and was nearly demolished by her efforts.

"Cavern creepers!" Thuria exclaimed as she threw her dagger, burying it deep in the wide, spiny back of the creature who still refused to release Bregna's hair. The first dagger was quickly followed by two more and the creeper collapsed with a wailing hiss, still holding the braid in its mouth full of innumerable teeth.

Witnessing Thuria's prowess caught Thogar totally by surprise, but he rushed forward to offer his assistance as there were several more of the creature swarming the campsite. Using his short sword, he hacked at the large, insect-like things that were charging the two maidens.

Thuria retrieved her daggers from the fallen creeper, then helped her friend pry the dead creature's teeth open. Accomplishing this, she returned to the battle with Thogar, who was still in wonder at the speed and accuracy of her daggers.

Bregna gave a disgusted grimace at the state of her hair, then flipping the braid behind her, joined her two champions in the fray. Evidently, the creepers wanted the trio's bedding as they kept trying to abscond with it. Being unarmed, Bregna fought to retrieve first one blanket then another as Thogar and Thuria battled the spiny creatures that remained. A few had managed to disappear into the rubble on the opposite side of the passageway from the standing wall, hissing and screeching over their wounds. Many more lay about where they had fallen, pierced by either short sword or dagger.

"Well, that was fun!" Thogar stated with a wry smile as the battle came to an end.

Bregna was far from laughing as she tried to cleanse the slimy goo from her hair. "Oh yes! Just lovely! Always wanted my hair to be part of a cavern creeper's nest or something."

Thogar began gathering up the carcasses and disposing of them in a large crack he found behind some of the rubble, while Thuria attempted to calm and cheer her friend.

"At least you saved your hair," she said as she patted Bregna on the back and handed her another rag that was all that was left of their blankets. "Have you taken a look at your poor basket?" She held the object mentioned up for inspection.

The sight of the wicker tangle in Thuria's hand caused Bregna to giggle in spite of herself.

"So much for using it to carry home all our treasure," she said with a grin.

"Look on the bright side," Thogar said as he rejoined the others, having finished his task. "Now we have some kindling if we need it."

"That's right! We could build a cookfire," Thuria agreed then leaned down closer to Bregna's ear. "Got any good recipes for cavern creeper?"

"What I want to know," Thogar said, looking on in wonder as Thuria began cleaning and replacing her collection of daggers, "is where did you learn to throw daggers like that?"

His tone of voice and look of wonder left Thuria speechless and blushing as she lowered her face to inspect the edge of the dagger in her hand.

"Oh, that was nothing!" Bregna piped up. "You should see what she can do to a composition assignment from Master Kurek!"

All three had a good laugh at this before they took stock of their shambles of a campsite. Their packs, though strung around, were still intact, so their provisions were safe. They were able to find one blanket that had survived the attack, so Thuria and Bregna could share that. The creepers had torn the corner off the cloak that Thogar had fastened to his pack, but he could use it as a covering. All three lanterns had been knocked about, but were still in working order. This fact made Thuria and Bregna extremely grateful. They had no desire to be in complete darkness knowing that they were not alone in the passageway.

"You two get some sleep and I will keep watch the rest of the night," Thogar said as he retrieved his crossbow from behind the rock it and his pack had been laying on. He set one of the lanterns, opened to its brightest, on a nearby tilted slab and prepared to guard his companions.

"You can't watch the rest of the night by yourself. You need rest too," Thuria stated. She raised a hand to stop his objection. "Bregna and I can take a turn at guard duty."

"Thuria, would it be all right if we took our turns together?" Bregna asked.

Thogar smiled, not only at Bregna's request, but also at how quickly Thuria agreed to it.

"Very well, I will take the next three hours, leaving the two of you with the last three. Will that please you?"

Before Thuria had a chance to answer, Bregna spoke up. "Not as much as having a squad of warriors here, but I guess it will have to do."

Thuria gave Thogar a smile and Bregna a hug as the two disheveled friends lay down to try and get some rest. To their surprise, they fell asleep quickly and slept soundly until Thogar woke them for their turn on watch.

The rest of the night passed without incident. After a quick breakfast, they were ready to continue their quest, hoping to reach the Thrushspire before night fell once again.

Most of their early morning travel went much like the day before, with only one difference. Bregna, now without her basket, made much better time in the tight spots and could not help needling Thuria a bit.

"Hurry up slow-poke! It would be so much easier for you without that lute holding you back."

"You better hope I hold the lute back," Thuria muttered to herself as she once again fought her way over and between a jumble of rocks. "Otherwise, there may be a couple of Dwarves with lute shaped lumps on their heads."

"What did you say?" Bregna asked as she turned after hopping nimbly through a cleft.

Thuria attempted to follow, her lute jamming between boulders and bringing her to a stop. "Nothing, nothing at all," she growled between clenched teeth.

Just as she came up even with her waiting friend, they heard Thogar call from up ahead.

"I think I see light ahead. It looks like sunlight."

The two friends gave each other wondering looks and hurried to catch up with the scout.

"See, up there?" he pointed up a steep incline in the passage. "That is sunlight. There must be a break in the side of the mountain. There should be no place for the sun to come through otherwise."

There were several larger boulders blocking the passage at this point, and the three Dwarves had to really work their way through. Thuria finally had to take her lute off of her back and carry it in her hand by the neck so that she could squirm through the openings as she brought up the rear of the line.

Having made much better time, Thuria's two companions took a brief rest and waited for her in the welcome sunlight filtering into the small cave. From the looks of it, Thogar had been correct and the cave had been formed when the mountainside collapsed. The continuation of the passageway could be clearly seen on the far side.

Bregna found a seat near the mouth of the cave and was enjoying the view out across the kingdom of Mansker that the Dwarfholt of Drost bordered. Thogar leaned against the edge of a rock near the crevice that Thuria was making her way through, so he could help her if need be—and if allowed. He turned toward Thuria as she finally emerged from the crack, her lute held out in front of her like a jousting lance.

"I was wondering if I would have to pry you out this time," he said with a smile. He raised his hands and ducked, his smile replaced by dismay as Thuria, with a fierce look in her eye, took a two-handed grip on her lute and swung it at his head with all her might.

There was a resounding SMACK accompanied by splintering wood as the round back of the lute connected with the head of the spotted mountain cat that was leaping down onto Thogar from the ledge it had been crouching on. The large cat flew across the cave and impacted against the wall not far from the opening where Bregna sat, her mouth hanging open in disbelief.

Quick to recover, Thogar drew his short sword and raced over to the inert body. He sheathed his weapon when he saw there was no need for it. The cat was very dead, its skull crushed by the blow from the musical instrument that now dangled by its strings in Thuria's hand.

"Master Kurek is going to *kill* me!" she said as she sunk down onto the ground, shaking her head. "At least the blasted thing was good for something!"

"I will be more than glad to take the blame," stated Thogar. "If you hadn't sacrificed your 'beloved' lute, that cat would have killed me!"

Bregna, her eyes still the size of saucers, nodded her head in agreement as she rushed to her friend's side. "And I will back him up on that! You are a hero, Thuria!"

Thuria rolled her eyes and began to shake her head, but Thogar stopped her by placing both hands on her shoulders as he knelt down beside her. He waited until she raised her eyes to meet his before he spoke.

"You *are* a hero, Thuria. If it were not for you and your quick reaction, I would have been badly mauled if not worse." He held her gaze for just a moment longer before regaining his feet. He moved back toward the cat as he continued. "Some scout I am! I know that a cave like this is the perfect lair for all kinds of wild creatures, and I failed to even check for inhabitants! I am just glad that it was a mountain cat and not something bigger and more dangerous."

Bregna's hand flew to her mouth, her eyes widening even more as the possibilities raced through her mind. "I think I am just about ready to return to my nice safe bakery," she stated. "The most dangerous thing I have to worry about there is not putting the spices back in the order the Mistress wants them in!"

"Sorry, Bregna." Thuria placed her arm around her friend's drooping shoulders. "I didn't think this would be quite this much of an adventure either when we started out. At least we have had no casualties other than your basket and my lute—"

"Along with our blankets," Bregna broke in.

"Yes, along with our blankets." Thuria ground her teeth slightly, but managed not to get angry with her worried friend. "So this is a good thing, right?"

"I guess so," Bregna agreed, perking up a bit.

Both maidens turned around to see Thogar deftly finishing up skinning the mountain cat. He then laid the skin out on the flat surface of a nearby boulder and began scraping it.

"Just what are you doing?" Bregna asked.

"He is scraping the hide to get it ready to be cured," Thuria stated before Thogar had a chance to answer. "The question is, why?" She raised an eyebrow and cocked her head sideways.

"You are correct. As to the why, I plan to make a shoulder cape for my beautiful rescuer. This golden fur will be a lovely contrast for your auburn hair." Thogar was careful to keep his eyes on his work, but both maidens saw the flush creeping up over his beard. "And these brown spots are just about the same color as your eyes." He refused to give into the urge to pull at his jacket; he had been doing that much too often here recently.

"Oh! What a wonderful idea!" Bregna clapped her hands in joy, her trepidation seemingly forgotten. "You will look wonderful in that, Thuria! And just think of the fun you will have telling the tale of how you got it!"

Thuria gave a shy smile, her eyes sparkling. "At least I will have evidence to back up my story on the demise of my lute for Master Kurek." She picked up the remains of the instrument in question, gave it a disgusted look, and flung it out through the opening of the cave.

"I will have no trouble keeping up with the two of you the rest of the way to the 'Spire now."

"This is true," Thogar agreed as he rolled the scraped skin and tied it to his pack. "Now, shall we make our way on to the 'treasure vault'?" he continued, waving his arm toward the remaining passageway with a bow and a flourish.

Thuria checked to make sure the necklace was still safely around her neck as both maidens came to their feet and straightened their packs, ready to finally reach their destination.

After a few more hours of the steepest climb they had faced yet, they reached the doorway at the end of the passage. The portal was closed, as it had been now for five centuries at least. Thogar reached for the large steel ring that functioned as the door knob and looked at his companions. At their nods, he pulled with all his might.

At first the door refused to move, and the trio was afraid that it might be locked, but then it finally began to open with a groan of very rusty hinges. Thogar proceeded to pull it as far open as possible, and Thuria had Bregna help her place a large rock in front of it to keep it from swinging closed.

"Good thinking," said Thogar as he rolled his shoulders to ease the strain from forcing the door open, "but I doubt it could go closed again without a good, hard push."

"I agree, but at this point I am not willing to take that chance," Thuria said as she brushed the dust from her hands. Bregna's braids bounced in agreement.

"Where the door was sealed, there should be no unwanted visitors in the chamber. Do you want to go first, Thuria, or would you rather I scouted out the premises?"

"That worked so well last time." Both maidens grinned at Thogar's discomfort before Thuria continued. "Sorry, couldn't resist. No, I think I will be fine going first, but stay close."

Thogar stepped aside to let his companions pass through the door and into the 'Spire.

Thuria took a deep breath before she stepped over the threshold. The chamber she entered was approximately fifty feet wide and twice that in length. She paused just a few feet into the room, her gaze passing all the way around. The walls, as far down as she could see, were covered with mosaic tile work. The murals were even more elaborate than what they had found in the passage-way.

Bregna wandered past her to the wall on the right, raising her lantern high to get a better look.

"Why, the whole wall is covered with birds!" she exclaimed.

"Not just birds," Thogar said as he joined her, "thrushes!"

"The 'Thrushspire,'" Thuria said breathlessly. She joined them for a brief look before continuing her visual tour of the room.

The tile floor was covered in thick dust and buckled in spots from the tremors that had closed the passageway, but remained mainly intact. In the center of the room was a round, raised platform about twenty-five feet in diameter which was reached by a flight of fifteen stone steps. In the middle of the platform was what appeared to be a small, dry fountain circled by a stone bench; otherwise the chamber was empty. Thuria could almost hear the tinkling of the water in her mind as she wandered over and climbed the steps to get a closer look at the fountain. She was lost in daydreams of what the 'Spire must have looked like long ago before the mountain shut it off from the rest of the 'Holt.

"Notice anything strange about the thrushes?" Thogar's question broke into her musings.

Thuria moved to join him on the left side of the chamber. She looked closely at the flights of thrushes, before turning to him in question.

"See, they are all flying toward the far end of the chamber."

"He's right, Thuria!" Bregna called from where she stood. "I just noticed that myself."

"All right then," Thuria transferred her lantern to her left hand and raised it high while her right hand slipped unconsciously to grip one of her many daggers by the hilt, "let's go see where they are all going, shall we?"

Her companions agreed, Thogar reaching his hand to his own short sword, and Bregna falling in close behind and between her friends. The trio carefully made their way to the far side of the chamber and found themselves up against an entire wall of moldering drapes.

Thogar reached up with his left hand and took a firm hold on the worn fabric. At Thuria's nod, he yanked it aside. The chamber was flooded with colorful light as the entire section of drapes fell away in a maelstrom of dust that left the Dwarves coughing, sneezing, and eyes streaming.

Blinking away her tears as best she could, Thuria gazed through the dust motes to behold a beautiful stained glass wall. The colorful design was composed of trees, flowers, and the ever-present thrushes. In the center of the wall were double doors that led out to a terrace beyond.

"Will you look at that!" Bregna managed to get out between sneezes. "Who would have thought?"

Clearing his own eyes with his tunic's sleeve, Thogar made his way to the doors. Gently he gave the handles a turn and to his surprise the door opened almost noiselessly.

"That's a surprise after the trouble we had with the chamber door," he stated as he cast a look at Thuria.

The minstrel's eyes were filled with wonder as she

stepped lightly out onto the terrace. She was startled as at her approach several birds flew up from hiding places near the mountainside that flanked the terrace on each side.

"Thrushes!" Bregna clapped her hands in delight as she moved to join her friend.

Thogar stopped her with a hand on her arm. "Let her have a look first," he said with a warm smile and a nod toward Thuria. Unable to hide the disappointment in her eyes, Bregna agreed and waited by his side as Thuria wandered about the terrace.

Sheltered near the mountainside, where the birds had taken flight, were what appeared to be ancient roosts and nests. There was a stone railing that ran from the mountain on one side around the circle of the terrace to the mountain on the other side. In one section, part of the handrail, along with a few balusters, was missing, but that which remained was still beautiful. Thuria ran her hand over the once polished surface of the granite, amazed at the smoothness that remained after all these years. The span of railing was lined with curved stone benches and planters. Most of the planters contained the remains of ornamental trees and shrubs, but a few still had spindly little plants striving to survive on their own.

After making her way around the perimeter of the terrace, Thuria turned toward the middle of the tiled floor. There was a larger version of the fountain that they had seen inside.

"Bregna, look!" she called to her waiting friend, who was more than happy to join her after flashing a smile at Thogar, who slowly followed her to Thuria's side. "There is still water in this fount, even though it is coming out in just the merest trickle."

Thogar placed a finger in the small stream. "Cold too!" he stated. "And fresh!" he added after tasting it.

Thuria took a seat near the fountain, gazing out across Mansker far below, her eyes shining. Thogar and Bregna silently joined her, allowing her time for contemplation. After a few moments of them sitting there quietly, the thrushes began to return. One, more stouthearted than his fellows, landed on the railing and burst into song. The Dwarves were thrilled and listened joyously for several minutes.

After the bird had finished his concert, he flew over to one of the dilapidated roosts as the sun slipped behind the western end of the mountain range.

"This is breath-taking and beautiful," said Bregna as she once again looked around the terrace. She made her way back inside the chamber and placed her hands on her hips. "But where is the 'immeasurable treasure that must be shared'?"

Thuria tore herself away from her daydreams and followed the young baker back inside.

"Right," she said, "back to business." She reached to her neck and pulled the pendant out and clasped it in her hand. "I have the 'key.' Let's see if we can find the keyhole. But where do we start?"

"There aren't that many choices really," Thogar answered, looking around the room. "All that is here is the terrace, the platform, and the bare walls."

"Well then, Thogar, you take the terrace."

The scout bowed and made his way back through the double doors.

"Bregna, you take the walls."

The baker shrugged and muttered as she turned to the nearest section, "What in the seven Dwarfholts am I going to find on a bare wall?"

Thuria chuckled at her friend as she made her way to the platform and up the steps. "Guess that leaves the platform to me."

The setting sun had disappeared behind the mountain range long before the searchers found anything.

"This is hopeless!" Bregna said with a huff as she plopped down on one of the benches near the fountain. "I studied every inch of these bare walls." She waved her hand around wildly as she spoke. "Do you know what I discovered?" Her two companions turned their attention toward her. "BARE WALLS!" She crossed her arms in disgust, her braids bouncing.

Thogar joined her on a bench nearby. "All I found were a bunch of disgruntled thrushes." He gave Bregna a lop-sided smile. "That and several hundred years of bird droppings."

Much to the scout's delight, Bregna had to giggle in spite of herself.

Thuria was now examining the sides of the platform and only gave her companions half of her attention. There had to be something here; she just knew it.

"More thinking and concentration and less fussing and fuming," she murmured to herself. The phrase had been going over and over in her mind ever since she began her search of the platform. She did not know why, but she felt like she was close to finding the treasure, if she could just think a little bit more clearly.

"The only thing of slight interest that I found—" said

Bregna, pulling some wafers from her pack and sharing one with an eager Thogar. She took a nibble before she continued, "—is that there is a border with raised diamonds that runs all the way around the whole room."

"I found the same pattern on the benches and planters on the terrace," Thogar said around a mouthful of wafer.

"Yes, I noticed that too," came the muffled reply from Thuria, who was still searching around the base of the platform and was now at the section directly opposite the staircase. "The diamond border runs all the way around the base here too. Except for this spot right here, where it seems the diamond is missing . . ." Her voice trailed off.

"What?" Bregna asked as she made her way to the railing over Thuria's head. "What did you say?"

Thuria's brow lowered in concentration. "There is a diamond missing here." She traced around the small indentation with one hand as she fingered the necklace with the other.

"No! It can't be!" her excited voice floated up to her companions.

"What can't be? What are you talking about?" Bregna hurried across the platform and down the stairs, Thogar close behind her.

They reached Thuria's side and watched expectantly as the young minstrel held her lantern up so that it would shine on the indentation.

"Here, let me hold that for you." Thogar took the lantern from her hand.

Thuria turned a grateful smile on the scout, then reached to remove her necklace. Thogar was glad for the failing light. That smile had caused his face to warm, but now it would not show.

Bregna was still somewhat in the dark until she saw Thuria lean closer and gently blow the centuries of dust out of the depression in the stone. Thuria then brought the necklace up and attempted to insert it in the cavity, lining the points of the diamond up with the rest of those in the border.

"It doesn't fit," she said in disappointment.

"More thought and concentration," Bregna quoted. "No fussing! Turn it a little bit and try it that way."

"Yes," said Thogar eagerly, "try turning it."

"Give me a moment!" After closer study of both the necklace and the indentation, Thuria turned the pendant a quarter turn and again attempted to insert it.

The pendant slipped into the indentation with a soft click. Thuria tried to turn the pendant to match the diamond on it to the pattern on the wall. First to the left. Nothing. The Dwarves all held their breath while she then tried turning it to the right. The pendant turned easily in this direction, accompanied by a louder click, a muffled thump, then a grating of stone on stone as a section of the platform wall sank back about a foot and slid to the right, revealing a hidden room.

Thogar shook his head as the two females squealed in delight. Then, once again, he held Bregna back to allow Thuria to enter first, earning himself a disgusted scowl.

Thuria carefully replaced the necklace around her throat before retrieving her lantern from Thogar. Holding the light out before her, she stepped into the low-ceilinged room. Unlike the main chamber, this small room was nearly dust-free and filled from wall to wall.

"Oh my!" she breathed, her wondering gaze taking in the contents of the room.

"What? *What* did you find?" Bregna jerked free of Thogar's grasp and rushed inside. Thogar followed, once again shaking his head. He would never figure out females!

Thuria did not answer Bregna's inquiry. She was busy lifting page after page from first a music stand and then a table or bookcase all around the treasure room. There were musical compositions for every instrument imaginable, but most were written for the lute.

"It just figures," she said with a smile, her eyes moving lovingly down each sheet and scroll.

"All I see is music!" Bregna said with disgust. "Where is the treasure?"

Taking one look at the bliss on Thuria's face, Thogar placed his hand on Bregna's arm, drawing her attention to her friend. "I do believe that the music is the treasure."

"Oh, yes!" agreed Thuria, pulling her eyes from the composition in her hands. "This music *is* the treasure. And music must be shared to reach its full worth."

"If you say so," Bregna responded, her exuberance somewhat deflated. "I would rather have some jewels or gold if you ask me."

Thogar came up to stand beside Thuria, taking her lantern once again so that she could use both hands to turn the pages she held. Bregna turned away, rolling her eyes and shaking her head in disbelief. They both seemed to be happy with the "treasure" they had found, though she failed to see why. There just had to be something more hidden away in here somewhere.

Bregna moved about from one place to another, poking here and prying there, moving stacks and stands full of music out of her way and trying to discover what was behind and beneath each one.

At the back of the room, in a small alcove formed by the outside staircase, Bregna's search was rewarded. She found an ornate chest tucked away under a piece of cloth and a stack of music that she quickly placed on the floor beside her.

"Thuria! Thuria! Look what I found!"

At the eagerness in the outburst, both Thuria and Thogar hurried through the music racks to Bregna's side.

"Look at this chest! It isn't very big, but it is big enough to hold a nice lot of gems or such."

Thogar stepped forward and lifted the chest out of the alcove. Bregna swept the stacks of music off of a small table in her eagerness to find a place for him to set it–an act that caused an anguished cry to escape from Thuria's lips.

"Oh," gasped Bregna when she saw the look on her friend's face, "I wasn't thinking! I was just so excited."

Thuria just shook her head in disgust and moved to look at the chest the young baker had discovered.

"I hope you are not disappointed, Bregna," Thogar said as he placed the chest down on the table with a soft thump. "This doesn't feel heavy enough to be filled with a pile of gems or gold."

"Well, maybe it's more jewelry nested in satin," said Bregna, still hoping for the best. "That would be fine with me too." She stood there rubbing her hands together in anticipation as she watched Thuria examine the outside.

Thuria, who was used to her friend's exuberance and was quite good at ignoring her when she wished, went over every inch of the chest. It was made of a beautifully finished wood with a swirled grain pattern that Thuria had never seen before. There were inlaid designs in both gold and silver on all sides, and it appeared the chest was Elven in design. She stroked her hand across the surface, marveling at how smooth and polished it still remained after the many years it had been hidden away. The top of the chest was covered with runes of inlaid gold.

"Look here," she said calling her companions' attention to a set of runes on the top of the chest. "I am sure this chest is Elven, but these runes are Dwarven."

Thogar leaned down closer to get a better look. "You are quite correct. I believe it's an inscription of some sort." He held his lantern closer to shed better light.

Thuria ran her finger over the inscription; the gold reflected the lantern light, but she was finally able to make out what was written there.

*A gift for Grand Master Drogi*
*The finest bard in all of Aaleria*
*In humble appreciation of his talent*

*Indariel of Valamar*
*Your friend*

The three young Dwarves looked at each other in slack-jawed wonder. Even Bregna knew that Indariel was the Lady of Valamar, one of the great Elf kingdoms.

Suddenly, Thuria grabbed her lantern and ran to one of the nearby music stands, snatched up a sheet of music, then quickly replaced it and leapt to another stack on top of a bookshelf.

"I can't believe it! I can't believe it!"

Thogar and Bregna looked at each other in confusion, then watched the auburn-haired whirlwind as she sped from one place to another.

"I can't believe it!" she repeated with each page or scroll she looked at.

"What can't you believe?" Bregna asked as Thuria flew to yet another stack. "Thuria!"

On her next pass by, Thogar caught the excited minstrel and drew her up against his chest in a not overly gentle embrace.

"Now, I have you! Bregna, try your question again while I have a hold of her."

"Thuria?" Bregna asked anxiously.

Thuria did not even hear her friend's pleading voice. In fact, she did not even notice that Thogar was holding her in his arms. She was busy looking at a sheet of music she had clutched in her hands. She gave every appearance of being in a world all her own.

Thogar was a very patient Dwarf, but he had had enough. He clasped Thuria with one strong arm and pulled the music out of her sight with the other.

"Answer your friend!" he nearly growled.

Thuria looked at him in confusion, then turned toward Bregna.

"Well?" the young baker prompted.

"Well? Well what?" Thuria was having trouble coming back to the real world it seemed. Thogar gave her a good squeeze. "She asked you what it was that you couldn't believe!"

"Oh. Oh!" Thuria's face shone with excitement, and the smile she gave Thogar took his breath away. Bregna was not impressed and was thinking of giving her friend a good pinch or punch in the arm, anything to find out what all the fuss was about.

"The name! The name on the chest!" Thuria held up

the music in her hand and waved it for her companions to see. "It's here on the music too! On *all* of it! Drogi! I can't believe it." She started to raise the music up to study once more.

Bregna pulled the sheet from her hands. "And Drogi is . . .?"

"I'm sorry, how rude of me. Please, Thogar release me, I am having trouble catching my breath."

The scout released her with a sheepish look, and Thuria stepped slightly away from her two friends, smoothing her rumpled dress. After attending to this, she held her arms extended to both sides and slowly turned in a circle.

"All of this! The chest, the music, even the Thrushspire itself. All of it must have belonged to Grand Master Drogi." Her two companions still gazed on her in confusion. "It is just as the inscription says! Drogi was the greatest bard who ever lived. *This* was his sanctuary! This is where all of his lost tunes have been for nearly an age! And I was given the key!"

Both Thogar and Bregna looked impressed then excited as they came to understand what this would mean to a minstrel like Thuria. They let her bask in her joy for a few moments more, then Bregna could stand it no longer.

"You have to open the chest! I will go as crazy as you are if you don't!"

The trio joined in laughter as Thuria made her way back to the table. She ran her fingers over Drogi's rune once more, then opened the latch on the chest. With Bregna leaning close on one side and Thogar on the other, she slowly raised the lid. There inside was the most beautiful lute that any of them had ever seen. It was made of the same wood as the chest, and, like it, was also inlaid with gold. The tuning pegs were even set with gems!

Reverently, Thuria lifted it out of its satin nest. She looked at first Bregna then at Thogar, her eyes filled with wonder. At their encouraging nods, she set her fingers and strummed a cord. The tone was magnificent, *and* it was still in tune! In disbelief, Thuria softly played a short tune, then just held the lute reverently and ran her hand across the smooth, polished wood.

"Well," she said with a rueful smile. "I guess Master Kurek will be quite pleased."

"What do you mean?" Bregna asked.

"Well, just look at all the music he now can make me learn." Thuria cradled the lute in her arms. "Mainly though, with the fact that he will never again have to *force* me to play the lute." Her dark eyes now shone with a mischievous light. "The harp on the other hand . . ." And all three friends burst out laughing.

## *A Pixie Rescue*

Becca Lynn Rudder

Eranea had changed. The peaks of the Gwindes Mountains no longer glimmered in the sunlight, for the sun itself was simply a baleful orb trying vainly to pierce through a colorless sky. There was no wind making the flowers dance, the brooks were dull and silent. All that had always been cheerful was now only gloomy. It had been an entire year since Princess Argessa had been kidnapped, and everyone was the picture of doom—except for a few.

I had finally gathered a small group of fairies who believed the same as I did—or at least trusted me enough to follow my lead, no matter how inexperienced I *definitely* was—that Dwimera had taken Argessa into the Black Forest. I looked at each face gathered around me there at Kileri's Clarkia, pursing my lips. All were my friends and very good fairies, but . . . well, we still weren't exactly what one would call "the best team one could find."

First up, the twins—Siemma and Tiemma. Both had hair like gold, eyes like sapphires—and tempers like fire-crackers. It doesn't take much to set them off, and when they go off, they go *off.* This could be good or bad. We'd have to wait and see. Right now they were calm enough, sitting with their legs crossed at the knee and their hands clasped over their kneecaps, staring at me like a couple of hawks. It wasn't nerve-racking . . . much.

Next there was Laryn, and beside her, Kileri. Laryn had reddish-brown hair, starting to frost white at the front, and beautiful amber eyes that still held their gleam, even after everything that had happened. She was pack-ing up flitter-cakes and dyru muffins, along with other foodstuffs, equipment, and . . . and weaponry . . . and ev-erything that we'd need on our excursion, humming soft-ly to herself. Her daughter cut a striking contrast to her. Kileri had jet-black hair flowing down over her shoul-ders, icy blue eyes, and a solemnity about her that was shocking to see in a young, teen-aged pixie. She leaned her slender form against the wall and silently watched her mother, expressionless.

On the opposite side of the room from them were Dinad and Jairik. The former was slight of build, *slight* of hair, and often wore a confused look on his face. Pres-ently, Dinad was milling around, trying to make sure he had all of his precious books packed—what good they would do him in the Forest, I didn't know, but it was pointless to ask. All I'd get was one of those confused looks he ought to be famous for, and then be ignored again as he went about his book-packing. Jairik, though, was a Royal Guardian—the only one we could get to listen to us. I still didn't know how we ever convinced him to join us, but I'll be forever grateful. He was looking through some old maps of the Black Forest he had helped us to obtain, trying to find the best point of entry. I watched him for a moment, not able to keep back a small smile. His concentration, determination, courage . . . chestnut hair, kind hazel eyes . . . Suddenly he glanced up at me, and I blushed and looked away. He had caught me staring—again. Why did I do that, anyway?

To my left, an annoying little giggle erupted. Why did my little sister have to do such irritating things at such already awkward moments? I glared down at her, and Eilia just sent me an ornery grin, a glimmer in those big emerald eyes of hers. She was one of the few, like Laryn, who hadn't been altered very much—if at all—in personality since the First-Flight gone horrifically wrong. She was just the same as she'd always been. Which could spell trouble for us, but . . . I couldn't just leave her there. Of course she had to come.

To my right, Markette softly chortled and patted my arm. I looked at the old nurse, hair silver-grey, eyes kind and filled as always with laughter. I smiled at her, shrugging a little. The twinkle in her eyes told me she probably knew something about my, ah, staring problem . . . thing, but I knew if I asked she'd just tell me something like, "Oh, you'll see, dearie. In time, you'll see." How did I know? Well, she'd said so before, so why wouldn't she now?

I wandered past Eilia and looked into the mirror on the wall. My dark auburn hair, pulled back into a wavy ponytail but curling out in the front, my tangerine-and-burnt orange dress coming down to my knees in points, my sienna slippers with the vine-like threaded border around the top . . . I couldn't see any of that. All I saw was the intense fear deeply showing in my amber eyes, and much more deeply *felt*. What was I thinking? How could I do this? I was a nobody, just a nurse for the Royal Nursery . . . how could I lead a rescue mission? Tears welled up in my eyes, but then I smiled faintly. That was why. My little princess . . . I would not, *could* not let Dwimera have her any longer. I *had* to get Argessa back!

"Ah, Clirena?" I heard Eilia say suddenly.

I blinked, then quickly wiped my hand over my eyes and turned around—to find everyone staring at me. I guess I must have been giving myself my little pep talk with the mirror longer than I thought, because each one of them wore Dinad's confused expression. Except for Markette—again, old Markette seemed to know exactly what I was doing. How? My guess is wisdom of old age, or maybe . . . hmm, maybe I remind her of herself at my age? I don't know; that might be it, I guess.

I took a quick, hopefully not very noticeable, breath, then tried a smile at Eilia. "Yes, Eilia? Do you . . . need something?" I attempted to "not know" why she and most of the others were looking at me like I had two heads.

She gave me a look that showed me how truly unconvincing I was, then shrugged. "I was just wondering if you could, um, help me get ready to go?" She nodded once in affirmation, sending me a quick grin.

I smiled a little more genuinely. "Of course I will." I gave a nod to the others, then took Eilia off to a corner of the room to help her. The others went about their own business again, hopefully just continuing to pack and not discussing my sanity or possible lack thereof.

Wait . . . what did Eilia need help with? "Um, all right, Eilia, is there anything you *actually* need me to do for you, or were you just helping me out of that . . . awkward whatever-it-was?"

Eilia grinned again. "Mostly the latter—you're welcome, by the way—but a little bit of the former, too." She held out a hair band. "I can't get my hair to stay in a ponytail like yours. I keep trying to put it up, but it won't stay!"

"You are remembering that you have to pull your hair through the band more than once, right? More like either three or four times, usually?"

Eilia gave me a sheepish little look. "Well . . . no."

I laughed a little, shaking my head and taking the hair band from her. "All right, I'll help you with it. Turn around."

Eilia complied and stood there silently for a few moments while I wrestled her thick sandy hair into a puffball-like ponytail. Then she sighed. "Clirena?"

I finished pulling her hair through the band one last time as I answered, "Yes, Eilia?"

She bit her lip, then turned toward me. "What's going to happen?"

I hesitated. "What do you mean?"

"Well . . . in the Forest, how are we going to get to the Fir without being caught by a . . . a Firanther, or a Ballaker, or something? And if—I-I mean *when*, of course—when we get there, how do we get past Dwimera and get the Princess, and then get past her again to get out, and . . . and . . . what're we going to do?"

Eilia was close to tears. I put my arm around her

and held her close. "I . . . I don't know yet, Eilia. But we'll do it; we have to."

After a moment, she nodded. "You're right, we do. I just . . . I just still wish I knew how," she murmured.

I gave her a squeeze. "You and me both," I replied with a faint sigh.

"Clirena," two voices said behind me in perfect unison.

I jumped and spun to face the twins. I hadn't even heard them fly over. "Oh, um, yes?"

Siemma and Tiemma clasped their hands in front of them and looked for all the world like they were about to give recitations. All this formality, just to tell me, "Laryn wants you." With that, they flittered off to another room.

I looked down at Eilia and we blinked at each other a couple times, then I shrugged. "I guess I ought to go see what Laryn wants. Are you okay?" I asked.

Eilia rolled her eyes at me. She was back to her usual self. "I'm *fine*, go see why you're wanted, silly. You don't need to be so worried about me all the time." She grinned and followed the "Emmas" to the other room.

I watched her flutter away, then shook my head and smiled. I would never understand my little sister. Never.

I flew over to where I had last seen Laryn packing, and sure enough, both she and Kileri were still there. I glanced at the Kileri, who didn't even to seem notice me. She just looked coldly out of her window, arms crossed, oblivious to the world around her at the moment. Then I looked at Laryn. She was looking at her daughter, too, worry in her eyes. After a moment, though, she shook her head and smiled at me. "Ah, there you are, Clirena."

I nodded, trying a smile back. "Emma and Emma said you wanted to see me?"

Laryn laughed softly. "Yes, with all their usual . . . flare? . . . too, I saw."

"They do have a thing for excessive drama, don't they?" I grinned, then tilted my head. "What do you need, Laryn?"

She gestured to the pile of bags beside her—one for each of us, of course. "I just figured you might want to take a quick look to make sure I didn't miss anything before we head out. The only one I don't have here is Dinad's. He's still trying to fit every last one of those books of his into it. I don't know how I'm going to fit even just a bit of food and maybe a knife in there with those silly things, but I guess we'll find out soon enough." She peered past my shoulder to watch him for a moment. "I don't *see* any more books after the one he's shoving in now, so hopefully we're about ready."

I looked through the eight bags she already had lined up as she talked, and simply nodded. My mind wasn't really on what she was saying—or on the bags, either. She seemed to notice this.

"Is . . . is everything all right, Clirena?" she asked, concern in her eyes. "Should we, maybe, wait till tomorrow to head out?"

I blinked, then shook my head adamantly. "No, we have to go today. A year's been way too long as it is, let alone a year *and* a day." I sighed and looked up at her. "I'm sorry, Laryn. I . . . I guess I am a bit . . . preoccupied, worried, don't really know what to do?" I bit my lip, then looked down at the floor.

Laryn gave a little smile and patted my arm. "All of

us are, and none of us do, Clirena," she replied. "But we still have to do *something*, anyway—and the sooner the better. I agree with you on that. We need to get the little princess back, and get things back to normal, somehow. If we can." She then put her hand under my chin and made me look up at her. "But we can't if we don't try. You stepped up to a big responsibility, Clirena. We're all following *you*. You have to get some things straightened out in *your* mind now or this might not work."

"I know, Laryn . . . I just don't know *how*." I sighed faintly.

Laryn nodded. "Well, I can't make all the decisions, but I can give a suggestion, if you want."

I nodded a bit more eagerly in return. "Yes, please."

"How about you *start* with, 'how are we going to get to the Forest?' The best starting points are *usually* at the beginning, anyway. Does that help?"

I looked over at Jairik, who was still concentrating on one of the maps. In fact, he was drawing something on it—probably marking the best route he could find. "I think our Royal Guardian has that down already," I replied with a little smile.

Laryn shook her head slightly. "I don't just mean finding a good way to get there. *How* are we going to get there?"

My brows furrowed. "I . . . thought we'd fly?" I answered.

Laryn sighed. "Well, yes, probably. But what if there are Guardians on the way there—besides Jairik. They don't want anyone going Forest-way, for whatever reason *that* is. Would you reason with them, or have Jairik or Markette try to, maybe? Or should we sneak around them, not come into contact with them at all. And even before we get to the Forest, there's always the risk of running into animals—some of a more unfriendly nature." She glanced at the window. "Especially at night, and that's closing in on us fast."

I sagged against the wall. "I hadn't really thought much about that," I murmured, biting my lip.

Laryn nodded. "You need to."

I was about to answer, when I heard someone clear his throat behind me. It was Dinad, clutching his bag tightly in front of him. "Oh, um, excuse me, I need to . . . give this to you, momentarily," he said, holding it out almost cautiously to Laryn. "Please, ah, be careful with my literary masterpieces, would you?"

She smiled. "Of course, Dinad. I will try my best not to tear or bend any of the pages of your priceless—" she grunted slightly upon taking the already over-stuffed bag from him, but still managed to keep up her smile and finish with, "collection."

Dinad nervously watched as she set it down, then nodded. "Well, all right. I . . . leave them with you. Do be careful, please, do!" His mouth twitched, then he fluttered off.

We both watched him leave and shook our heads. "I don't get it, " I murmured.

Laryn nodded. "Me neither. How can he even carry this?" She lifted it again and held it for a moment, with some strain. Then she set it back down, letting out a breath. "I'm amazed he's not two or three times his size, if he carries loads like this all the time—and it sure seemed like he wasn't having much trouble with it."

along the lines of, "I wonder if Jairik ever smiles?" Then I blinked at myself and shook my head. That's not important . . . no, it's not. I sighed, then tried to start thinking about how to get to the Forest.

It didn't seem like a lot of time had passed—and yet like a decade had, too, in some weird way—when Laryn and Markette came in.

"Ready and rarin' to go when ye are!" the latter said cheerily.

I swallowed, then nodded to her. "As-as ready as I'll ever be," I replied, adding in a murmur to myself, "I hope . . . ."

\* \* \* \*

It was about an hour after we left the Clarkia before we flew into any trouble. Well, if you can call a nosey old pixie sweeping off her porch *trouble*, considering what we'd more than likely be facing down the road.

"Where're you going in such a hurry, eh?" she called, leaning on her broom. "Nothing much down this here path but a couple more berry bushes and some patrolling Guardians."

The slightly more rambunctious twin snorted. "None of your—"

Markette clapped a hand gently, but firmly, over her mouth. "We're goin' to . . . ." She thought for a moment, then pulled one of the dyru muffins from her bag. "We're goin' to drop off a couple o' treats to the Guardians. They work so hard, ye know, deservin' o' a little appreciativeness, hrm?"

The old lady twitched her nose slightly, then nodded. "That's true, that is. Not appreciated enough fer all they do fer us, that's what. Go on ahead, then!" She waved us off, smiling faintly to herself and going back to her sweeping.

We flew out of earshot, then I let out a breath. "Thanks, Markette."

She chuckled quietly. "No worries, dearie. Just had to get out o' that, and that's what I did." She nodded once.

Someone cleared her throat softly. "Um, Markette? Sorry I . . . was like I was," a cooled off Emma murmured a bit grudgingly.

Markette smiled at her. "No harm done, Siemma (how could she tell?), not this time anyways. Ye just need to be workin' on that, or ye'll be gettin' the lot o' us in a heap o' trouble before we even get where we're goin'. All right?"

Siemma nodded quickly. "Yes, ma'am," she replied, and then she flitted off to rejoin her sister.

We fluttered along the path for another couple hours or so, dusk fading into the gloaming, dodging Guardians here, there, and everywhere—were there even any still at the Sequoia with the King and Queen? I'm still not sure; there were so many!—until we came to a narrow pass. The Forest was beyond the Gwindes Mountains, and there were many of these passes and clefts that we would have to fly through to get to the other side, because the Gwindes are very tall and the air is too thin and cold to fly over them.

Right in the middle of the pass, with no way around him, was one of the Guardians. I recognized this one as Ruleon. Now what? If we tried to fly over him, he would spot our shadows, and there was no way to bypass him on either side.

I looked over at Markette, hoping for some words of

wisdom. For a moment she just squinted straight ahead at Ruleon, then she beckoned to Jairik. They exchanged a short, whispered conversation, then Markette lead the rest of us to the cliff wall, behind a portion of the cliff that was jutting out.

We stayed there, as silently as possible, for what seemed like forever—in reality, probably no more than eight to ten minutes—and then we saw Ruleon soar away as fast as he could. After another cautionary minute, Jairik came around the corner and gave the "all clear" for us to go on.

As we continued through pass after pass, I asked Jairik how he got us through. "I told him that King Carlor requested his presence, and that I was there to deliver the message and take over his post," he replied.

I tilted my head. "Am I right to think he wasn't entirely convinced to start off with? It doesn't seem like that should have taken so long."

Jairik nodded. "Yes, you are correct. He seemed . . . extremely reluctant to leave his post, no matter what. But, when I told him this was so urgent that he would probably lose his place among the Royal Guardians if he did not go to the King's Sequoia, he snapped out of it enough to leave quite speedily, as I am sure you saw."

I smiled stupidly for a moment. I could listen to him talk forever . . . wait, what? I blinked at myself, then nodded to him. "Good work. Thank you."

He glanced away, probably letting out a silent sigh because of me, then looked at me and dipped his head. "You are welcome, Clirena." With that, he flew ahead to help Siemma and Tiemma scout out the correct paths and clefts we'd need to follow to get out of the Mountains.

At least, that was part of it. The pessimistic side of me figured he was just trying to get away from me and my awkward self.

We were about halfway through the Gwindes range now, and everything looked the same—dark, jagged, hard, rock. A few stars peeked out above us, but there were so many ledges and such in the cliffs that they didn't offer us much light. The shadows of the twilight spooked us. On several occasions we thought we saw some wild animal or another that was going to get us, but there never was one, that I know of. They were all tricks of the mind.

What wasn't a trick was the boulder that rolled down into a cleft we were traversing. Eilia spotted it first, and the poor young pixie let out quite the scream. Those of us who were almost past its path hurried forward, and the rest zipped back. It landed with a CRASH, and then the danger was past. The ones who flew back now fluttered over the boulder to rejoin the rest of us. The only loss was Eilia's bag, which she had dropped in her terror and was now crushed beneath the boulder. Ah, well; she was safe. I had *no* problem sharing what I had with my little sister as long as she was all right.

Midnight rolled around, and as I looked around at our little group, I could tell that each and every one of us was getting tired. Even our Royal Guardian was starting to look half-asleep. I fluttered alongside Markette and whispered, "Should we, um, stop for a little while, and get some rest?"

Even in the darkness of the night, I could see her eyes twinkle at me. "Well, that'd be your decision, now wouldn't it, dearie?"

I sighed . . . and the sigh turned into a yawn. I pursed my lips. "I guess we'd better, " I murmured.

Markette patted my shoulder. "Don't ye worry about it, Clirena. A little rest now is better than bein' exhausted when it'd be better not to be, now isn't it?"

It took me a minute to process that (I really did need some sleep!) but then I smiled faintly and nodded. "You're right. Everyone," I said a little louder, so they hopefully would hear me, "I think we need to find a good place to camp for the night. Any suggestions?" I tried to sound like I was in authority—well, I was, of course, but . . . the sounding like it was still kind of an issue for me.

One of the twins (I think it was Tiemma; she seemed a little more mild-mannered right then) flew straight up a little ways to get a broader glimpse of our surroundings. I heard a faint cheer before she flittered back down. "We're almost out of the Gwindes! Past that curve," she pointed in the direction we were presently headed, "it's only about fifteen minutes to the edge, I think. There's a little copse of trees just beyond that would make a good campsite, don't you think?"

I glanced at Jairik and Markette, hoping for a little advice, but they only looked at me in return. I gulped, then said, "Yes, it probably would." I half expected to have heads shaken at me, but instead everyone nodded and a few even smiled.

All except Eilia, who had fallen asleep on a rock beside me while we were talking. I couldn't help a small chuckle to myself. I reached down and shook her arm a little. "Come on, Eilia, we don't have much farther to go tonight." I got a sleepy little "m'hm" in response, and ended up half-dragging, half-carrying her to the campsite.

Luckily for her and me both, Tiemma got the timing wrong—it only took about *five* minutes, not *fifteen*, to reach the edge of the Gwindes, and about a minute to get to the trees. These turned out to be four or five blue oaks and quaking aspens clustered together, a smattering of evening primroses around them. We fluttered into the middle of the copse of trees and chose the biggest primrose we could find on short notice, then flittered inside. After a few minutes we had our blankets out of our packs—I shared mine with Eilia, of course—and we drifted off to sleep. Except for Jairik, who insisted on taking the first watch.

Morning came way too quickly, and we all knew when it did—the primrose just suddenly wilted and spilled us onto the ground. It might not have been the best sleeping place, after all. Oh well. At least we didn't have a chance of over-sleeping!

As I stood up, I looked around. Surrounding us now was a field full of snowy-white and green lacepods, pretty pink pinedrops, and golden yellow arrowleaf groundsel. The last of the evening primroses, pale pink in hue, were wilting away for the day, and the morning wind rustled the leaves of the oaks and the aspens. It really was a beautiful place, now that I think about it, although I didn't really pay much attention at the time. It wasn't important right then.

What *was* important was getting back on our way to the Princess. I looked toward the west, where the Black Forest would be, and I could see it in the distance. It looked so close, and yet . . . still so far. Between this field and the Forest, we still had to go through the Mustang Meadows. Don't get your hopes up; it's not named for horses. It's named for the mustang *clover* that fills it to overflowing, little flowers either white or pink with darker dots on the petals. The Meadows weren't very far from here; only an hour's flight away, maybe two. But they were big. It could take quite a while to cross them and get to the edge of the Forest.

I bit my lip, then looked back at the others. They were sitting in a semicircle, taking a meager breakfast. We weren't running out of food—not even close, yet— we just didn't know how long the journey would be and were trying to make it last as long as possible. Once in the Forest, I personally wouldn't trust the food and water that could be found *there*. Who knows? Maybe that's how all the animals there were turned . . . weird. They ate and drank in the Forest.

I took a place beside Eilia and took two small dyrus out of my bag, one for her and one for me. She looked up at me and tried to smile when I handed her hers, but I could tell she was still scared. Maybe . . . maybe I shouldn't have brought her along. I thought she'd be safer with me, but . . . that boulder almost . . . It was too late. She was here now, and I wasn't about to send her back through those mountains by herself.

Once we had finished eating, we donned our bags and started out through a patch of the groundsel. We tried to fly under the flowers as much as we could as a precaution. Dwimera might have spell-bound birds as well as animals; we didn't know. Better safe than sorry.

Of course, the animals would be on the ground, so no place was really safe, but we thought it was a good idea at the time. Until we reached the Meadows a while later, and—wouldn't you know it?—a Ballaker smelled us out.

What is a Ballaker, you ask? It resembles a light brown bear, on the small-ish side compared to a grizzly. But they're still *humongous* to a group of nine little fairies like us. It was also one of Dwimera's spell-bound animals, sent abroad to keep nosey little fairies out of her way. Ballakers used to be half-way friendly to fairies, until Dwimera warped them. We had called them Faer Bears. They would help us sometimes, and when not helping us, they would just stay away usually, unless you found a particularly friendly one.

This one wasn't one of those. Not by a long-shot. This was a Ballaker—by definition, a Rend-and-Tear Bear. That was it's only purpose in life, other than to make more of its kind for Dwimera's use. Why couldn't she leave the poor Bears alone?

We heard its growl to our left, and everyone's eyes grew huge. We had figured that it wouldn't be until we were closer to the Forest that we would have to worry too much about this; we weren't really prepared for it.

Instantly, all of our wings started fluttering as fast as we could get them to. The Ballaker kept lumbering after us, growling and snarling. Markette started to lag behind— her wings weren't as young as they once were, of course, and couldn't flutter as quickly as ours—and I looped my arm through one of hers, and Kileri, surprisingly to me, grabbed the other one to help Markette keep up with us.

I could faintly hear Eilia starting to go into a bout of hysterics a little ways ahead of me, and bit my lip. I looked over my shoulder; the Ballaker was gaining. How was it going so fast? As we started to pass poor little Eilia I slipped my free arm around her and tried my best to drag her along.

We flew like that for ages (all right, in reality, probably more like a few minutes, but it sure seems longer when you're fleeing for your life!) until we finally reached the lone oak tree marking the half-way point through the Meadows. We made our way to the top of that tree as quick as lightning, and then we waited. The Ballaker pummeled itself against the tree for a bit, shaking it and us terribly, before letting out an indignant snort and skulking away.

Everyone seemed to let out their breath at the same time. I held Eilia close for a while, Laryn doing the same with Kileri, just trying to calm down enough to venture back out there. Now, at least, we would know we were in danger already. I just wish we could have learned that without being chased half-way through the Meadows. Oh well, I suppose we did get to that point faster than we would have otherwise.

Finally, I cleared my throat. "Is . . . is everyone all right?"

I got answers varying from a simple 'yes,' 'I think so,' or even just a nod to a frightened but angry Siemma exclaiming, "All right? *All right*? What do you mean all right? We were nearly mauled just now, but oh yes, we're doing dandy, Clirena!"

"Now, ye just calm down, Siemma," Markette reprimanded the young spitfire. "Yes, Clirena, we're all here and fine. How're ye doin'?" She looked at me closely.

I shied away from Siemma slightly, and nodded to Markette. "I'm all right," I replied, then looked out between the oak branches, and pursed my lips. There was the Black Forest, plain as day, straight ahead. We still had a ways to go, but it was much closer. I was glad of that, of course, but at the same time, it was . . . well, ominous to think about.

I felt a hand on my shoulder. "Clirena," Laryn said quietly. "We need to get moving, don't we?"

I blinked, then nodded. "Right, um . . ." I took a breath, then tried to sound leaderly again. "Come on everybody! Let's get back out there."

I got a couple groans in reply, but we all ventured at least semi-willingly back into the Meadows. We were even more cautious this time—some, namely Dinad and Eilia, perhaps overly so, if that was possible—and stayed as close to the clover as we could for cover. We zipped along through the Meadows until evening started coming on. We weren't covering as much ground as quickly now that we didn't have a Ballaker chasing us. That made me nervous; I wanted to get there, and get there *now*. Finally, though, we made it to the far edge of the Meadows. There was a small open space immediately before us, and then . . . the Forest. There it was, glaring at us in the fading sunset.

I gulped, and looked at Jairik. "Where do we go from here?" I asked—remember, he had picked out the best entry point on his map.

He turned his back to the Forest to catch the last glimpses of the sun on his map for a moment, looking at it closely, then pointed to the south. "We need to go that way for a while, and we will come upon a narrow path into the Forest. The Guardians made several of them as they tried to find the Fir, after Dwimera's spell was broken the last time. That way they could come across it again more easily if need be. I believe this one will be the closest to the mark."

I nodded silent thanks, then beckoned to the others. "Are you ready?"

Siemma sighed. "We've been flying *all* day."

"Yes, I know," I replied a little bit curtly. "We need to cover as much ground as we can in as short a time as we can. There's a lot riding on this, remember?"

She nodded slowly, then hung her head. "Sorry."

I gave her a little smile. "Thank you. Don't worry, we'll probably stop for the night before too long. I just want to reach the path, first. That way—"

"We can start the real adventure in the morning, right?" Tiemma chimed in.

"Ah . . . yes, exactly," I replied with a nod.

With that out of the way, we fluttered onward into the night, reaching the entrance Jairik had mapped out (or at least, we hoped it was the right entrance; it's hard to tell in the dark!) by about midnight. At that point we were all pretty much ready to fall over, so we flittered just a little ways back past the edge of the clover and fell asleep on some little rocks for the night, after eating a small meal. Rocks aren't as comfortable as flowers, of course, but we didn't have to worry about falling on our heads in the morning this way!

I woke up first the next morning, closely followed by Dinad—the one who was *supposed* to be on watch during the night, but who I found sleeping and gave a soft whack upside the head shortly after getting up. After we got the others up, we ate another small, not completely satisfying but enough to keep us going, breakfast, and wandered back to the edge of the Meadows. Each fairy peeked out at the Forest, the dark, ominous, dreadful place we were preparing to enter. Most, if not all, gulped slightly, and we looked at each other. This was it. We were finally there. All we had to do now was find the Old Fir!

And then, well, the actual, *actual* hard part would begin . . . .

I took a shaky breath, then stepped out into the open space between the clover and the Forest—trying to look calm and courageous, even though I *really* didn't want to go first, but nobody else did either, and *somebody* had to. The others followed after a moment, the youth of our group—plus Dinad—all huddled together, and the rest still following hesitantly. I led the way to the edge of the Forest, then stopped. I *really* did *not* want to go in there anymore. In fact, I wanted to turn back and go home. I even started to turn around, but I caught a look from Markette that made me stop and realize this was exactly what Dwimera wanted. Her spell was messing with my mind. I shook my head, cleared my throat, and beckoned for the others to follow me into the Forest.

It seemed to get darker the further we went. We stuck to the path, as near as we could tell, but it wasn't as well defined now for lack of use. Off and on a ray of sun would somehow break through the pine needle barrier above us, and when it did Jairik checked his map—the first few times.

Until we lost all sense of direction and just had to wing it (no pun intended) to stick to the path.

The only incident that occurred during the first few hours of Forest-travel is actually kind of funny to recall. We were flying along the overgrown Guardian-made lane, following each wind and twist silently, when suddenly we heard a rustling in the undergrowth to our right.

The twins shared a gasp, and we all backed away from it. Jairik pulled a Guardian-issue knife from its sheath at his side, Laryn taking a small dagger from her bag simultaneously. We all held our breath as the rustling came closer. Jairik and Laryn went into a battle stance—and then the diabolical creature emerged!

It was a perfectly untainted chipmunk, who just kind of looked at Jairik and Laryn, bewildered. I caught my breath, then let out a little laugh. "Keep calm, everyone; it can probably smell fear."

After a few seconds, most of the others joined in with my laughter, except for Dinad—too busy grumbling—Kileri—too busy being her current, too serious for a normal teen-aged fairy self—and Jairik—too busy being a Guardian, I guess? I flittered over to give the chipmunk a reassuring little pat, and found myself wondering if Jairik ever laughed. I shook my head (not the time or place, Clirena) and stroked the chipmunk a couple more times before it zipped off into the trees.

"Well, that was a close one." Eilia grinned.

"Oh, yes, extremely," Kileri said with a grimace. "Let's just keep going, huh? This place gives me the creeps."

Eilia hung her head and fluttered closer to me as we continued onward. I pursed my lips, wondering what was getting Kileri's goat's beard. And then I remembered. Oh, right. Dwimera.

Hours later, we were still flittering along this never-ending pathway. I hadn't realized that the Black Forest was so huge! I figured it would only take us *maybe* this long to reach the Old White Fir . . . but, no. We were *still* trying to find it.

The day was growing old, the bursts of sunlight coming through the needles becoming fewer and fewer. Still the path went on; I thought we would never get to the Fir. Until suddenly—there it was.

It stood tall, probably twenty feet high. It was not the tallest tree in the Forest, but perhaps the saddest-looking. Two-thirds of the pale trunk was completely barren of needles, a large clump that looked like a bad hairdo crowning the top third like a sort of canopy or awning. We shrank back closer to the aspen on our left as we surveyed the terrible tree. There were various barred windows scattered here and there on the trunk and a huge, ornate door at the base of it. The Fir didn't seem to be guarded very well (I only saw a few birds near the top of it), but it still gave me an ominous feeling in the pit of my stomach as I gazed at it.

When I finally tore my eyes away from the Fir itself, I could see that it was in a small clearing, close to the opposite edge from where we were. The rest of the clearing was almost bare, with only tufts of dead or dying grass scattered across it, and maybe a few dried-up weeds here and there. Overall, it was as dismal a place as I have ever seen . . . no wonder nobody wanted to look there. Even without the help of a spell, this was simply an incredibly bleak, dreary location. Which of course made it the perfect place for Dwimera to have taken the princess.

The last thing I noticed was how the sunlight still filled the clearing, even though it was starting to dim. I bit my lip. We were *so* painfully close, but I knew that those birds would most definitely still see us in this light. I didn't know for sure that they were Dwimera's foul fowls, but I knew we shouldn't take the chance and push on right then.

Apparently, the thought hadn't occurred to the twins. "There it is!" one hissed between clenched teeth.

"What are we waiting for? Let's do what we came here to do!" the other Emma—Siemma, I think—exclaimed, perhaps a little too loudly.

"Shh!" Laryn admonished them. "Be quiet, and wait for your leader's decision."

She put a hand on my shoulder, and everyone looked at me. I started to sweat a bit as I looked at all of their faces; some scared, some worried, some halfway excited, some knowing what I would say. All looking to me for the answer to their unanimously unspoken question. And all good—no, *wonderful*—fairies, and friends that I didn't want to see get hurt because I made the wrong choice.

Finally, after a long period of silence—or maybe it was only a few seconds, I don't know—I spoke. "We're going to wait for nightfall. It could be more dangerous, but at least we'll have the darkness to help us sneak in." I held up my hand as Siemma opened her mouth to complain. "I have made my decision," I said in the most authoritative tone I had ever used—*I* was even surprised at myself. Siemma shut her mouth and bowed her head slightly in respect of my decision.

"All right. So," Tiemma looked up at the sky, then back at me. "What do we do till then?"

"I think we need to come up with some sort of strategy," Laryn offered.

"Strategy? We already know what we're here to do," Eilia said, looking confused.

"Yes, but how are we going to do it?"

"Oh," Eilia blushed.

Laryn smiled and gave her a pat on the shoulder, then looked up at me. "Have you been thinking about the *'how's*, Clirena?" she reminded me of our talk before we started out.

The authority figure in me had about worn down then. "Well . . . yes. Some."

Laryn nodded slightly, sighing to herself. "Well, what have you got?"

I grimaced. "Mostly just nightfall. I'm still working on how we'll get in and . . . after that . . . ."

"For getting in, the bars on the windows look far enough apart for Kileri and Eilia to squeeze through," Jairik suggested. "Then they could make their way down to the door and unlock it for the rest of us."

Laryn and I glanced at the barred windows again. He wasn't wrong, but . . . "We don't know what might be behind those windows, though," I pointed out. "Would sending the kids to discover that be a good idea?"

"Perhaps not, but it may be our only choice. There is no way to unlock the door from the outside, and we cannot all fit between those bars."

I looked at Laryn, then Markette, both of whom nodded at me in turn. "All right then," I consented, casting a somewhat worried look in Eilia's direction, but knowing it had to be this way. "After we get in, where will we find Dwimera, and how will we get there?"

"E-e-excuse me, but I think I might possibly know where she will be."

Our gazes shot to Dinad all at once. Unknown to us until then, he had apparently been sifting through his over-filled bag of books. About eight or ten others laying around him, he held a large burgundy book in one hand, the index finger of his other hand marking a place on a page. His balding head grew a little red as we just stared at him for a moment.

Finally, Kileri broke the silence. "Well, tell us. What's your idea?"

Laryn shot Kileri a little look, then turned back to Dinad with a smile. "Yes, please tell us," she said, in a much nicer tone than her daughter.

"Well . . . not so much an idea as a finding," Dinad corrected.

I nodded. "What did you find, Dinad?" I asked, offering him a small smile.

He looked down into his book. "This is all about the Royal Guardians capturing Dwimera the first time she used the Fir as a hideout. It says here that she was found near the top of the bare portion of the trunk, two windows down from the needles. It was a large room, with a sort of platform at one side, a window with a balcony." He looked over his shoulder, nodding when he spotted it, then looked back to his book. "Where was I? Oh, yes . . . window with a balcony, and . . . and . . . interesting."

Eilia broke in. "What's interesting, Mr. Dinad?"

He looked at the page silently for a moment, a thoughtful look on his face. "This is very peculiar," he said, picking up a smaller green book and thumbing through it. "It says there was a design on one wall, behind the platform, that had only appeared in the myths of Faery-lore. Well, until then, anyway."

"What kind of design?" Eilia asked again, clearly intrigued by Dinad's having found a use for those books.

"Um . . . huh?" He stared at a page for a moment, then checked the title on the spine. "Oh, that could be the reason . . ." he muttered to himself, laying that book off to one side and picking up a blue one. He checked its spine and nodded. "Ah, this is the one." He thumbed through it speedily, then placed a finger on a page. "This kind of design," he replied, turning the book so we could see it.

Each one of us gazed at it intently. It was a beautiful depiction of a fairy's wing, intricately detailed—almost as if it were the wing of an actual fairy, and a *specific* one at that. For the most part, a fairy wing is a fairy wing, but each individual fairy has a difference, whether subtle or drastic, in their wings from all others. What surprised me the most was that the wing design looked almost . . . familiar. Maybe I had just looked at the myth books when I was little. I always liked looking at pretty pictures, and there were definitely plenty of them in the books of Faery-lore.

"Well," I said finally, "what's the myth behind this wing?"

He turned the book back toward himself, flipping the page. "This artistic and apparently *architectural* wonder, being as it is carved into the wall, is said to be a mark of hiding, whether yourself, items, or in this case, quite possibly a pixie princess. Hmm . . ." His gaze swept down the page. "We might have a problem, however," he said, pursing his lips.

My eyes widened. "What might that be, Dinad?"

"Well, it says here—and I quote—'If ever this could be found, only the one-winged fairy could unlock what is hid therein.' It . . . seems to me that we all have . . . *two* wings." His signature confused expression surfaced on his face. "I don't believe I have ever even *seen* a fairy with a single wing. What now?"

We all looked at each other. I gulped. "I have no idea," I admitted truthfully.

"I don't believe any o' us do, dearie," Markette agreed solemnly. Everyone else simply nodded in response to her assessment of the situation.

"This is great," Siemma grumbled. "We almost maybe know where she'll be, and we can't get to her!"

I shook my head adamantly. "No. We're *going* to get to her . . . we have to. We'll figure out a way. Maybe when we see the wall in person, we'll come up with something."

Dinad looked skeptical. "Well . . . this *is* a book of myth-lore; perhaps the masters did not include every detail about it. You can never be sure. Some liked to play mind-games and riddles with their 'lore', and most are, well, long-dead. Still, there might be something we just do not understand about it, having not lived in the time this was written in. It is quite an ancient myth, you know."

Eilia tilted her head, studying the book in Dinad's hands. "It doesn't look that old to me, Mr. Dinad."

He sighed, but then managed a faint smile. "It is hand-copied into a new book now and again, because as books age, the words and pictures fade." He looked thoughtful. "That . . . that could also explain why we cannot understand it entirely. It is possible that something may have been copied wrongly because of the faded text."

I nodded slowly. "Well, at least we still have something more to go on, now." I looked up into the sky above the clearing. The sun had set behind the trees, but the sky still glowed with its last farewell of the day.

I sat down on a small rock by our aspen. "Just a little while longer, and we can start making our way in."

\* \* \* \*

"Clirena, Clirena, Clirena! Wake up! It's daylight again!"

I blinked my eyes open in sleep-induced grogginess. "Huh?" I muttered as Eilia shook me a couple more times. Then realization hit me like a ton of burs. "What? No!" My eyes widened as I looked up at the sky, then squinted as I managed to look straight into the sun.

"Yes," I heard Jairik's voice behind me. He sounded bitter. "We *all* fell asleep and missed our opening to get in."

I pressed a hand to my head. "How did we . . . ?" I couldn't even finish my sentence, I was in such disbelief.

"My theory is Dwimera's spell on this stupid Forest," Kileri responded dryly behind my shoulder.

Markette sighed. "Aye, I'll second that, dearie. I'd bet anythin' she knows we're here. Probably one o' them birdies saw us and told her."

I stared at the Fir, trying very hard not to let the tears escape my eyes. What could we do? It still seemed foolish to try to get inside in broad daylight, but . . . could we really wait another day? Who knows what she'd do to us—or Argessa, for that matter—if we didn't try to do something right away? My heart and mind raced as I tried to think of what to do, but I just couldn't. All I could think about was how wrong I was to try to rescue her. I was just a little nobody nurse; I wasn't special. I couldn't do anything . . . .

Wait a stinkin' minute!

I grabbed my head, shaking it hard. "That's enough of that," I muttered through clenched teeth.

"What are you talking about?" Eilia's worried voice completed the breaking of Dwimera's hold on my thoughts.

I looked up at each of my eight friends' faces, most staring at me like I was cracked. I shot a look of utter contempt at the Fir, then stood up. "Nothing . . . now."

Markette patted my shoulder, once again understanding the situation. "She'll be fine, don't any o' ye worry 'bout that. We're all bein' messed with, I'm sure. She's just attackin' our leader with a little more spitfire than the rest o' us."

Dinad agreed right away. "Ah, yes . . . a similar thing happened to you when you were in Clirena's stead, I believe."

"Aye, truth be told," Markette affirmed, shaking her head. "Still up to all her ol' tricks, even if she may have some new ones to boot."

The Emmas pulled their unison trick again, first in nodding at the same time, then with synchronized speaking. "So, what do we do now?"

I cast an uncertain glance at the sky, then the birds, and finally the Fir. I shook my head and clenched my fists, turning to face the others. "We can't wait anymore. We have to make a move *now*."

"I concur," Dinad agreed immediately, though his voice faltered.

"Works for us," the twins chimed in.

"We're here, aren't we?" was Kileri's response, followed by a soft reprimand from her mother.

"Excuse her," Laryn apologized. "And I agree with you," she added a little hesitantly, stroking her daughter's hair.

I looked at Eilia. That's right; they had to push through first. And those birds . . . I'd made my decision. I couldn't back down now.

"Clirena," Eilia cut in as I was about to say something. "Just don't. You know I have to do it, and I'm going. Just tell me and Kileri when." She tried a little grin. I knew she was just as nervous as I was, but she was brave as well. She seemed to have grown up a lot in the past few days. She didn't seem quite so little anymore—even if she was only eleven.

"They'll be fine, dearie. I'm sure o' it," Markette's encouraging tone relaxed me some, though I still felt frightened. We all did.

"It is decided then," Jairik completed the vote, casting his own gaze in the direction of the Fir. I followed it back, surprised to see only a few birds in view. "This seems to be as good a chance for them as any. Clirena?"

I swallowed once, then looked at the girls and nodded. "Be careful," I pleaded.

Kileri turned to make a flitter for it, but Eilia smiled at me before following suit. "You, too," she replied, then she sped off to catch up with Kileri.

We watched the two youngest of our group steal away to the Fir, then Tiemma turned toward me. "What do the rest of us do? Keep waiting?"

I looked around briefly, thinking for a moment. "No," I said finally. "We need to move to a position closer to the door." I glanced to the edge of the Forest nearest the door. "Let's make for that," I pointed toward it. "Then we can just zip inside once the girls get the door open."

"We will also be able to stay out of sight longer if we keep just inside the edge," Jairik pointed out.

I smiled faintly. "Exactly." I cast one last glance in the girls' direction. They had nearly made it to the Fir; we needed to act fast. "Is . . . everybody ready?"

I got several nods, 'yes's, and a 'i-if you are'—that last one being from Dinad—in response. I took a breath, then led the group twisting and winding through the trees. About halfway to our destination, I *really* started to wish I had let one of the scouts of our party—Jairik or one of the Emmas—lead the way.

We fluttered along at a good pace, over this branch, between those trees, and so on. It all seemed to be going fine, when I heard the fierce, ghastly, telltale howl we all dreaded.

A Firanther had spotted us—and was readying its attack.

Once it was one of the kindest, bravest, most beautiful protectors of fairy-lands. A cousin of the wolf, its coat was purest ebony, a sheen shimmering across it in sunlight or starlight. The Firanther, then called the Calucian—the beauteous paladin—helped the Royal Guardians in all of their scouting, patrolling, and Guarding duties, and all of the other fairies when they needed aid. That could include anything from lifting something too heavy for a little fairy, to transportation of supplies or messages—or even tired fairies who had been flitting about all day—to just a need of companionship from one who wouldn't pick on them or argue. Best of all, they would protect us no matter what the cost. We could trust them in every situation.

Until an insane Dwimera got a hold of them. Now, their fur was dusty coal—what wasn't ripped and shredded from their apparent in-fighting, now that she had twisted them—and their eyes, once sparkling blue, now held an evil, reddish tinge. They were brutal, just barely protectors of Dwimera herself, and that only because she forced them in the harshest of ways. Those that we had trusted with our lives, now made us fear for our lives. Our best friends were now our worst nightmares. Well, second-worst. What Dwimera might have done to the Princess still took first-place.

The howl had sounded close, but I didn't realize how close it was until I just barely escaped having my foot bit off by the slobbering, growling hound. I felt sweat beading up on me as I tried my best to keep away from the beast—and ended up nearly flying right into the hungered maw of a second. A scream wanted to escape my throat, but I held it back as I flew straight upward, trying to get just far enough away to assess the entire situation without being eaten.

The twins seemed to be doing their part in keeping one of the now *three* Firanthers dogging our heels—*no* pun intended, *at all!*—busy chasing them around. Jairik and Laryn, the only two in our group with halfway extensive weapons training—Jairik having the most, of course, as the Guardian—tried to discourage the others from coming after Markette and Dinad. Dinad came up to join me at a surprising speed, but Markette just couldn't keep up anymore. Laryn lost the attention of her Firanther and it bounded toward Markette, ready to pounce on her.

I must have momentarily lost my mind in panic, or at least that was the only explanation I could think of at the time. I made a dive straight at the creature's head, terror gripping me lest it should get Markette. I didn't take the dagger out of my bag that Laryn had packed for me. It never even came to mind right then. I just had to get the creature away from Markette; she deserved better than to be a hound's noon-time snack. I jabbed my tiny fists into its head, for all the good it did. Maybe it annoyed it a bit. No, it definitely did. The creature snarled, then chomped at me. "Go!" I shouted to Markette through gritting teeth before swooping to the ground and tossing a whole little handful of dirt into the Firanther's eye. That sealed it— with a growling bark it sprang after me.

I stole away as fast as I could, keeping just inside the Forest's edge, sometimes zipping around the Firanther's head, sometimes sweeping underneath the creature, all the time trying to keep its attention on me and away from the others. I heard an anguished yelp from back where I had left them. One of their two Firanthers must have been subdued. That left one for them, and then mine. The latter lifted its head and listened briefly, as if thinking of going back. I pulled its tail—well, a few hairs of its tail—and that thought vanished from its mind. We were at it again.

We kept at it for . . . it must have been fifteen minutes, at least. It couldn't have been any less, surely. All the time it seemed that *I* was wearing out, while it was just getting started. Suddenly, I missed a moment when I should have swooped or swerved, and it gave me a good *whack!* with its large, ratty-looking paw.

I did let out a scream then, pain surging through my left wing, until all of a sudden, it went completely numb and limp. The Firanther didn't come to finish me off— why I didn't know right then—but I knew it was still the end for me. A fairy can't fly with a broken wing; it just can't be done. I was spiraling, around and around, desperately trying to catch enough of the air pressure ahead of me to slow down with my good wing, but I couldn't do it. In another pitiful moment, I would crash head-first into a monstrous lodgepole pine. I squeezed my eyes shut, bracing myself for the impact that would spell my doom.

Except that it didn't. There was an impact, but it directed me straight up a little ways before I slowed to a stop. A gentle stop, not a crushing one. I couldn't make myself open my eyes for a moment. I couldn't figure out what had happened. Something was under me . . . around me . . . something strong. There weren't vines in an evergreen forest, were there? No, I knew there weren't. I was against something wide, warm, maybe a little damp. Perhaps from sweat. I could feel someone's gaze on me. After a little while, I realized that the only way I would get an answer would be to open my eyes, so I slowly did so.

And found Jairik's face above mine, staring down at me—and looking concerned. Really concerned . . . actually showing a deep emotion. I'd never seen him like that before. He had rescued me, he had caught me before I could be killed. He hovered there, cradling me in his arms, deeply concerned, and . . . and . . . "You saved my life," I somehow managed to whisper through my shock.

I could just barely tell that he let out a breath he'd been holding. He then gripped me firmly, yet still gently, as he brought me down to the others.

By the time we got to them, enough of my shock had worn away that I could think semi-clearly again. Most of the shock left over wasn't even about nearly dying. It was still about seeing how Jairik was *really* feeling for the very first time. I tried to get that out of my mind as much as possible when I saw the worried faces of my five waiting fairy friends. "Clirena!" they gasped unanimously once we reached them.

I tried a small smile at them. I'm not sure how successful I was, but . . . I tried it. Jairik started to lower me to my feet, then stopped almost uncertainly. I hesitated, then looked up at him and nodded. He inhaled slowly, then set me down. I was surprised at how balanced I was standing, thinking that having the broken wing would make me perhaps lean toward the good one. I guess not.

Markette looked at my broken wing, letting out a low whistle. "Are ye all right, dearie? Aside from . . . the obvious?" She sighed sadly.

I took a couple steps; my legs were fine. I moved my arms and neck slightly. Nothing hurt, and nothing else was numb. I could move just fine. "I think so." I looked over my shoulder at my drooping wing. "Is that . . . permanent?" I couldn't help but ask—could you have?

Markette shook her head slightly. "I'm not at all certain, dearie. It will be if ye don't get it looked at soon, truth be told, but . . . not much we can do on that note, I s'pose." She shook her head again, looking down at the ground.

To my own surprise, I didn't take that news too hard. My flying ability just didn't matter right at that moment. "All right, we'll get to that, I guess. Are all the . . ." My voice trailed off as I noticed the two dead Firanthers not ten feet away from me. "Oh. Never mind, then. Let's get to the . . . door." I had turned around as I was talking, and there it was. My flight had gotten us just about to the spot we'd been making for.

"Are you sure you still want to go in there?" Tiemma looked at me skeptically.

My eyes widened as I turned to look at her. "Princess Argessa is in there, as well as Kileri and my little sister, now. I have to. We all do. This," I waved my hand almost dismissively at my wing, "this is no excuse to give up and leave them alone in there. If I . . . if I slow you down, I'll just be rear-guard, or something. Anything! But I *have* to go in there with you."

Dinad, of all people, spoke up. "Clirena is right. She led us here, she should stay with us to the end. Whatever that may be."

I smiled at him, then glanced around at the others. Before anyone else could comment on whether or not I should go with them, however, the door suddenly opened with an overly loud *clang!* We all spun to face it, gaping.

Eilia hovered just inside the door, a sheepish little grin on her face. "Well . . . we got it open! Come on in?"

Most of us—myself included—couldn't help but laugh softly at her discomfort. Then we drifted in. Well, most of us did. I, of course, walked. Which alarmed my little sister.

"Clirena, why aren't you flying? Something wro—" She gasped. "Your wing!"

I glanced at it, then shook my head at her. "I'll be fine. Where's Kileri?" I looked around, not seeing our second-youngest invader.

Eilia sighed at me, then pointed upward. "She went back up a few levels once we had the door unlocked. It might not have made quite as much of a crash if we were both working on opening it, but, oh well, I suppose."

My brow furrowed. "Why did she leave you here by yourself—let alone go off by *her*self?"

"I don't know. I guess she figured I could have the door open pretty quickly without her—and I did—and wanted to try her own hand at scouting?" Eilia shrugged.

"She should have stayed with you," Laryn broke in, clearly not happy with her daughter's going off on her own.

"I agree, believe me. It's kind of creepy in here." Eilia glanced around, shuddering slightly.

I gave her arm a little squeeze, then looked at the rest of the group. "Onward and upward?" I gave a tight smile.

The Emmas showed their agreement by zipping off immediately, Dinad, Laryn, and Markette following a little more slowly. Jairik put a hand on my shoulder to grab my attention. "There is a staircase over there, Clirena," he said quietly, nodding in its direction.

I smiled at him a little more genuinely. "Thank you, Jairik." He stayed near me, a little bit ahead and to one side, as I started my climb up the stairs. Eilia grasped my hand, half-pulling me up them. I'm not sure if she was doing that intentionally or not, but it did make it interesting. One arm might be a bit longer than my other one now; I'm not sure.

We made it up the first three or four levels uneventfully and found Kileri waiting for us on a landing between staircases. All of us were surprised to see scratches and peck marks all over her face, neck, and arms. Laryn, most of all.

"Are-are you all right? What happened?"

Kileri sighed. "Let's just say I found a bird nest." She pulled a feather out of her hair with a wince. "And its occupants didn't like being found," she finished in disgust, tossing the feather aside.

I looked around, not having seen any signs of a bird or a nest on the way up. I didn't see anything besides Kileri's appearance that pointed to their being in here, either. "Where were you, when that happened?"

"Outside. Eilia made it in before they spotted me, and then—"

"Wait." Laryn looked at Eilia with disbelief. "Why didn't you tell me that my daughter looked liked she'd been used as a pin cushion?"

Eilia blushed. "I . . . I was going to, but I got distracted . . ." She sent a fleeting glance toward my wing, then looked back up at Laryn. "I'm sorry."

Laryn stared at her for a moment more, then shook her head and smiled gently. "It's all right. I understand." She looked back to Kileri. "Well, as long as you're all right, mostly, I suppose that can't be helped, now. Why did you leave Eilia by herself, though? You know you shouldn't have come up here on your own."

Kileri shrugged a shoulder. "You're letting the twins scout for us. Why can't I?"

Eilia tugged on my sleeve. When I bent down, she whispered, "I guessed right!"

I shook my head, sighing at her with a smile. "What am I going to do with . . . you . . . oh, no." I ran a hand down my face.

Eilia looked confused. "What?"

I looked around one more time to make sure I hadn't just missed them. Nope. "Where are the twins?"

"Oh, they kept going after they found me here. Said scouting was *their* job, in their annoying, little bit hot-tempered, unison sort of way, and to wait here." Kileri rolled her eyes.

I felt my own little bit of a hot temper start to simmer. "Why would they . . .?" I sighed. "Dwimera's trying to split us up, isn't she?"

Markette nodded. "Seems likely. We'll need to catch up to 'em right quick, I reckon."

I couldn't have agreed more. I gave a brief nod in return, then started climbing the next set of steps as fast as I could without tripping on them. Even so, all of the others easily passed me. I was just too slow, being grounded. Jairik looked over his shoulder, realizing this fact, and drifted back down to me.

I shook my head. "Don't worry about me. I'm just slowing you down."

Jairik shook his own head in response. "If we do not want the group split, we certainly cannot leave our leader behind." With that, he swooped behind me and literally swept me off my feet, speedily carrying me up to the rest of the group.

Said group had caught up with and detained the twins. They looked a little bit sulky when I first saw them, but then they saw me and Jairik and smirked childishly to one another. "Clirena and Jairik sittin' in a lily . . ." they started to chant quietly.

Laryn actually bopped both of them. "Not the time," she admonished them.

"Yes'm," they said, though they couldn't help a grin.

I looked at Jairik, and he looked back at me, and we just kind of shrugged at each other. I, at least, really didn't know what else to do.

"*Anywho* . . ." Markette cut into the awkwardness, "It seems to me that we might've reached our level now, what d'ye think, Mr. Dinad?"

I looked over toward the two, surprised to see another door—a double-door, this time. There hadn't been doors between levels before. I would guess that Markette was right. Still, I looked to Dinad for confirmation as well.

He nodded. "I-I would say so," he stammered nervously.

I nodded to Jairik, who gently set me on the dingy, dusty, greenish-brown floor. I stepped to the doors, studying them. Each one was still bigger than a normal fairy's door, though not anywhere near as big as the one at the base of the Fir. They were dark brown, scarred up a bit, with tarnished brass handles formed like long, drooping leaves. Surprisingly, there was no keyhole on either of these like on that other door. Did that mean they weren't even locked? Why would Dwimera hole herself up in a room without a lock? I began to be even more afraid of what all might be behind those doors—not that I wasn't already scared half-to-death before.

I looked back at the others. Each one of them—some a good bit more than the rest—wore frightened, nervous, or at the very least anxious expressions on their faces. I swallowed, feeling like the epitome of all the above. Then I turned back to the doors, took a breath, and reached for one of the handles.

Being grounded, I of course couldn't reach it, but

apparently it was the thought that counted. Both doors swung wide open into the room with such shrill squeaks and squalls as to make one feel half deaf for a moment or two afterward. I bit my lip slightly, then slowly crept a little ways into the room, beckoning for the others to follow.

It was empty.

The place looked like Dinad had read it would: platform, window and balcony, even the design on the wall. But no one was there—not Dwimera, not a single Firanther, *no one*.

I had made my way to about the center of the room, searching for any sign of life, and now looked around at the others. "This-this has to be some twisted joke. They have to be here . . ."

Markette pursed her lips. "Maybe we were wrong, dearie. They don't seem ta be, that I can see."

"No." A determined expression plastered itself on my face. "No, they're here. I *know* it. Show yourself!"

My command echoed through the room over and over, seeming to bounce off every wall. Just before the reverberation died away, a laugh joined it from somewhere just above us. Suddenly, Dwimera floated down toward us, landing just five or six feet from me.

"Well, well, don't we have a clever little sprite? A nobody nurse just *had* to follow some pathetic instincts and lead you all here to die, didn't she? It wasn't enough to just die 'valiantly' by herself. No, she needs her friends with her. Too miserable for one to die alone, I suppose."

Markette huffed. "Now, Dwimmy, ye just stop it—"

"'Dwimmy'?" Dwimera laughed again. "*Dwimmy*?

You really brought that one back out of its bag? Fine. Oh, *Ketti*, how long it's been. Want to 'catch up' before your end finally finds you?" An evil smirk touched her lips.

I blinked slightly when I heard Kileri let out an irritated groan. "Just show us where the princess is, will you?"

"The princess?" Dwimera fluttered a little closer to Kileri. "Why, you know where she is. A little birdie told me so." She shot a smirk at Dinad, then looked back at Kileri. "So, you don't really need my help there, now do you? Or do you mean, let you in—or, her out?" She tsked. "I'm afraid I cannot do that—and you knew that from those books, too. I could open the portal to let her in, but only one fairy can ever open it again to get her out. And that fairy is the real myth, so . . ." She shrugged, clearly enjoying herself.

"Wait, you just kidnapped her so you could stuff her in a room and she'd never see daylight again? I'm confused."

We all—Dwimera included—just kind of *looked* at Siemma once she'd said that. Finally, Dwimera said what we were all thinking: "What kind of an *idiot* do you think I am? Of course that wasn't the reason, you bumble-bee!"

I took a breath. "Then . . . then what *was*?"

"You think I'm really going to tell you?" Dwimera started to laugh, then seemed to think a moment. "Well, you *are* going to be dead soon enough, anyway. I guess I might as well."

"Then, by all means, enlighten us," Laryn interjected into her musings.

Dwimera shot her a dark glare. "Fine. Oh, where to begin? I suppose at the beginning is usually preferred. Ah, Cilendra, dearest niece." She smirked as most of us gasped. "No one ever told you that? Doesn't surprise me. We middle kids are more easily forgotten, no matter what we do, it seems. I was the third of four. When my older sisters had children before me, I didn't take that so hard. That's how it usually happens, isn't it? No big deal. When my younger sister had a little girl before I had any kids, I was . . . a little jealous then, but after a while that didn't faze me so much, either. But when my little sister's *daughter* had her precious little brat, Niriel . . . well, I suppose you could say—heh, have said—I lost it. I had never even found love, and here my niece had just made me a great-aunt!"

Dwimera's near-black eyes smoldered angrily for a moment, then she tossed her head back with a faint smile, as if remembering something fondly. "That sealed it for me. I was going to have my revenge—"

"Your revenge for what? What did your sister, niece, or Queen Niriel ever do to you?" Siemma broke in sharply.

"Caladia stole my life. I realized that then," Dwimera snapped in response. "The youngest shouldn't have had children before her older sister. It should go down the line, and I was skipped! And Cilendra, oh, Cilendra. So prim and perfect, never did a thing wrong. Mother always preferred all of her other children and all her grandchildren over me. *I* could only do things wrong. Mereth does this better, little Ryken did that better, why don't you watch your sister Callie and her daughter, and follow their examples! I couldn't take it anymore!"

"Now, wait a blinkin' minute!" Markette exclaimed. "Ye weren't treated that way much, if at all, by anybody—and ye certainly didn't feel at all that way when Niriel was *first* born. Ye couldn't've been more excited about it all, for the first few *months*, even! Ye were the picture-perfect great-aunt if ever there was and'll ever be one!"

Dwimera's boiling temper suddenly faded drastically. "I don't . . . remember that . . . ."

"What d'ye mean ye don't?!"

That temper rekindled again with a passion. "Exactly what I said, Ketti!"

"Wait!" I cried, staring at Dwimera. "So you did all of this out of pure jealousy?"

"Not so pure—!" Markette started to cut in, but I held up my hand and stopped her.

"All right, maybe not 'pure' jealousy, then. But, you kidnapped Cilendra and put a spell on most in Eranea because she had a little girl before you? And when that didn't pan out how you wanted it to, you tried later with Queen Niriel when she had . . . found love . . . and now *she* has a daughter." I looked over at the wing design on the wall. "You took Argessa because she made you a great-*great*-aunt."

"And you don't even look any older than twenty-five . . . *maybe*," Eilia said in confusion, tilting her head.

Dwimera smirked at my little sister. "Thank you; I try." She then looked over at me. "You're smarter than you look, though it's not getting you much, now is it?" She shook her head. "I've had enough of this, haven't you? I think it's time for some, heh, fun."

Before any of us could even make a sound, she began

fluttering her wings at that tremendous rate she demonstrated the year before at the Sequoia. All of us were sent flying—with no one using their wings to do so—all over the room. Kileri and Dinad both crashed into a wall, lying unconscious on the floor—at least, I sure hoped they were just unconscious.

Dwimera wore a mock-sheepish expression on her face as she looked around at all of us, slowing her wings again. "Oh, sorry. That happens when I get worked up," she said sarcastically.

I scrambled to my feet, just in time to see both Emmas really start to boil. "Oh, you're going to be sorry!" they snapped, whipping their knives out of their bags and lunging at her.

Dwimera easily dodged their attack, pulling out her own thin blue-black blade and laughing at them. "So, this is how you want to do it, huh? Works for me."

The twins flew back to her, trying to get on both sides and flank her, but that didn't faze Dwimera one bit. She only had one blade against their two, but she was *fast*. No matter what they did, she was always one step ahead of them and could block it easily. Siemma tried to slash at her a bit wildly; Dwimera parried it and nearly spun her around. Tiemma made a slightly more calculated thrust; Dwimera just smirked and locked cross-guards with her. She skillfully flipped Tiemma's knife out of her grasp and blocked another stab from Siemma—with both her own knife *and* Tiemma's, having caught the latter when wrenching it away!

Tiemma was not happy at all. When Dwimera's attention was more on Siemma than on her, she leapt at Dwimera and tried to tackle her. Her reward was catching her own blade in the shoulder and sinking to the floor. She clutched her wound, watching her sister with wide eyes.

Siemma just about lost it entirely. Instead of any normal almost-maybe-halfway-calculated moves, she started sort of hacking at Dwimera with her knife. She did manage a few cuts—a couple of those on herself— before Dwimera knocked the knife out of her hand and slugged her in the side of the head with the pommel of her blade.

"Four . . ." Dwimera murmured with an ominous grin, looking at the rest of us. "Who's next, I wonder—wait." She counted us. "Four down . . . one, two, three . . . four here. Where's the little one?"

My eyes widened. Where *was* Eilia? I looked around as well—hopefully a little less conspicuously than Dwimera was—trying to find her. It didn't take me too long. She was behind Dwimera, on the platform. She had crept along it and was by the wing design on the wall, looking like she was trying to find a way in. According to the books, there wasn't one besides the one-winged fairy, but I wasn't about to stop her, just the same. I looked back to Dwimera after a few seconds, shrugging a little. "Maybe she went for help?"

Dwimera stared at me a moment, then just laughed. "Even if she did, it would be pointless! You know that. These are the only people you could get to listen. And you're not a little kid! She would get even less attention, I'd bet."

I glanced briefly at Eilia again. She was starting to get a little flustered. *Oh, please keep quiet,* I thought at her before quickly bringing my gaze back to Dwimera. "You don't know her like I do. I think she can be very persuasive, when she wants to be."

Dwimera shrugged. "Perhaps. Not that I have any reason to, you know, care."

While I had kept her attention mostly on me, Laryn and Jairik had managed to get around behind her, Laryn with her dagger and Jairik with his knife. Suddenly, Jairik took hold of her from behind, bringing his knife to her throat. "Drop your weapon, Dwimera."

The villain glanced down at his knife-hand, then up at Laryn, now in front of her in a subtle battle-ready stance, and just smirked. "All right," she said, letting the blade slip from her grasp. For a moment, I thought we had beaten her. Then, all of a sudden, Jairik went flying into the platform. I didn't even see what happened, but now Dwimera and Laryn were struggling for control of Laryn's dagger.

"You can't beat me. You can only dream of it—and that, hardly!" Dwimera laughed, having driven Laryn to the ground. Laryn still had a hold of the dagger, but Dwimera had a grip on her wrist and was trying to force her to cut into her own throat.

Just at that moment, Eilia looked back in our direction—and screamed.

Dwimera looked over at her. "Oh, that's where the little pixie wandered off to. I'll need to . . . attend to her, in a moment."

That single moment of Dwimera's distraction was all that Laryn needed. She wrenched her wrist away from Dwimera and knocked her off of her.

That didn't make Dwimera very happy. "Think

you're so smart, hmm? Let's test that, shall we?" She grabbed for something on the floor beside her, clearly thinking she'd find her blade—except that she didn't.

"Now, ye just stop, Dwimmy," Markette said slowly, holding the searched-for blade in her hand. "We don't need to go on like this. Just help—"

"Just help you? Just help *you*?" Dwimera's laugh echoed throughout the room. "Never again, Ketti." She rose to her feet. "I'm not that deranged girl that believed in helping others beside herself anymore, like you seem to think."

"No, ye're just a deranged ol' bat what doesn't know which way be up no more!" Markette shot back indignantly.

"Up? Hmm, perhaps not." An evil glint came into Dwimera's eyes. "But *down*—that I am most definitely familiar with. As in, that's where you're going, dearest Ketti. *Now*." With that, she fluttered a gale at poor Markette, driving her into the opposite wall from where Kileri and Dinad lay. Then, she flew over and swept Eilia up from her spot by the wall, zipping right back to me and Laryn. "Now, what should I do with this little *pest*, I wonder?"

"Leave her alone!"

"Oh, really, Clirena, you don't seem to understand me at all."

I tried to fly straight at Dwimera like an angry yellowjacket, but only ended up falling on my face. Right; broken wing. I sighed heavily at myself, glaring at Dwimera.

Who just laughed. "Oh, so heroic, aren't you?" she gibed at me. "I'm just all a-flutter over it, can't you tell?"

She started to get her wings up to speed once more, but Laryn suddenly dived toward her, aiming a careful stab into Dwimera's arm so that she wouldn't hurt Eilia. She lost her grip on Eilia as she cried out—a rather horrible sound—and my little sister flitted over to me instantly as Dwimera and Laryn went at it again.

"Are you all right, Eilia?" I whispered, watching the other two carefully while holding her tight.

"I think so . . . except for the ribs you're now crushing," she whispered hoarsely in return.

I blushed, loosening my hold on her. "Sorry." I looked at the platform. "I need to get up there. I don't know what good it'll do, but . . . I just feel like I need to. Think you can help me?"

Eilia looked at me a little skeptically. "The eleven-year-old can carry the twenty-year-old. Sure."

"No, that's not what I meant," I replied, shaking my head. "I can get over *to* the platform just fine. I'm just going to need a quick boost onto it. Think you can do that?"

She pursed her lips. "I . . . I don't know." She glanced at Laryn and Dwimera, then back at me. "But I can try," she finished decisively.

I gave my little sister a small smile, then broke off in a run toward the platform. I don't think Laryn or Dwimera either one even noticed us. When we got to it, I studied it closely. It was only four or five inches higher than I could jump. It shouldn't be too much for Eilia—I hoped.

I looked up at her and held my arms up. "It's now or never. You can do it."

Eilia swallowed. "R-r-right. I can do it." She grasped each of my hands in hers. "I can . . . do it." she reassured herself one more time before pulling me up with all her might.

And we *just* made it. In fact, the only way that we did make it was because, just as I was halfway above the edge of the platform, Eilia fell over backwards and kept hold of me long enough to bring me along with her. She shook her head. "Well, I did it. Kind of," she murmured.

I smiled at her. "You did *just* fine, Eilia." I held out my hand and helped her up, then looked down at Dwimera and Laryn. The latter no longer held her dagger either, but neither did Dwimera, so that was fine. It lay beside Laryn. What *wasn't* fine was that Dwimera wasn't down there anymore—just Laryn with a wood-scraped gash on one side of her forehead, lying on the floor beside her dagger. *Uh-oh* . . . .

I grabbed Eilia's arm and turned to run for the back platform wall—and that's where Dwimera now stood. "Well, well. A nothing nurse and her little pesky sister. Quite the 'rescue' team left, huh?"

I tried to keep a cringing Eilia behind me as I slowly made my way to the center of the platform, and Dwimera followed suit. "This can end now, Dwimera. You don't have to do this," I said once we were only a few feet apart. Probably not the best distance to be between us, but, really, there was no such thing as a 'good' distance, if I could still see her. Even if I couldn't . . . it would be iffy.

"I don't?" She looked mock-surprised. "Whatever gave you that idea?"

Eilia decided this was the time to say something incredibly stupid to somebody incredibly delusional. "I don't know, common sense, maybe?" she sniped at her, perhaps even more stupidly stepping out from behind me and putting her hands on her hips.

268

"Hmm." Dwimera looked faintly amused—I knew that could mean nothing good. "Is that so, huh? Common sense . . . is that really a thing? I thought it was a myth, like how to save the dear little princess is," she responded with a smirk.

"I don't believe it is," Eilia replied, sounding like she just had a sudden realization.

"You . . . don't?" Dwimera asked warily, tilting her head curiously.

"No, I don't! Clirena, I think I just—Aaah!"

Just as Eilia was about to tell me, Dwimera backhanded her hard, sending her to the floor. Eilia looked up, wiping blood from her nose, a few tears welling up in her eyes—the only evidence she let show of any pain. "You're nothing more than a monster, no matter how nice Markette says you used to be!"

"No need to pay me any compliments, my dear little pest," Dwimera replied dryly.

"I wasn't trying to."

Dwimera gave her a smile, then a disgusted, I'm-done-with-this look took over her features, and she just blew Eilia completely off the platform with her wings, all the way out to the balcony. I was surprised—though relieved—that she didn't go flying completely out of the tree.

"That just leaves a stupid little sprite with only one useful wing," Dwimera pointed out the obvious. "This has been easier than I thought—and I thought it would be overly easy to begin with! Really, what do I have to fear from a fairy with a broken wing?"

I stared at my sister, then at Dwimera, dumb-founded. Was this it? Was this all I came to do—get myself and my friends destroyed by this villainous wasp? All my hopes were gone; all my fears stared me in the face in the form of those cruel near-black eyes looking back at me. Everything was lost . . . wait.

One useful wing . . . one-winged fairy. One-winged fairy! Was I the one-winged fairy in that book? I glanced at the design on the wall, then over my shoulder at my own wing, then at the floor. The wall's wing and mine couldn't have been more alike if mine had been used as a mold for it. Maybe I hadn't looked in that book—just in the mirror! I could hardly believe it!

"Ahem," Dwimera's voice startled me out of my epiphany. "I don't think that patch of floor is very interesting; why do you?" She stared at the same spot, then looked up at me when I looked over at her.

"I don't. It just seems to be a good thinking spot."

Dwimera frowned. "What . . . do you mean?"

I gave her a tight grin. "I mean, thank you for giving me my answer, Dwimera."

"What? No!"

She leapt at me, but I was able dodge out of her way and ran straight to the design as she scrambled back to her feet. "What can *you* do?" she cried, reaching her boiling point once more. "You can do *nothing*!"

For a second, I almost believed her again. Then, my thoughts went back to "mold" and "carved into the wall". I took a breath—and a chance—and turned away from Dwimera, pressing my one good wing against the design. At first, nothing happened. I shifted, just slightly—and I felt an odd tingling.

"What-what's happening?" Dwimera's flustered voice carried over to me.

270

I didn't move, except for my eyes. I looked back as far as I could without moving any more than that—and it was *amazing*. First the design glowed, then *my wing* actually glowed, too. Just faintly to start with, but it steadily grew brighter and brighter until I had to look away, even close my eyes as it completely filled the room.

"No! It can't be. It's impossible! NO!" came a distraught, raspy shriek from Dwimera.

The tingling went all through my body now. It wasn't unpleasant, as tingling usually is, just . . . oh, I may as well say it. Magical.

The light slowly faded out of the room, and just before it did, I heard a soft *click*. It puzzled me for a moment, then I stepped away from the design as it suddenly slid upward, revealing the room inside. The hideaway contained a fountain, a pantry, a few pieces of furniture, and . . . and . . . .

A little princess, now six-years-old, jumping up from a small, ratty-looking chair excitedly. "Clirena!" she exclaimed, zipping out of the room as quickly as possible, straight into my arms, so that she wouldn't have a chance to be trapped in there again. We all hoped.

I held onto her tightly, trying to calm her down. I looked over at Dwimera when she started moaning.

"No. She won't be happy with me . . . no . . . ."

I gulped. "Wh-who won't be happy with you?"

"That would be *me*."

My eyes widened as I looked around for the source of the new voice, one I had never heard before. One that sent chills running up and down my spine and made the hair stand up on the back of my neck. A dark cloud suddenly filled the room, making it hard to see anything. It

dissipated with a frightening *poof!* as its ominous instiga-
tor landed beside a now quivering Dwimera. If *Dwimera*
was afraid of this new arrival . . . *uh-oh*, again.

She was pale-skinned, with deep mahogany hair
made up in a tight bun. She wore a long black, strapless
gown, and an intricate necklace of pure onyx. Her light
green eyes bore into Dwimera. "How could you let this
happen?" she shot at her.

Dwimera shrank away. "It wasn't . . . I didn't . . . how
could I know she was the one?"

"Well, it seemed like you told her how to open the
room and let your niece out!"

"U-um, great-great-niece, actually, Erngarha—"

"Are you correcting me?" Erngarha bristled. "After
what you've already done, you're *correcting me*?" She
straightened. "You are no longer required, you incompe-
tent *fool*."

Erngarha swept her hand up, and Dwimera shrieked.
All the years that had been taken from Dwimera, giving her long-lived youth, suddenly struck her. Her hair
turned dull grey, her face and form taking on that of an
old lady—which she actually was. Older than Markette,
even, I now remembered as I stared at them.

Dwimera, cast out from the hold of evil, looked
around at all of my friends, then me, and finally, Argessa.
She burst into tears. "What have I done . . . what did you
make me do?" she cried, her aged voice cracking with
grief.

"What I could not do, as I cannot leave this accursed
Forest!" Erngarha answered, making a growling sound
in the back of her throat.

Jairik, Eilia, and Siemma had now come soundlessly

up by me and Princess Argessa, while the true villain was distracted by her contempt for Dwimera. "Now what?" a miffed Siemma "whispered" rather loudly in my ear.

I really didn't know. Erngarha, however—after knocking a blubbering Dwimera to the floor—turned toward us with a pretty-ish, yet frightening, smile. "Now, you are mine."

"No."

Everyone stared at Dinad. Did that really just come out of *his* mouth? After a moment, Erngarha chuckled ominously. "No? My dear, you have no idea who you are dealing with."

He straightened up. "But of course I do. Erngarha, Maid of the 'Mire. The Cindermire, if I remember correctly. A dabbler in the darker arts of Fairy-dust, exiled to the Black Forest ten years before Dwimera came to live in the Fir. That being about two months before she turned evil—except that she quite obviously did not. Well, not of her own accord."

Erngarha made that growling sound in her throat again. "There had to be a bookworm in their little group."

Dinad gave a quick smile, disappearing seconds after it came.

Erngarha grinned darkly. "All right. At least you will know who killed you. Any last requests?" she inquired, though she knew the answer.

"Why have you been going after Dwimera and Argessa's family?" I replied.

"*Glad* you asked, little fool. You may as well know." She smiled again, even more pretty-but-frightening than before. "It was all Dwimera's mother's fault, really. Liana was the one who discovered my . . . shall

273

we say, practice . . . and told the Royal Guardians, who in turn told the King, of course. She was the reason they found me and threw me in this blasted Forest, never to see a person again. Or at least, so they thought. Who would have guessed that her third daughter would come to live here, long after I had been forgotten by all but the bookworms and librarians." She sneered at Dinad. "I found her those afore-mentioned two months after she took residence here, and, well, much of the rest of the story you know. Need I say more?"

"No," I replied. "I think that covers it fine."

"And makes much more sense than Dwimera's story did, too," Eilia threw in.

"Ah, yes, I suppose that is true. I guess I just never thought she would ever have a need to tell it, so it did not matter so much. I will take the blame for that." Erngarha shrugged. "Now, as there will be no further questions to answer . . . farewell."

Dark clouds suddenly swirled between her hands. She gave a laugh just as she started to stretch her arms forward and make an end of us, but that laugh turned into a scream as she was suddenly knocked forward into her own spell. A whirlwind-like swirl and another sickening scream filled the air, and then . . . it was quiet.

I opened my eyes, having closed them as the swirl came up, and couldn't believe them. Erngarha was nowhere to be seen—and neither was Dwimera. The villain who had tried to destroy us, saved us from the one true villain who had been controlling her.

The old, kindest fairy in all of Eranea used that re-kindled kindness to keep Eranea safe. And she had won.

I continued staring at where they had been for a

moment, then Eilia and Argessa each tugged on a sleeve. "Is it over? Can we go home?" they perfectly mimicked the twins without meaning to.

I looked at each one in turn, then smiled. "It's over. Let's go home."

\*　\*　\*　\*

As we passed the edge of the Forest, we were met by an army of Royal Guardians, now broken from all spells. While in the Forest and in the Meadows, we came across several Firanthers and Ballakers—no, I should say Calucians and Faer Bears—also broken from their spells, who carried us back to the Sequoia. They still didn't look like they were supposed to, but that would come in time. They were our friends again; that's all that mattered.

All ten of us that had been in the Forest spent a while in the infirmary—some of us more than others. Not all of us had been incredibly hurt, but all of us stayed for at least a day or two, just in case. Kileri suffered a concussion, but healed up nicely, as did her mother's wounds from struggling with Dwimera. Tiemma still has limited use of one arm, but seems to shrug it off. Markette was forced to retire from the Head Nurse position because of her injuries, but she still cares about the children and will tell them stories and play with them as much as she can. Most of the others just suffered from bumps and bruises—or, in Argessa's case, lack of love and good food. Most of them have recovered quickly and nicely. As for me? Well, my wing was set and bandaged thoroughly. Only time will tell as to whether I'll really regain much use of it or not.

Now the kingdom finally felt at peace, joyous celebrations occurring all over the place—many times at the

Sequoia itself. The King and Queen's relief, as well as everyone else's, showed itself in all of the feasts, shows . . . just everything, in every way.

I stood at the infirmary balcony one night, gazing at all of the festivities below and around me. I wasn't able to participate yet (I'm not sure I was even *supposed to be* out of my bed) but I just had to watch. I smiled as I saw all of the children playing—especially Eilia, Princess Argessa, and Kileri, who was finally back to being herself instead of that somber, annoying teen that she had become. It was amazing to see them playing together again, all laughing and smiling. I could have watched them for hours.

That is, if someone hadn't come up behind me at just that moment. "How are you feeling, Clirena?"

I turned toward the person speaking, a little surprised that it was Jairik. "O-oh, um . . . all right, I think. Mostly. A-and you?" I stammered like an idiot.

He didn't seem to notice. "I am glad of that. I am fine as well. I just wanted to . . . check on you. Your sister, especially, has been worried about you. She has not been able to come up to see you herself for the past couple days. It is a little hectic down there."

I couldn't help noticing a difference in him. It wasn't like him to hesitate like that, and the sudden change from checking on me because he wanted to, to because Eilia needed him to, was a little . . . suspicious. To me, anyway. "I can see that. At least it's a good kind of hectic, now," I said with a smile.

Jairik nodded. "That is a blessing, after everything that has happened."

I nodded in return. "Yes, it is."

There was a lull in the conversation, and I could feel my face warm as I started to blush. I looked away from him for a moment, biting my lip a little. Out of the corner of my eye, I saw him start to look around a bit restlessly. Both of us seemed to be feeling the awkward silence we had plunged into. Then, all of a sudden, a firework burst in the sky above us. I whirled around. There came another—and another! Soon, the sky was absolutely filled with blazing, colorful fireworks.

I took hold of the balcony railing, gazing up at the display in awe for a few moments. Suddenly, a strong, kind hand slipped over my own. I looked up at Jairik; he looked down at me. . . .

And that was the first time I ever saw him smile.

## About the Authors

**C. K. Deatherage** earned her B.A. and M.A. from Southern Illinois University at Edwardsville in English and her Ph.D. from Purdue University in Old and Middle English Language and Literature. Her previous publications include *Waysmeet: Poems and Tales of Fantasy and Wonder*, "Niall MacDonaugh and the Leipreachan" in *The RudderHaven Science Fiction and Fantasy Anthology I*, "Final Entry" in *Star Trek: Strange New Worlds V*, and various poems in anthologies and journals. She won the 2013 Poet of the Year and the 2013 Vardis Fisher Award for Most Humorous Piece by the Idaho Writers League. She currently resides in Idaho with her husband, two kids, two large dogs, and four cats—and an occasional very temporary field mouse.

**C.S. Marks** has often been described as a Renaissance woman. Artist, songwriter, author, illustrator, educator, field biologist, and avid horsewoman, Chris holds a BS in Zoology from Butler, a MA in Zoology from Southern Illinois University at Carbondale, and a PhD in Life Sciences from Indiana State University.

Dr. Marks recently retired from SMWC, where she served as chair of Equine Studies for over twenty years, attaining the rank of Full Professor and earning the Pomeroy award for excellence in teaching. She is now in demand as a lecturer and presenter at conventions, academic fairs, equestrian events, and publishing workshops.

She has competed both nationally and internationally in the sport of endurance riding. One of only a handful of Americans to have completed the grueling "Tom Quilty"

Australian National Championship hundred-mile ride, she has described that moment as her "finest hour."

The child of an English professor, she has always loved classic literature as well as epic fantasy, and decided to try her hand at writing and illustrating an epic series. The result: The very successful *Elfhunter* trilogy (Parthian Press), which has sold over 50,000 copies both in print and e-book form. This epic trilogy has garnered awards (Reviewer's Choice Best Fantasy, Best Series) and over 200 reviews. She is now hard at work on an exciting new Alterran series, the *Undiscovered Realms*.

**Becca Lynn Rudder** is teen-aged girl with a dream of writing a story—and actually finishing one, finally. She is the daughter of Douglas and Sheri Rudder, both of which are also *RudderHaven* authors. They, as well as other members of her family, helped her with the polishing phases of her story. She knows that she couldn't have finished it without their help. Becca lives in southern Illinois with her parents and their dog, Shadow Star. She enjoys MMOs and PC games, movies and TV shows (especially older ones), reading, and just plain talking. She likes Barbies and Princesses—and *really* likes super-heroes, Star Trek/Star Wars, and Lord of the Rings as well.

**Douglas Rudder** is a St. Louis area science fiction and fantasy author and Managing Editor for RudderHaven. He currently resides in southern Illinois, where he often battles Orcs, Aliens, and Super-Villains with his wife and daughter. An avid reader of science fiction and fantasy since childhood, Doug's first book, *Tolkien: Roncevaux, Ethandune, and Middle-earth*, is a work of literary criticism. He is also an author and editor for *The RudderHaven Science Fiction and Fantasy Anthology* series. Current creative endeavors include three novels in various stages of mayhem and several short stories for upcoming anthologies.

**Sheri Lynn Rudder**, a fortunate stay at home wife and mother, grew up in rural, southeast Iowa. Thanks to her mother and grandfather, she learned at an early age that the best place to find adventures was in books. Almost twenty-five years ago, when she married her knight-in-shining-armour (known to most as Douglas) she was introduced to the wonderful worlds of sci-fi and fantasy, mainly through the writings of JRR Tolkien, Michael Stackpole, and Timothy Zahn. Now, with her husband's encouragement and the quick-clicking editing pen of her teenaged daughter, she is trying her hand at sharing her adventures with you.

**B. David Spicer** lives in Ohio, where he earned a B. A. in English from Ohio University. He has always been an avid reader and one day woke up and started writing fiction of his own. Along with crime fiction, science fiction and horror fiction he'll occasionally jot down a prose poem or two, though he'll probably deny that in court. He sometimes writes scripts for independent comic book publishers, but short stories are his favorite subjects. He likes board and role-playing games and attending gaming conventions.

www.ingramcontent.com/pod-product-compliance
Lightning Source LLC
Chambersburg PA
CBHW050713180626
46814CB00002B/414